GOOD HEART

ALAN NEWMAN

This is a work of fiction. Names, characters, businesses, places, events, locales, and incidents are either the products of the author's imagination or used in a fictitious manner. Any resemblance to actual persons, living or dead, or actual events is purely coincidental.

Quotations from *The Prime Ministers*, by Yehuda Avner, with permission from The Toby Press.

Cover Design: Dragan Bilic – Upwork.com
Cover Artwork: Arthur Schreibman
Typesetting: Optume Technologies

ISBN: 978-965-229-955-0

3 5 7 9 8 6 4 2

Gefen Publishing House Ltd.
6 Hatzvi Street
Jerusalem 9438614, Israel
972-2-538-0247
orders@gefenpublishing.com

Gefen Books
140 Fieldcrest Ave.
Edison NJ, 08837
516-593-1234
orders@gefenpublishing.com

www.gefenpublishing.com
Printed in Israel

Library of Congress Cataloging-in-Publication Data

Names: Newman, Alan B. (Alan Bernard), 1944- author.
Title: Good heart / by Alan B. Newman.
Description: Jerusalem, Israel ; Edison, New Jersey : Gefen Books, [2018]
Identifiers: LCCN 2017059206| ISBN 9789652299444 | ISBN 9789652299550
Subjects: LCSH: Jews--Fiction. | Christians--Fiction. | Families--Fiction. | Friendship--Fiction. | Religious tolerance--Fiction. | Indiana--Fiction. | Israel--Fiction. | Jewish fiction.
Classification: LCC PS3614.E62 G66 2018 | DDC 813/.6--dc23 LC record available at https://lccn.loc.gov/2017059206

To friends of Israel

When the heart yearns for something, the distance one has to go to get it matters not at all.

From the teachings of Rebbe Nachman of Breslov

Forgetfulness leads to exile while remembrance is the secret of redemption.

From the Baal Shem Tov,
chiseled in stone at Yad Vashem,
Jerusalem

I say to you that many will come from the east and the west, and will take their places at the feast with Abraham, Isaac and Jacob in the kingdom of heaven.

Matthew 8:11

1
Purple Rain

Lieutenant Tal Omri raised his arm signaling forward and led Corporal Yoni Baranson and the rest of the Israel Defense Forces platoon through the three-foot-wide gap cut out of the coiled barbed-wire barrier separating Israel from Gaza. Just before they stepped across, each soldier handed half of his dog tag to the squat, red-cheeked corporal responsible for tracking who was heading into harm's way. Another dog tag had been split in two with one piece wedged into each combat boot.

On the other side of the squirrelly tangle of razor wire plastered with windblown paper, the platoon divided into two lines and marched guardedly down a rutted dirt road. They shuffled ahead at a quickened pace without any chatter, carrying their heavy gear across several unkempt and unprotected fields, trying to reach the first low walls bounding the Gaza town.

Earlier in the day, the Southern Command received the order to cross the frontier into Gaza. The Givati battalions quickly deployed their infantry's tactical plans with synchronized armor, engineering, and artillery. The Israeli Air Force added its mix of deadly F-16s and agile Apache helicopter gunships to provide dominant air firepower.

It was late 2008, and Yoni's battalion was the first ground unit into Gaza since Israel's unilateral disengagement in August and September 2005. When Hamas came to power six months later, the frequency of the Qassam rocket and mortar attacks escalated, as did the threat from tunnel digging. Israeli schools and residential areas were targeted, and kidnapping attempts were barely thwarted. The

Givati Brigade was sent in to capture Hamas leaders and to ensure the rocket-launching areas were fully destroyed.

They had less than a mile to reach the low walls of the urban area. The noises from the heavy armor weapons, gunship rockets, and machine gun bursts screamed in Yoni's ears. The cacophony exceeded anything he had experienced during training and two years of service. Funnels of sooty smoke and rounded clouds of dust tossed up from shelling craters obscured the clear blue sky. Yoni imagined that some of these housing units had a view of the beach and the Mediterranean beyond.

He felt his heart race and heard his own labored breathing as he relied on sight to keep in touch with his team. With half a mile to the wall, Lieutenant Omri stopped, turned, and barked out "GESHEM SEGOL!" Literally translating to purple rain, that was the code for incoming mortar fire. He then dove away from the road and flattened onto his stomach into the slightest of a dusty depression. Fifty yards away, the mortar hit, jolting the ground and sending up a burst of dirt, rocks, and shrapnel. Nobody was hit. The lieutenant gauged the timing and the distance to cover, and called for them to move up. With sixty pounds of weapons and supplies on their backs, they raced the rest of the way to the safety of the wall.

It had been only a few months before that Yoni and his pal Doron had visited their friend Benji Mizrachi in Sderot, an Israeli town near the Gaza border. Thousands of rockets had rained down on the city and on nearby Kibbutz Kfar Aza. In the Sderot police parking lot, hundreds of crated boxes of projectile remnants were there for all to see. The rocket terror had come to define the town of Sderot.

Their car pulled up next to one of Kibbutz Kfar Aza's many bomb shelters. It was a small, concrete shell standing adjacent to a colorfully painted school bus stop. Kfar Aza, about two miles or eight precious incoming warning seconds from the Gaza Strip, had been a frequent target of rocket and mortar fire. Benji, a third-generation resident, led Yoni and Doron on a tour of the concrete-reinforced youth nurseries, the repaired shrapnel pockmarks, and the new razor-wire–topped electrified fences.

As they headed to a pastoral overlook of Gaza, they walked past the flower garden where Jacob, an eighty-year-old Holocaust survivor, was killed. Benji added, with a touch of cynicism, that he was optimistic that someday the kids wouldn't suffer from trauma and the parents wouldn't have to choose which baby to grab from the playground before sprinting for cover.

The staging area for the Givati battalion near where the incursion would eventually take place was an open, mostly flat field, stubbly with cut-down wheat stalks. The closest Gaza cities were Beit Lahia and Beit Hanoun, and they were the source of the deadly rocket fire.

Yoni and his platoon assembled in the fields with the larger force preparing to go to war. Already the engineers had created a firing range, and an olive-green city of tents arose to house the soldiers and communications equipment. Latrines and mess tents were there for creature comfort, and larger tents for meetings and intelligence stood tall. Ample stores of supplies and ammunition were stacked for distribution.

Further away, the rows and columns of aggressive-looking Merkava tanks had chewed their way into place. They now stood shoulder-to-shoulder with aligned low-slung turrets and lethal cannons. Transports continued to bring in more bulldozers, APC's, self-propelled artillery, and 4X4's. The forest of whip-like antennae, along with Israeli flags, poked skyward.

Over the past few days, Yoni had sorted through his possessions, whittling them down to just what he would carry with him into battle. Now that he was nearer to the place and closer to the time, he was even more selective. Out went the running shoes that he had thought would be useful for a quick conditioning jog; out went a bound diary. He substituted extra ammunition and water. He would, at the last minute, jam in a few Kabanos meat sticks.

He made just one small sentimental sacrifice of his valuable backpack space. Years before, his Grandpa David had given him *The Abridged Prayer Book for Jews in the Armed Forces of the United States.* It was the same size as an index card. On the first page was inscribed the name Seaman David Baranson, and curiously, in parentheses, Borinski. In 1944 and 1945, David prayed from it while serving on the USS *Massachusetts* in the Pacific.

Yoni remembered stories about his Austrian ancestors, the Borinskis; he had heard the travails of his great-grandfather Isaac and the tragedies of Leon and Stefan. His little tan prayer book had been published by the Jewish Welfare Board in 1941. Now wrapped in a sandwich bag, it symbolized the sweep of his family's history, from escaping Nazi Austria to defending Israel.

Just before the familiar Hebrew prayers in the tan book was a preface. Yoni would often glance at the first paragraph and marvel at its relevance and prescience.

> *May this prayer book, small enough in size to be carried in a pocket over the heart, bear the spiritual message of Israel's ancient prayers to the heart of the American Jewish soldiers and sailors serving their country. The prayers here gathered together speak to the eternal aspirations of the Jewish people, and, indeed, all mankind. They lift the soul above the immediate cares and interests of the daily round to the sphere of tenderness, purity and faith that is divine. They link those far away from home with some of the most beautiful and uplifting associations of family life. They quicken the loyalty to loved ones and to all one's fellow men. They strengthen against temptation and give courage to spurn evil and hold fast to faith in the ultimate triumph of the good. In furthering this high purpose, this little volume of*

> *devotion serves not only the men who use it, but the highest ideal of America.*

But today as he packed, Yoni wasn't thinking about the words in his prayer book. He had too many distractions clouding his mind.

Most of the characteristic good-natured army banter had slowly petered out as they approached the border staging area. One guy from Haifa, Ilan, put up a sign: "To all the virgins up there in heaven, we just wanted to let you know an especially rough month awaits you," referencing the Muslim belief of what awaits martyrs in the afterlife. Nobody reacted to the braggadocio.

The youthful bravado, built on a sense of immortality and reinforced by surviving intense IDF training, was being replaced by the realization of the possibility of injury and death. In spite of the overwhelming military advantage, random events occur in war. People suffer grievous injuries, and people die. The possibility of causing harm to noncombatants or harming a fellow soldier worried most of the young men.

During the day, Yoni and his team attended briefings in which officers would rattle off a long list of warnings and tips about what was coming up. In a darkened tent, lectures about camouflage booby traps, mines, and sniper locations were given.

Yoni's buddy from San Francisco couldn't help but continually repeat a joke to all who would listen, "My commander growled at me, 'I didn't see you at camouflage training this morning,' and I said, 'Thank you very much, sir.'" Maybe it was nervous energy.

Protocols for communications, medical treatment, and resupply were reviewed. For every twelve combatants, there was one assigned medic, and combat doctors would cross over into Gaza. A stern officer advised, "Boys, when you have secured the area, make sure the enemy knows it too."

Yoni was slowly coming to realize that in spite of all the rugged IDF training, this was the real thing, and he would never be the same. He was about to face the moment when the basics of his moral code would be shifted. Now it was his job to kill. Like all IDF soldiers, he had been schooled in the IDF code of ethics. It made clear the dual responsibility to defend the state while at the same time following the traditions of the Jewish people and respecting universal moral values regarding the value and dignity of human life.

At sunrise and sunset, when he woke and went to sleep, Yoni asked himself if this day would be his last. There was poignancy to life's simpler acts. Like his pals, he wrote a letter to his parents that they should only read upon his death. Yoni had dated several girls back in Indiana before he moved to Israel to join the army, but none warranted a last will and testament reference. His letter was short on distribution decisions, but very clear in declaring that by serving in the IDF he was doing just what he had always wanted to do. He thanked his parents for sharing their values.

He watched the religious soldiers don their tefillin, wrapping the leather straps around their arms as they prepared for morning prayers. Standing together in uniform next to lethal machinery, these young, tanned men held their prayer books with their white prayer shawls billowing around their shoulders in the shallow breeze. Even with the drama all around them, their observance didn't change.

On top of all of his concerns, Yoni had to lie to his parents. Maya and Danny had been following the escalating violence, and he knew they needed his reassurance, or at least to hear his voice. Yoni was fully aware that his mom knew the ropes. She knew that every anxious Israeli parent who sent a child off to the IDF to protect the country felt death circling above. Every phone call, doorbell ring, and knock on the door carried the portent of disaster.

No matter how many times his mother told him about her dad, Yonatan, being called up to defend Israel on a Yom Kippur morning and about receiving the shocking notification of his death days later, the story gave him chills. He understood that to protect her, he must go through a long-distance charade. He knew it was his job to diminish the reality of war and to instill confidence that, yes, in a few more days, he and his parents would chat and all would be fine. Unlike soldiers whose families were in Israel, lone soldiers couldn't make frequent, quick calls to their parents to let them know that all was okay.

Yoni had to be especially careful with his dad's feelings when they spoke. Yoni's Indiana-raised dad had fought against the pull of Israel on his son. But when he saw the inevitability, he reluctantly gave him his support. This was in contrast to his mom, who worried but totally understood the mission as she came from an Israeli background.

About two months before, Yoni had sent Maya an inspirational quote from Israel's first prime minister, David Ben-Gurion: "May every Jewish mother know that she has put her son under the care of commanders who are up to the task." Maya had acknowledged the intent, but dryly advised that her mother, Dahlia, would have been highly critical of David Ben-Gurion's successor, Golda Meir, and her preparedness for the 1973 Yom Kippur War.

When Yoni called home from the base, he told his parents that he got a letter from Susanne Langford, Danny's pal Bobby's daughter. She was about to travel to Israel to work with a Christian Zionist organization.

Yoni asked, "When Susanne comes over, could you send her with some of my thick hunting socks? I still have one more winter to serve, and I'm tired of having cold feet." He hoped referring to the future might put them more at ease.

Maya answered with a little more cheer, “Of course. How many pairs?”

Danny, also on the phone line and sitting in their kitchen, pressed Yoni to share some details about whether Givati would be called into action. He told Yoni that the papers talk about all the rockets and threatening words from both sides.

Yoni carefully replied, “Dad, if I knew, I wouldn’t say, I couldn’t say.”

He didn’t want to sound irritable. He decided to fib, “But I’m guessing it will all blow over, because Hamas knows better. It’s all a lot of posturing.”

Yoni suffered through these exchanges and did his best to soothe their nerves. It was a challenge, since every indication said that the Southern Command and Givati would be the point of that spear. After all, the motto of Givati was “Any place, any time, any mission.”

In their green and tan battle gear, with gray-black straps and weapons, the patrol slid along the cinderblock wall. Their moves, with some positioned low and some high, were choreographed to provide 360-degree bubble coverage. Watching out for angles where snipers could find them and checking telltale trip wires or circular land mines just below the dust, they moved left toward the knocked-in opening. Hunched up next to the wall’s breach, Yoni and Yair used scopes to look up and down the alleyway on the other side of the wall. When it looked clear, they sprinted through to the side of the first apartments.

Wrecked cars with windshields blurred by muddy concentric arcs scored from once-operating wipers were scattered about. Several cars were burned out with blistering blackened paint. Garbage and shards of building blocks knocked down from the upper floors and caved-in balconies littered the streets. Electrical lines, many cut, hung in disarray like forest vines. Twisted iron reinforcing rods, no longer holding fast to poured concrete, pointed skyward.

Lieutenant Omri checked his map and directed the team southwest to find the buildings likely to hold the hidden rocket cache and provide shelter for Hamas fighters. Yoni heard the footfalls of his fellow soldiers crunching through the debris and rubble as he listened for commands from Omri. He knew they would have to move into the apartment maze about three blocks into the town, and that the further they got from the wall and the support teams, the more precarious were their positions.

The other Givati teams were also moving in the area, and they communicated constantly to ensure no friendly fire accidents occurred. Yoni heard all around him the Tavor assault rifles' *crack-crack-crack*. The burst of growls and ricochet zings of a firefight echoed in the alleyways. It was followed by messages that bad guys were found and cleared out. The slow building-by-building exploration, each room an excruciating test, moved forward. It seemed the warning leaflets dropped by the Israeli Air Force had been heeded, and, so far, few civilians had been seen.

Lieutenant Omri told them that they'd reached the two apartment buildings they were assigned to investigate, and if necessary, destroy. Just across the next narrow street, they saw a mosque and a school already dinged with shrapnel, but still standing. Yoni guessed that the proximity was the reason both for the intelligence's suspicion and for the caution against the apartment's aerial destruction. The team blew in the apartment's metal door and worked their way up the two flights.

Qassam rocket launching frames sat piled in one corner. Tables covered with stained cups and dishes stood in another. This was the place. Here was the building that they'd destroy.

The demolition team was radioed as they waited for an expected ten-minute delay. Lieutenant Omri began pulling his team out of the two buildings, deploying them in a defensive semicircle close to the adjacent apartments. Yoni sat back for a moment at the building's corner and drank from his canteen. Over the last hour, he had only taken one long slurp of water to clear out the dust. He had fired only a few dozen shots. Now, the pressure from the danger and the strain from his heavy load sunk in.

As he replaced the stopper, he felt a massive concussion from somewhere behind the apartment. The apocalyptic noise overwhelmed his senses. The ground moving under him failed to register as something very unusual. The apartment that he had just left seemed to puff up, the walls bowing out and disintegrating. In his mind's eye, Yoni watched himself drifting along in slow motion.

For a moment, he blacked out. With one or two steps, he staggered away from the bursting building's walls. As he tried to react, he pivoted back and saw the cantilevered balconies just above him snap off and collapse onto him.

Yoni was sure that he had not passed out, but he couldn't recall the moment when the crushing weight landed on him. He was perplexed thinking he should have remembered, and he realized he might be in shock. He found himself lying faceup, staring at a building that was now just a waffle of floors and supporting columns. Swirling dust filled the air. There were no windows or walls, but the floors remained. Wires and pipes dangled in profusion.

Yoni didn't even attempt to sit up, knowing that he was pinned firmly between his backpack and jagged shards of what were once two balconies. Now, the pain in his left arm and right leg registered. It was not bad at first, but it grew steadily worse. He knew that the pressure on his shoulder was from his arm getting twisted at an odd angle, and the rhythmic throbbing was accompanied by a sense of wetness.

Lieutenant Omri, through a cloud of dust, stooped down close to Yoni. "My friend, you are going to be fine. You were very, very lucky."

After another moment, Omri asked, "Can you give us a minute to get you out?"

Yoni reverted to his jocular way, replying, "We need to discuss building codes with Hamas."

Instinctively, Yoni knew that he would be evacuated and that he would survive. He wouldn't die; he wouldn't be left there. He rotated his head around, trying to see what had happened to the rest of his platoon.

Yoni asked, "Omri, what happened? Did we blow up the building?"

"No, we didn't. I don't think so. The blast came from the next building. Probably a booby trap that just went off. Please relax, stay still. You have a broken arm and leg, maybe a broken collarbone. Nothing more. Not even a shot in the rear… 'the million-dollar wound,' as you Americans like to say."

A swarm of fellow soldiers used all their strength and cleverly leveraged reinforcing rods to extract him from the blanket of broken building slabs. Medic Dodi Liebler oversaw the cleaning and wrapping of the wounds, and four men hustled Yoni on a stretcher back across the wall, back through the field. He would be taken to the armored transport and the medical ward.

The soldiers jogged with Yoni's stretcher, turning left and right, paralleling a worn footpath he couldn't see. To help manage the pain, he focused on the deep blue sky bounded by his towering IDF brothers, one at each corner. Later, he would remember the bouncing ride, sagging safely and comfortably into the canvas's middle. It crossed his mind that the stretcher resembled a wedding chuppah.

Yoni's thoughts drifted away from his injuries, and the thunderous sounds of the military maneuver now faded. He was acutely aware of the sway and softness of the stretcher's fabric. He was suddenly overtaken by an innocent wonderment at it all. How did an Indiana-born boy end up fighting with the IDF, now wounded in Gaza? His ideals, dreams, and plans clashed with the reality of his injuries.

He was flooded with remembrances: a collage of family faces, bits of stories, and familiar voices called out. Yoni began to dispassionately reconsider his journey. He had always taken pride in his commitment and decisiveness. But now, with less confidence, he pondered how all this had come to pass. He considered his multinational family history and how it had led him to become a lone soldier. What came before?

While he recovered from his near catastrophe, Yoni would have time to puzzle over his unique story.

2 The Attic

Back around 1920, alongside of what was once a quiet, ambling country road, the sturdy house that the Langfords now lived in was built. The rolling fields of Indiana hadn't yet been divided up into housing plots for returning World War II veterans like John Langford. Whoever lived there at that time enjoyed an unobstructed view of miles of farmers' fields and stands of tightly clustered woods.

Although the cold-in-the-winter and hot-in-the-summer attic could have been turned into a livable second floor, the builder only completed the skeletal wall studs, properly spaced and braced, revealing where two bedrooms and a bathroom could be. A few low-wattage bulbs, one for each of the uncompleted rooms, provided dim light; the wooden two-by-fours sliced the weak luminance. Angled shadows chased over the accumulated boxes across the roofing's underbelly and rough floor planking.

John Langford's family found that they, too, had more than enough living space on the first floor. There was a sizable master bedroom for him and his wife, Nancy. For the three children, Bobby, the youngest, was given his own room, while Claire and Polly shared the middle-sized bedroom.

The one noteworthy improvement made to the attic space by the Langfords was a cedarwood closet. The spicy smell of cedar kept moths away and eliminated the stale, moldy odor of stored clothing. The smooth cedar planks, with reddish and yellow striations, came with tongue-in-groove edges. With some measuring, sawing, and nailing, John easily completed the closet's construction.

When the prairie winds picked up, nature's forces would press on John Langford's Indiana home. Wood rubbed against wood, and builder's spikes, long ago pounded into the structural pine, edged in and out from their tight, dry crevices. On these windy nights, little seven-year-old Bobby Langford hid beneath a thick quilted cover, trying to ignore this cacophony of eerie sounds. All the creaking, moaning, and grinding noises above his bedroom ceiling disturbed him. He fought to control his imagination, and he developed a reverence for the source of it all: the attic.

In his sepia-hued, pinewood-paneled den, John Langford would slouch back in his worn leather lounge chair and rest his long legs on the matching ottoman. His prematurely graying dark brown hair contrasted with his still youthful appearance, featuring a square-jawed face, aquiline nose, and broad shoulders.

Tartan plaid drapes, covering almost half of the two den windows, restricted the afternoon light, while a miasma of cigarette smoke filled the air. The butted remains of half a pack crumpled into a brass ashtray, adding to the room's sour smell. A single lamp glowed in the otherwise dim space. John frequently sat here in his lounger to read books or listen to the radio. It was where he could relax and consider things past.

Adjacent to John's desk, in a cherrywood frame hung from the paneled wall, was a picture of nine young men in U.S. Army uniforms. They stood in front of a muddy truck. These soldiers, in olive drab, all had the same divisional insignias. Some smoked cigarettes and all were unshaven, and they held their long, brown weapons with ease. With helmets cocked back atop their youthful, smiling faces, at least for the moment the photo was taken, it seemed they had forgotten the death and destruction they'd witnessed.

Over the years, Bobby outgrew his attic fears. For him, and less so for his older sisters Polly and Claire, the attic's accumulated clutter became a rich treasure trove of things from the past worth exploring.

Bobby would occasionally retrieve something for his mother. Sometimes, his dad asked him to find something, but he was given instruction not to dawdle in the attic. John would call out, "Bobby, hey buddy, please get me the box with the fishing reels, and then come right down. No fooling around up there."

From time to time, John Langford, sitting in his den, would hear footfalls above in the attic. He'd look upward and call out something like, "Bobby, is that you, what are you doing? Don't create a big mess up there. Careful, it's all dusty, and I don't want you tracking dirt all over the house. Come on down."

Bobby would typically call back, "Okay, Dad, be right down, let me finish, be right down."

He was a good-looking boy, sharing his dad's strong face and his mother's lighter coloration. John came to learn just how much of an explorer his boy was compared to his two sisters. John surely adored the two girls, but he relished the opportunity to roughhouse and play sports with little Bobby.

On a late afternoon in early April 1970, Bobby decided it was time to take out his dust-covered Rawlings baseball glove, Louisville Slugger bats, and shoebox of scuffed baseballs. The winter had been harsh, and only now could he get back to his favorite sport. The schoolyard baseball diamond was due for its first mowing of the season, and the muddy base paths and pitcher's mound were finally drying out.

He was alone in the house. As he headed up the attic stairs, he flicked on the lights. Stepping over two sets of his dad's boots, he bounded to the top.

Bobby found the baseball gear just where he had left it. His left hand comfortably slipped back into the glove, and he reflexively pounded his fist into the oily palm's center. This was where a ball's flight ended, the inning came to a close, and pats on the back began. Bobby was a good outfielder. He reveled in the crack of the bat, following the ball's upward trajectory, and racing to intercept it with his glove splayed opened at the end of his outstretched arm. In his mind's eye, it was a cloudless day in Yankee Stadium, the masses roared for him, and he had the chance to be a hero. Above the Bronx din, he heard his dad and all his pals screaming "Wayyyyy to go, Bobb-eeeee!"

Just before heading back down the steps, he heard scraping and tapping near the cedar closet. Stepping around the studded walls into what was built to be a small bedroom, he saw next to the south-facing window a brown robin building a nest. The noises came from the bird's frenetic pushing and pulling of small twigs to craft her new home. Bobby, through the pane, watched the bird's fluttering actions – wings, beak, and bony little legs – all twitching around.

It was then that he first noticed, between the floor joists and beneath the staggered end of the unfinished floorboards, just next to the cedar closet's outer wall, the corner of a grey cardboard box. He bent over and pulled it out from its hiding place. The box was about three feet long and one foot wide, and it was tied tightly with a thin braided hemp rope. With a swipe of his hand, he removed the box lid's accumulated dust. He saw the box was stenciled in thick lettering with the words "Sgt. John C. Langford."

Over the years, Bobby had not seen much of his dad's World War II memorabilia. Even with his son's repetitive requests, John had not recounted exciting tales of desperate, smoky battles. John had shared detailed memories of a boyhood working on a farm, hunting, and fishing. He shared bits and pieces of the family tree, of immigrants, settlers, and hard-earned victory together with frustrating, futile enterprises. Mom had stories of her Midwestern adventures, but it was dad's war stories that Bobby wanted to hear.

Nancy had shared with Bobby's two giggling sisters the stories of her and John's first date, the romance and courtship, and the wedding. She had saved her wedding dress, and the girls loved to look at it. Between the stories, stolen kisses, and handholding, John and Nancy's love for each other was obvious to their young children.

Bobby yearned for a father-son travelogue of John's 1944–1945 exploits in wartime Europe. John spoke broadly about the training, shipping off with his friends, and "seeing action," but after that, details were modest and sparse. When Bobby would try to press on, his dad's eyes would narrow, his jaw would tighten, and he would change the subject.

John Langford was the good, attentive father that any kid would want. He was a well-liked neighbor and a community man building a respected business. John had come marching home from the war with millions of others who had little choice but to make the transition from military service to getting on with life. Despite the challenges, the building blocks of his postwar life – marriage, children, and career – somehow fell into place.

Nancy was a steadying influence, as she blended relaxed manners with consistent messaging of right and wrong. When the kids got into their small troubles, she was careful not to force John to be the disciplinarian. There was time for play, church, homework help, and answering the endless stream of "why?" questions kids ask.

Hollywood, magazines, and history books, to a lesser and drier extent, painted the landscape of the great Allied triumph that excited the imagination of little boys. In Indiana's backyard battlefields, the kids crafted foxholes in wheat fields, and cornrows were turned into Normandy hedgerows and volcanic islands. Bobby and his pals sometimes played "war" in the nearby woods, imitating the high drama of close combat in Europe and the Pacific. They fired toy rifles and made improvised sounds of shots, explosions, and ricochets. There were clever ambushes and brave charges to capture cardboard pillboxes and rusty washing machine tanks. Deaths were dramatized tumbles over fallen trees into soft piles of leaves. The good guys always won.

Bobby's curiosity about the box in the attic was supercharged. He figured if his dad would not tell all, then it was a mystery he should solve. The rope, wrapped around it twice on the longer side, was finished off with a square knot. Although the box was tightly bound, Bobby, concerned about hiding his sleuthing, was careful not to damage the box so it could later be resealed.

Within a few moments, the ropes were undone, and the box sat there defenseless.

The top easily slid back and revealed a sight that shocked him. He was frozen in place, his wide eyes focused on a folded red Nazi armband, affixed with a well-stitched white circle and a methodically sewn black cloth swastika.

His face felt a hot flush, and his mouth fell slightly ajar. His lips were dry. He was lightheaded. He could feel his heart pounding.

Details slowly emerged from the blur. The armband's red color was still vivid, the white was too stark and too perfectly round, and the narrow, black streaks chilling. There were two armbands.

In all the movies, magazines, and newsreels, it was this broken cross, the swastika, that so clearly symbolized the evil of the Third Reich, the German enemy. He had seen the emblem painted on the sides of German planes and smaller versions inscribed as "kill" notches under the canopy of American and British flying ace's planes.

Bobby saw there were also several pistols, daggers, and a bayonet. The weapons looked clean, oiled, and ready to use. The daggers housed in metallic scabbards with ringed hangers were emblazoned with swastika and eagle emblems. A more utilitarian scabbard housed the bayonet. The pistol, hard and industrial, with a few nicks and scratches, had a crosshatched grip.

In the corner of the box was a yellowed, folded V-mail envelope. Bobby, concerned that the old, curling paper might tear, pulled it out with two fingers and opened the flap. Inside, he saw a four-inch-long, three-inch-wide torn and threadbare strip of coarse cloth. It was grey and blue striped. Bobby returned the envelope with its cloth swatch back to the box.

Bobby was weak from the shock of the discovery, of uncovering something he couldn't fully grasp. He knew that these weapons were real; they weren't the cap pistols or rubber knives used in their war games. These weren't the tools of local hunters. They weren't intended for rabbits, pheasants, or deer. It was a wrenching shift from the vague, imagined past to a three-dimensional, touch-with-your-hands reality. It was proof positive of something important, but what?

His head swam with questions about the box, the objects, and his dad's war experiences. Also, why hadn't his dad trusted him with the story?

With care, he retied the rope so it all looked like it was when he found it. He wedged the box back into the corner and walked back down the stairs. He felt alone, even embarrassed. What he couldn't put away was the need to understand why all those Nazi weapons and relics were there resting in his family's attic.

3
Route 231

As John Langford drove home on Route 231, Bobby looked stiffly out the rolled-down passenger window. They were returning from the man-made lake where their green and white twenty-foot-long flat-bottomed boat was kept. Looking downward as they powered forward, Bobby studied the remainder of the painted white line where the highway's edge ended and the road's grassy shoulder began. Small chunks of asphalt had broken off, carrying fragments of the white line with it.

The recent winter's freezing and defrosting added to the overall decay of the local country road. Along the edge, the spring's sun and rain allowed new grass and weeds to punch through and encroach on the road's cracking surface.

They had about an hour drive remaining, and now was the chance Bobby had waited for. Now, he'd ask his dad about the box in the attic. He'd soon have the answer to the nagging mystery.

The ride from the lake took them past woods, farms, and homes. On these long drives, Bobby would daydream, nearly hypnotized by the repetition of sounds and sights. The late afternoon sun's light, interrupted by trees, would flicker through the car's window, and the fading light of dusk would lull Bobby to sleep. On other rides, he would be distracted with the sights of tilled fields and their warped, three-dimensional patterns. He'd piece the landscape together like a patchwork quilt. Some rectangles were interrupted with ponds, feeding troughs, and rusting, outdated farming equipment. Others had been plowed back and forth with satisfying precision.

Closer to the road, dented mailboxes and weathered telephone poles would fly by. He would read the remainders of the peeling billboards that displayed Madison Avenue's best advice for what to buy or what to do. Faces on the billboards were disfigured as panels of paper disintegrated and the fragments of prior advertising campaigns reappeared. He'd look at sparse woods interrupted with dead, drooping trees.

But today, Bobby couldn't slip into any of these daydreaming routines or take comfort from familiar mileposts. Today he was alone, feeling pressed down into the front seat bearing the weight of his dilemma, and he had to ponder what to say and when to say it.

If he was honest, he would admit that his dad wasn't the easiest person to ask tough, personal questions – not about girls and not about the fears of standing up to Brad, the big kid in the seventh grade who was looking for a fight. His dad would say that he could ask him anything, and maybe he could, but most of the time he'd rather figure it out for himself. His guess was that his dad would rather talk about the goings-on around the home, a fix-it project, local sports, and homework. He was more than happy to compare and contrast the batting prowess of today's players to Stan Musial, Mickey Mantle, and Duke Snider.

Sometimes Bobby's mom would quietly reason with him about one thing or another. She'd face him, put her hands on his knees, and then patiently listen to the problem. She'd share a story from her past that at first didn't seem relevant to his situation. But with a few more words or with a little time for him to think, he would see how it showed him a path forward. He could also turn to his two older sisters every once in a while, when they would stop bickering long enough to talk like friends, like equals. Their few extra years of experience were just enough to help him out.

Over the last three weeks, he hadn't been able to stop thinking about the attic and the discovery of the box of Nazi armbands, knives, and pistols. The weapons and the envelope with the torn fabric were evidence of something significant from the past, something from the war, something his dad wanted to keep to himself.

Maybe his dad was waiting to share what happened when the time was right or when he was older, but the mystery gnawed at Bobby. Maybe his dad always knew that it would be found, and at that time he'd tell his family all about the life of young Sergeant John Langford, serving in the army and fighting in France and Germany. After all, Bobby reasoned, he could have thrown the box's contents away, and he never would have had to face any questions.

After the discovery, every time Bobby saw his dad, he carefully considered whether it was the right time and the right place to ask. The shock of the attic images wouldn't go away and returned full force every time they met. He replayed the discovery in slow motion, assessing whether some evidence had been overlooked. Bobby wondered if John would be angry that he'd been sneaking around the house looking for something that wasn't any of his business.

About a week before, John had asked why Bobby was so quiet at dinner, and he had almost mentioned the discovery. But he felt this was between the two of them. His mom and sisters were at the table, and he couldn't imagine how they would react. Did they already know about it? Was he the only one who didn't know, perhaps because he was too young? Bobby wanted his dad to tell him, father to son.

With a deep breath, he hitched up his courage and asked, "Dad, can I ask you a question, a tough question?" Bobby pivoted around on the vinyl seat so that instead of looking out the passenger window, he turned to face his dad.

To Bobby, John looked a lot like Burt Lancaster, with his close-cropped, thick hair, bushy eyebrows, and strong chin.. Because of John's characteristic poker-player facial steadiness, Bobby noticed his brow scrunch slightly.

While keeping his head steadily fixed on the two-lane road ahead, John easily responded, "Sure, Bobby. What's on your mind?"

Bobby was sure that until now, his dad had been using the driving time to think about his business, or an upcoming vacation, or the decision to repair or replace the water heater. He couldn't have known what was bothering his son.

To buy another few seconds and to ensure his challenging words would be heard, Bobby reached over to the dashboard and turned the radio's volume down, but not completely off. That would have been too dramatic. His dad was the pilot, and all the car's controls, including the radio's volume and station selector buttons, belonged to him. Riding in the passenger seat, Bobby knew his place in the automobile hierarchy. He clarified, "It was a little loud. Just wanted it quieter."

His head was now swimming as he considered the different ways to start. Pushing out the first word felt like trying to budge a boulder. He could feel his heart pounding, and his mouth was dry. He had practiced several opening statements, and he had imagined a wide range of his dad's possible reactions. His dad might be very angry. It would be a discussion like none they had ever had. It was adult business, it was personal, and it was scary.

Bobby began apologetically, "Dad, I hope, really hope, you won't be mad at me."

John took his eyes off the road, tilting his head to see his son's worried face. "Bobby, what's up? Let's hear it. Must be a big deal."

All he could now do was answer, "Dad, I was in the attic and I found…I found a box."

Bobby felt just a little relieved; it was as if that humongous rock had finally given in and moved. His dad's head rose back up, eyes narrowed and mouth opened just a little as he again stared ahead at the road. Bobby went on. "Dad, I found a box of yours, and I opened it. There was war stuff in it." His dad didn't say a word but a barely audible "mmm." Oddly, he seemed to relax ever so slightly. He drove on in silence for two or three minutes.

Ahead was an intersection with a two-pump Sunoco gas station wedged into the near corner. Diagonally across was a used car dealer, and empty lots occupied the other corners. His dad slowed, stopped, and looked all ways. Maybe he was considering each corner for a possible place to stop and talk. Instead, he accelerated forward across the intersection and drove another minute or two.

Finally, John carefully pulled off the road and onto an entranceway to someone's farm. He shifted the car into park, and the motor quieted. Dust from the gravel drifted up and swirled around the two aluminum mailboxes resting on graying, warped boards nailed to a thick brown post.

Another moment passed, and his dad, still looking straight ahead, began, "Bobby, please let's wait until tonight. Let's wait until after dinner, and we'll all...you, me, Mom, Claire, and Polly...we will all talk. I know that I need to tell you about the war. And I want us to be together when we talk."

Just before he put the car back into gear and edged from the farmer's driveway back onto Route 231, John Langford reached over and put his big hand on top of Bobby's head. It sat there just a little longer than a pat. He tousled his son's hair, turned the radio's volume back up, and they drove on home.

4 Witness

After dinner, John walked into his large country kitchen and sat down at the far end of the worn rectangular oak table. Tucked under his right elbow was the box from the attic. He held in his left hand the black-and-white framed photograph of his army buddies. The box was still tied as Bobby had left it. The framed picture, at first lying face down against the box, was now propped up and sat on top. He set the box down and fiddled with the corner of a woven wicker placemat as he waited for the four other Langfords to settle in.

Nancy, after she had taken off her high-waisted apron, slid into her chair at the far end, opposite John. Claire and Polly drifted in, taking their places on one long side. Both girls wore their old blue jeans and sweatshirts. Claire was a clone of her blond mother Nancy, and Polly had John's darker complexion and sturdy frame.

From the kitchen table, Bobby looked out through the wide-screened windows to their backyard to see the day's fading light. He was on the other long side facing his sisters. Although he was the youngest, the girls always grouped together, so one side of the table was all his. The dishes were now stacked in the sink, soaking in soapy water; a soft breeze filtered through the window screen, carrying the smell of freshly cut grass from the neighbor's lawn. The savory aroma of tonight's meatloaf and onion gravy added to the domestic fragrances.

John broke the unusual household silence and began in a soft-spoken, stiff tone. "Earlier today, Bobby asked me to talk about my experiences in World War II."

The family greeted his introduction with encouraging nods and smiles.

He paused and then proceeded. "We've talked a little about my army time, sometimes before parades, maybe on the fourth of July, maybe after a Hollywood war flick. But I've not shared much of what happened over there...what I did."

John skipped over the part of the story revealing Bobby's discovery in the attic, and he didn't refer to their labored car-ride conversation. Bobby felt relieved about that. He could see that despite this becoming a shared family exchange, they could have their own private father-son moments.

John inhaled and continued. "It's still hard to talk about... about the war." John pictured how many of the local bank's calendars had arrived in the mail since then. "It's been over twenty years since I was discharged, since I sailed home into New York harbor. More than that since volunteering, going through basic training, and shipping out to Ireland and then on to England, then to Normandy."

He paused and added, "Claire, when I joined the army, I was only two years older than you are now. Imagine that. I think I had been outside of Indiana only twice before I left for boot camp."

"After boot camp and before the fighting, we traveled by troop ship across the North Atlantic to Ireland. I got sick as a dog from the rough seas... I remember the starry nights and the long phosphorescent wake the ship stirred up...no trouble with U-boats."

Pointing to the fingers on his left hand, he ticked off his stops as he recalled the journey. "I remember staying in a little town called Lurgan for about two months. We transferred again to Oxford, England, to finish our training, and then we were repositioned near Southampton."

In an almost apologetic tone, he went on, "I was not part of D-Day, the June sixth invasion. I crossed the channel on the twelfth." He wanted to be clear that he hadn't faced the withering fire that killed so many on the Normandy beaches.

He struggled to describe the personal cost of war. "First, it's tough to talk about the actual combat...what it was like to be in the middle of all the chaos. I'd wonder, am I going to make it out alive? Will I be brave enough?"

He fumbled for words. "I saw friends killed...horrible sights... hard to forget. One minute they are there, the next, they're gone."

He returned to his journey. "We were part of the breakout at the Falaise Pocket, and then we fought our way across France and Belgium. We were in a series of small battles, firefights for villages, hedgerows, bridges, and intersections." Again, he used his fingers to count how many times he'd faced enemy fire.

Trivial details and poignant moments flooded back into his mind. He worried that his retelling sounded impersonal and generic. "There are so many stories I can tell you. When I think of the training, meeting guys from across the States, when I think about the skirmishes and close calls, and when I think about the daily living conditions in France and Germany, I have a hard time picking out what are the most important or interesting stories."

He pressed on. "The winter in France and the Battle of the Bulge were terrible, and we were tested daily...the cold, the snipers, the German artillery. But as the weather improved, we attacked in Alsace-Lorraine, moved ahead to the Siegfried Line, and then crossed the Rhine in March. Our battles were now on German soil, and the fighting was vicious...Nuremberg, Worms, Bamberg. And we finally crossed the Danube in April."

He looked down again at the framed picture and the box. Slowly, he turned to each of them the framed picture so they could all look at it. "These guys, the nine of us, were together for almost all of the time over there. There's Biff Parker, me, Tony Antonetti, Ellis Cass, and Tim Curry," he said, pointing to each of the kneeling soldiers. "There are Lewis Clinton, Neeves Jackson, and Stan Goldman. They were part of the original gang. They didn't make it to the end, to Bavaria and to the end of the war. I miss them. I mean, I miss all of them, not just Clinton, Jackson, Goldman."

John was speaking slower and more deliberately than they were used to. It was a John Langford they hardly knew. They could see that he was trying to choose his words carefully.

He fumbled on. "It's funny…about time. We were fighting in Europe for less than one year, just about eleven months. And it was a long time ago. Sometimes, I can't remember what I did just last weekend, but I think I can remember every day of the war. When I came back, I went off to college, met Mom, and got married. I started a business, we raised a family…but the noises, smells and sights, the people, the places, the landscapes, I can still remember. And I can tell you that even now, the images of some of those days in France and Germany are as if they happened yesterday. These guys, the guys in the picture, they saw what I saw; they went through what I went through. They were the family I had over there."

John's eyes were cast mostly on the framed picture, but he looked up between sentences to consider his family's reaction. He saw that they were locked on his every word, and they knew he was committed to telling his story accurately.

This was not the Langfords' typical time after dinner when they scattered to finish homework or talk on the phone. Usually, the television would be on by now, and they'd lie on the floor or the plaid sofa with pretzels and drinks. Tonight, nobody spoke but John.

Taking in another big gulp of air, he moved ahead. "Okay, I think you can, sort of, imagine the fighting in the countryside, in the smashed villages, the rubble, the homelessness and the burnt houses. You've seen pictures of Omaha Beach, fleets of B-17 bombers overhead. The movies try to tell the story, but they don't come close to capturing the chaos, fear, boredom, violence, and sudden death. Nothing can explain the sounds of artillery barrages or too-close rifle fire.

"You can picture the endless walking, the freezing cold nights, the wet blankets. Some of those experiences are like when we go camping."

Blowing out his cheeks and exhaling, he continued. "It would take me a very long time to tell you about all of the fighting…the dead and dying…the worst living conditions, the officers, the mistakes, the good luck and the bad luck, the heroes, the injuries, and losing your best friends." His solemn face shifted into a small smile. "There were also pranks, performances sponsored by the USO, cognac, and letters from home.

"We can talk more at some other time," he promised. "We will if you want. Not tonight. I promise I will tell some of the stories, and I will tell you because I'm very proud of what we accomplished – what we fought for. But not tonight."

Now, he settled deeper into the armchair and wriggled on the seat cushion, as if he expected a bumpy road. He said, "Tonight, I want to tell you about Dachau. I want to tell you about how we liberated the German concentration camp, Dachau, on April 29, 1945."

John, with a tightened jaw, looked directly at Bobby. He said deliberately, "In the box on the table are weapons and some other German things. And Bobby knows that there is an envelope, and it holds a small piece of cloth."

He received back encouraging nods from his family, but it was clear that it would be a monologue. Questions or interruptions would be out of place.

Now, he slowed his movements and his words were further drawn out, but he looked only at the box. "This is the time that has stuck with me the longest, and it is the memory with the most painful details. My telling you about those times is something I've thought hard about, and I've debated whether you would be better off not knowing."

Growing even more somber, he continued, "I've wondered if I'd be better off keeping it to myself. But we're going to talk about it tonight. So here it is."

Cautiously John pressed on, recalling the details. "We bivouacked, set up a camp, and went to sleep the night before, April 28, in a field just outside of a small town in a pretty part of Germany. We all knew that the war was coming to an end. Our captain confirmed the scuttlebutt, the rumors, that the next day we would be moving forward to take hold of a prison in the town of Dachau.

"We knew that the Nazis had concentration camps. It's where they imprisoned captured soldiers, people from conquered countries, communists, and political enemies of Germany. We had heard about people being kept in camps, the enemies of the state. And we knew how Hitler despised the Jews.

"The next day, after a quick breakfast of K-rations, we assembled and, like always, moved forward to the east."

John shifted in his chair. "We walked in two files, one on each side of a paved road. The guys in the picture were in the front, and we marched on for a few miles. We began to smell something different in the air. It wasn't the normal smell of cordite...it wasn't the metallic, acrid, and sulfur burning odors, not ammonia, and it wasn't gasoline or sweat."

John uncomfortably went on. "It was more like a sickening rot."

He paused, and then began again. "About an hour later, we came to the prison's brick walls. There was barbed wire on top and guard towers."

John looked out the window to his right and saw pink buds, where in a few months, green apples would grow. "Already some other guys had gotten into a small firefight, a shootout, and after a few minutes they managed to open the gate. We expected a battle, but it was over quickly. Several dead Nazi soldiers were sprawled on the ground and near the towers."

His family could sense his careful calculation of what they had already learned about versus what he needed to share from his personal recall.

He declared, "I'm not going to tell you what I saw in any detail because it was so terrible, so troubling, so horrifying. You will need to trust me that it was madness...a nightmare...a view into hell that was beyond anything I had seen in all the months of fighting."

John was filtering from his memory what he could tell his family. He recalled visions too terrible to be spoken around his kitchen table. John would not share the worst that emerged in vivid detail from the darkness of his memory. He tried to press back into the recesses of his mind the contorted greenish bodies, the tangle of limbs and sightless eyes whose last vision of the world couldn't be described. He couldn't talk about it. Ever.

He looked back to the box as if it were the lone witness that could corroborate his story. It would be the fading box that ensured all he recalled would be true and faithful to the living and the dead.

"The prisoners wore gray-and-blue-striped clothing, work suits, like moth-eaten pajamas. The clothing – many sizes too big – hung off their shoulders. The fabric was torn and fouled. And the prisoners were thin, like living skeletons, really corpses."

He tried harder to find the words. "They looked like skinny birds. Everywhere we saw naked, broken bodies...even worse sights...in the buildings, in the road, against the fence. Train cars, small wooden freight cars with sliding doors were open, and there were bodies there, too."

Like he was surrendering to his remembrances, he said, "There was a stench from the rot, the decay and, and...some of the prisoners had died just that day, probably because the Nazi guards wanted to finish their job."

John now looked directly at Bobby. "As we walked through the camp, we came to a young man lying against a wooden building. He was struggling for air...wheezing and choking. I knelt down next to him and held his shoulder. His breathing was rapid and shallow. He tilted his head and looked up at me with a gaunt face, protruding teeth, hollow eyes; he was too weak to stand and could only lean forward on one elbow."

John's eyes moistened. "His tattered prison uniform had a yellow star sewn onto the front, and he spoke only a few words." John said. "It could have been a question. I couldn't understand what he was asking, and it didn't sound like German. I guess he wondered why the rescue took so long."

John lifted his right hand from the edge of the box, imitating the young man's lethargic actions recalled from decades before. The gesture conveyed the effort and strain, "As I reached down to him, he stretched out to me his bony arm and hand. He was filthy...his lips were cracked. I looked right into his filmy eyes."

He returned his hand to the table and finished, "The very edge of his grey and white sleeve tore away and he fell back slowly... almost drifting to the ground...and died before me."

With steady and audible inhaling and exhaling, John said, "I tucked that piece of his garment into my jacket pocket. For some reason, I couldn't leave it in the decay, mud, and dirt. And later, I put the shred of his garment into an envelope and into the box that you found in the attic."

Nancy and the girls had tears running down their faces, and they tried to wipe them away. They didn't have any tissues or handkerchiefs on hand.

John asked, "Should I go on?"

Nancy simply nodded yes. She wanted John to finish what he'd begun.

John went on now, trying to finish his catharsis. "I don't know who the young man was, and I don't know what happened to his remains. We'll never know about him or his family. I now know that he was Jewish because of the yellow star patch."

John tried to explain, "We GIs didn't even know what the patches meant as we worked our way through the camp. It was the identifying badge that the Germans forced all the Jews to wear. There were dead and dying people everywhere, just like him...thousands and thousands."

With this darkest recollection now shared, they felt John's tension ease just a bit. He said, "This wasn't at all like the dead German soldiers we'd pass along the road, next to a burned-out tank or in a trench. These weren't the soldiers who we fought. These were the captives…victims of the Nazis."

He looked up and out the window again. The sunlight had completely disappeared, replaced by night. "In Dachau I saw awful things, I saw the ovens and the piles, the stacks of the dead…twisted and naked."

He paused longer than before, and with a blank stare said, "I think that is enough tonight."

Bobby guessed his dad was relieved, knowing that he had finally told his story about Dachau to his wife and children and had completed a task that he had long considered. Bobby imagined John had felt he owed the young man who died in his arms a eulogy, and now it had been delivered in a farmhouse kitchen in Indiana.

Bobby thought that his mom was probably aware of his dad's war experiences, and she could appreciate the load he'd just taken off his shoulders. She seemed proud that he had so courageously overcome his trepidations.

"Two more things that I want to tell you about," he went on. "The next day, before we marched east, our army rounded up people from the town of Dachau and made them walk right through the middle of the camp. These people, who lived within a mile of the sights, sounds, and smells of Dachau, in their suits and ties, and dresses and pocketbooks, saw full evidence of the atrocities. They saw what we saw. Now, they were witnesses too.

"Second: back here, when the war began, and even before, we saw newsreels about Germany's conquest of France, Czechoslovakia, and Poland. I even remembered a story about Kristallnacht, an early attack on German Jews, and we knew how much Hitler hated them."

John looked pensive, rubbing his finger on the tabletop. "When Pearl Harbor was bombed…we, my buddies and me, were all caught up in patriotism, we felt a real sense of wanting to fight for our country. The Germans, Japs, and Italians were the enemy. We didn't know much about anti-Semitism, nothing about a Holocaust.

"When we liberated Dachau, we really didn't know who the prisoners were. So little was understood, and the drama and chaos were overwhelming."

John, still rubbing the table's edge, stood up and prepared to end the intense evening.

Looking out the window, he quietly explained, "I didn't understand anti-Semitism. Not as a kid, not even as a soldier. Sure, I heard Jews called names, not often, but I did. It wasn't something my parents did."

John added, "It was only after the war that we learned about the six million."

Retired sergeant John Langford nodded to his beloved family, then walked up the stairs to the attic and put the box back on a shelf. The framed picture of his pals, though, he took to his office.

Bobby never asked his dad for more details about Dachau, but that night, he began to see how his father's war experience had affected his family. Facing the horror of war, John chose to keep faith with one young man who died in his arms. That anonymous man's legacy was theirs, too.

5
Toboggan Run

In the overheated eighth-grade classroom, Bobby Langford sat back gazing out at the falling snow. What had begun as a few lazy, random flakes was now blowing steadily and sideways. He whispered across the aisle, "Matt, do you see it piling up? The road is already covered!"

Matt twisted his blue flannel shirt collar and mouthed almost silently, "You bet, yeah."

All the kids were peeking out through the tall, four-pane windows at the accumulating white. They were hopeful the morning forecast and the 1971 almanac's prediction of a brutal winter would come true. If that was the case, school would be closed tomorrow, and the prospects for a three-day weekend looked good.

Tommy and Warren, buddies of Bobby and Matt, heard the snow tapping harder against the glass. The wind, now whistling under the eaves, proved that it was no flurry, but rather the beginning of a big Midwestern storm. Tommy, sitting a few seats ahead, rolled his head back and opened his eyes wide, signaling his wholehearted support for a world-ending blizzard.

Mr. McDowell's geography class was one of Bobby's favorites, and the discussion about the Panama Canal with the raising and lowering of the boats through the locks was interesting. All of Bobby's classmates now had to balance their weather-related curiosity with the need to focus on the Culebra Cut and Lake Miraflores.

Teachers could hit – and a hardwood ruler to the knuckles was not uncommon. Mr. McDowell, one of the few male teachers and much tougher than the women they'd had in the past, continued with the lesson. His hawk-like eyes darted behind wire-rimmed glasses, watching for the provocative, distracted, or dozing student.

A popular rumor was that he had been a military prison guard. While not much taller than some of the boys, his barrel chest, brawny forearms, and small, deep scar on his forehead made him a convincing bull. The boys feared him. In their daydreams, they found themselves in his crosshairs as they made an imaginary break over the wall to freedom.

Despite his intimidating demeanor, he was a very good teacher and wanted his efforts to be appreciated. Around the town, he was quick with a hello and would readily engage in cordial small talk. But in his cellblock, the classic red brick schoolhouse with a bell on top, you knew you'd better stay in line.

The air in the aging school building was redolent with a fresh coat of preservative oil treatment on the wooden floors and the mimeograph's sweet-smelling ink.

The coal fire stove, roaring below in the dark basement, warmed the black cast iron grates that sat in the center of the room. Bobby was careful walking on the grate with its curlicue design. Ever since he'd seen the floor louvers in the first- and second-grade classrooms, he'd imagined one giving way to his hundred pounds, causing him to slide down sooty pipes and onto red-hot coals.

The plastered walls held pull-down maps, blackboards, President Nixon's portrait, and framed bulletin boards. Coats, hats, and scarves hung on curved hooks screwed into a board topping the wainscot along the walls in the anteroom. Lunches, eaten an hour ago, had been stored in dented pails or brown bags under a long bench along with the students' boots. When the yellow school bus came over the long hill and pulled to a stop, the kids would stream into the anteroom, gather their belongings, and race out the door.

The black rotary phone on the front wall rang twice. Everybody guessed it was the snowstorm announcement, and they quieted, listening for hints. Mr. McDowell stepped away from his desk, put down his pointer stick, and lifted the phone from its cradle. The class heard him say, "Hello. Okay, okay, sure, sure, we'll be ready. Thank you. Goodbye."

It was only an hour before school would normally end, but the district superintendent had decided to shorten the day. Backed-up, slippery country roads were a danger. It was too soon for plowing or sand spreading, and the administration wanted all home before dark.

Mr. McDowell put the phone back and slowly said with a raised voice, "Announcement. Announcement. We're shortening the day; buses will be here soon, and schools will be closed tomorrow. Get ready."

The classroom broke out in happy chatter, but he didn't object. Already, Bobby had gotten up and was looking out the window at the disappearing horizon. The trees along the road began to disappear into the white landscape.

"Class, back to your seats," Mr. McDowell instructed. "It's your lucky day, and your long weekend," Mr. McDowell confirmed. "Okay, grab your belongings, and the buses will be here in about twenty minutes."

It was going to be a long weekend for the teachers as well as the schoolkids. Mr. McDowell began wedging papers into a worn, dark brown leather case. An uneaten banana blocked the way.

The snowstorm would mean that tomorrow the kids would be out shoveling snow from driveways and sidewalks. Some would earn a few dollars from older neighbors, and some would just help their parents. Bobby would be busy in town collecting some decent cash for his shoveling efforts. As a player on the Pop Warner football and Little League teams, he already was recognized as dependable. Because of his size, nobody doubted his ability to do the hard work.

For years, Bobby and his buddies had enjoyed sledding on nearby hills. Between the cemetery and the fruit tree nursery, there were steep slopes leading down from the road to a frozen creek bed.

When the snow was packed down, their Flexible Flyer sleds could zoom and weave over the frozen white at remarkable speeds.

However, the guys had a nagging feeling that they were getting too old for this kind of wintery fun, so they planned to step it up a notch. Bobby and his pals had been working on a downhill variation that would increase their speed. The grand plan also involved sneaking some alcohol from their parents' liquor cabinets.

Some of the guys had already tasted swigs of whiskey from their fathers' glasses or sneaked beers from a refrigerator. The notion of forbidden fruit stoked their curiosity and added a new dimension to their adventures. Maybe they preferred the taste of root beer or a malted milk shake, but they yearned to try the hard stuff.

During Tommy's dad's Christmas party, Tommy had attentively watched the stack of gift boxes accumulate near the tree in the den. He carefully hid one tall and skinny one deep in the back of his closet and waited to see if it would be missed. It wasn't. Tommy opened the box and saw a Jameson whiskey bottle, which he stashed away for the right moment.

Bobby came up with the idea to trek through the snow to the top of Dawkins Hill. It was an idea that predated today's snowfall, but now the significant accumulation turned the idea into a plan. At the summit, the five of them planned to share a full bottle of whiskey.

Two weeks before, Bobby's dad John had driven him over to meet the Baransons and their son Daniel. The family was new in town, and John had met David and Shelley at the last Town Merchants Association meeting. On the way over, John explained, "The family is new to Indiana. David bought some kind of tool-manufacturing business out here. I'm pretty sure they're Jewish, and they have a son and daughter. The son, Daniel, is your age, and I understand he also plays football."

Daniel being Jewish wasn't an issue for Bobby. His mom and dad were both active Christians, and the pastor had talked about anti-Semitism. Over the years, the Holocaust, the Eichmann trial, the movie and book *Exodus*, and the Six-Day War were discussed at church. The pastor gave sermons about their Jewish Jesus and the ancient and modern gifts of the Jews. Most significantly, Bobby vividly recalled his conversation with his dad about Jewish victims in the Holocaust.

When they were introduced, Bobby noticed Daniel was a little shorter than average, but was broad-shouldered and moved agilely like a good athlete. He had wavy black hair, a slight cleft in his chin, and dark, intense eyes. Mr. Baranson, after a few moments, introduced his son. "Bobby, here's Danny, he prefers it over Daniel."

Bobby nodded his head and shook Danny's hand. "Hey, Danny, nice to meet you, welcome."

Danny smiled and nodded politely. "Glad to meet you too."

Bobby and Danny explored the new home's property. The backyard had a few bare apple trees, and there was a retaining wall that melded with a small, weathering barn's foundation. They slid the barn door to the left and poked in. Bobby noticed in the back of the barn that now served as a garage a long, honey-colored, multi-slat toboggan. It sat shoulder to shoulder with garden tools, skis, and a set of golf clubs.

The middle slat was painted red, making it look like a British racing car. It had a curved front that turned back on itself like a *j* and looked long enough to hold about five or six people. There was a knotted rope that the riders could use to pull it up a hill, over the snow to its launching site.

"Hey, that toboggan is neat," Bobby said. "Have you used it before?"

Danny answered, "My dad and I rode it twice, when we lived in New Jersey. Lots of fun…it can really fly."

Although Danny was going to another school closer to his home, the boys shyly shared words about getting together soon as they parted.

Bobby, when he next saw Tommy, mentioned his introduction to the Baransons. He told him, "Danny seemed like a good guy." He described Danny's new house, the old barn, and the toboggan. He added, "I'm betting that Danny joins the junior varsity football team in the fall."

That piqued Tommy's interest. "What position would he play? Think he could be a running back?"

On the way home from school, while the school bus cautiously wound its way through the dim, blustery countryside, Tommy and Bobby sat together. Bobby outlined the grand plan. He described it in quick phrases. "All of the guys, after our shoveling is done, somehow gather up at Dawkins Hill." Bobby added, "We can get Danny to bring the toboggan."

Tommy contributed, "I'll bring the hooch. It'll be a wild toboggan ride down the long hill." Tommy and Bobby jumped out of their seats and shared the grand plan with Matt and Warren. The bus driver admonished, "Sit down, come on, you know the rules."

As soon as he got home, Bobby would call Danny, and their plans would be set.

The snow continued all Thursday night and into Friday morning. It was a wet, dense snow that quickly packed down and was hard to shovel. It wasn't the light, flaky kind that you could just push away or that blew around into drifts. With every shovelful you could feel the weight of its wet, almost sticky composition.

Bobby, Tommy, Matt, and Warren carved out pathways and driveways, digging down to concrete, asphalt, or grey slate stones. One by one, cars started up, and when the street plows came through, they were liberated. Drivers and passengers could head out on errands or go to work.

The guys exchanged calls and agreed to meet at Memorial Park at the edge of town before walking the last half-mile to the foot of Dawkins Hill. Danny would bring the toboggan, and Tommy would have the Jameson carefully protected inside his two sweaters.

In the late afternoon dusk, they all met. Bobby was relieved to see Danny with the rope in his gloved hand pulling the yellow toboggan. Bobby made the introduction, saying, "Guys, this is Daniel, er, Danny, he's new to Dawkins."

The boys exchanged quick, friendly greetings.

"Nice to meet ya."

"Hey, great sled."

"Welcome."

Tommy spoke up, "Really nice of you to haul over the toboggan, glad you came to Dawkins." Tommy reached into his coat, showing off the green-tinted bottle with its parchment label. "Here it is, boys, want a taste to warm up?"

The park was deserted, but still he looked around to see if anyone might wander through. Danny was the only one who didn't know about the drinking aspect of the evening's agenda, but he was not put off. With a smile, he readily joined in on the conspiracy.

The Jameson cork stopper pried out easily. The bottle was passed around. Grimaces betrayed the shock of the whiskey's bite. Like good actors, they each followed the swallow with a satisfied "ahhh." Now, all five turned together and headed east and upward to the top of the hill.

In twenty minutes, they reached the peak, and a second round of Jameson was shared as a reward. It was cold, and the esophageal warmth that the whiskey delivered was comforting. Tommy parked the bottle in the fresh snow next to the big pine tree. He wasn't going to risk breaking it during the ride to the bottom. Looking for the steepest gradient, the guys pointed the toboggan to the west and clumsily climbed on. Danny called a brief halt to the action and showed the others how to sit nested together, each boy with his legs around the person in front of him. It now looked right.

On over two feet of fresh snow, the toboggan slid downhill, but the ride was tame. Their combined weight held the sled deep into the snow, so the curved front struggled to push ahead through it. Looking back up at the carved path, the three-hundred-foot depression was easy to see. Danny promised, "It will be easier, faster on the next run."

Up the guys climbed, back to the top and back to the Jameson. Again, with the ritual now established, the bottle came out, the top twisted off, and around it went. "Good, very good," they fibbed. Again, the guys maneuvered the toboggan into place, and they climbed on with legs placed properly. This time, the toboggan picked up more speed on its previous tracks, and the groove got a little deeper.

"Wow, that's better."

"Wonder just how fast we can go?"

"Getting good."

At the bottom, just before the toboggan stopped, the five rolled out to the right and into the small snow bank pushed up by the toboggan's edge.

They spent the next hour sledding down over and over again. The whiskey now tasted better, their stomachs felt warmer, and a very nice, amusing dizziness was coming over everyone. The guys could smell the sweet, smoky whiskey on each other's breaths. The speed of the downhill racers increased on each descent. Now the groove that the toboggan raced in was almost a foot and a half deep, the bottom of the trench icy smooth.

When Tommy tilted the Jameson bottle to gauge its content, he saw there was just a one-inch-high wedge sloshing around. Tommy hollered, "Laaassst round, buddies."

The boys each took one last drink. Tommy returned the empty bottle into its cold, cylindrical place of honor in the drifted snow next to the pine. This would be the final run. Words were now slurred, movement less graceful, and getting aboard the wooden rocket was awkward.

Down they came, and the speed seemed even more out of control. Trees whizzed by now, the grey snowy shapes bereft of details.

Bobby, sitting third from the front, felt his right leg loosen its hold in Warren's lap. There was nothing he could do. They were about two-thirds of the way down, and the speed was at its maximum. Bobby's leg sprung outward and jammed into the snow bank, which in the freezing temperature had hardened into a concrete channel. The momentum of the five boys flying down the hill catapulted Bobby out of the toboggan. Unbalanced, the toboggan nosedived to the left and spat the boys out above the channel.

Immediately, Bobby felt a sharp, hot pain in his right knee. Facedown in the snow, Bobby almost vomited from the searing pain. Maybe the whiskey had dulled other senses, but the throbbing, stabbing sensation was too real. Light-headed and disoriented, Bobby tried to stand up. He couldn't put weight on the leg. It burned.

Tommy came running back up the hill to Bobby. He cried out, "Yikes. What happened? I saw you fly out. What a crash!"

Bobby almost couldn't speak. "My knee, my knee…I must have broken something."

Some of the guys were laughing hysterically, not realizing that Bobby had been hurt. The slapstick crash was the perfect way to end the boozy mayhem. But one by one, they noticed Bobby writhing in agony in the snow.

Matt edged in and asked, "Did you hit a tree or a rock?"

Danny and Tommy saw Bobby bent at the waist holding his lower leg. It looked bad, and they guessed he had badly twisted his knee. The reality of their problem was beginning to emerge through the cold and the whiskey. Slowly, they each realized now that they were in trouble. The group grew silent. They all knew the storyline was going to include drinking, getting caught sneaking around, recklessness, and someone getting hurt. Not good.

Danny squatted down close to Bobby's head and surveyed the situation. He saw the only way forward. He told the group, "Look, I'll take Bobby back to my house on the toboggan. My house is the closest."

Because of the snow and the waxed boards, hauling Bobby half a mile would not be a problem. The toboggan now became a stretcher. Danny said, "I'm sure my dad will know what to do. Maybe you'll have to go the hospital."

Danny reassured them, "Guys, I can take care of this. You head home and tell your family the story, but try to skip the part about the Jameson. Sober up. It was an accident, and nobody did anything wrong. Not too wrong, anyway."

The boys headed back to the main road toward home. With heads down, they felt the light-headed, swimming effects of the alcohol. They processed the day's combination of adventure, mayhem, and sudden consequences. Walking in the cold would soon sober them up.

Danny dragged Bobby home.

It took almost forty minutes, since he was still tipsy. Bobby and Danny, in spite of not knowing each other much before that night, chatted the entire trip. They were trying to convince themselves that it was a bad dream and all would turn out fine. Who would have pictured Danny, like a sled dog, dragging a wounded pal home from their mission?

Bobby sighed, "God, I really hope a banged-up knee won't keep me from playing football."

Danny could hear the fear in Bobby's voice. He tried to sound as optimistic as he could. "Bobby, I'm sure the doctors can repair anything that's wrong. Lots of the pros get hurt, and they come back the next season. Let's wait and see."

Finally, they made it to Danny's house. When Danny's dad, David, looked at Bobby's deeply discolored knee, he knew Bobby had to see an orthopedist right away. He called Bobby's parents, who said they would be right over to pick him up. Inside Danny's house, not much else was said. Bobby just lay back on the sofa, looked up at the still ceiling fan, and wished that useless wish that the past hadn't happened. He knew his parents would take the drinking very seriously. He'd be grounded for a very long time.

As he sat sadly in the backseat of their station wagon with his leg straightened out, Bobby told his parents the entire story – the Jameson, the toboggan, and the crash. John and Nancy Langford were unpleasantly surprised, but they understood. John silently played back in his mind silliness, mistakes, and adventures from his boyhood, and he recalled how quickly ideas that seemed great could go wrong.

Bobby, shifting his weight looking for a comfortable position, sat quietly for a few minutes. He rolled down the window for a little fresh air.

Bobby broke the silence. "I was impressed with Danny. He stepped up, and he just knew what to do."

John and Nancy listened to Bobby go on about how Danny quickly and wisely handled the situation. They decided that now was not the time to address the drinking. They would wait until after the medical emergency was handled.

The next day, the doctor wedged the x-ray results onto the illuminated glass frame for the family to see. He explained that a lot of damage had been done to Bobby's right knee, to both cartilage and ligaments. He pointed to the shadowy evidence of a ruined joint.

There would be an operation, a cast, and months of rehabilitation. This injury would not allow Bobby to continue playing football. Bobby's parents concluded that this consequence was more than enough punishment for their son's misbehavior.

While it seemed at the time that only misfortune had come from that night in the snow, it was also the beginning of Bobby's lifelong friendship with Danny.

6 Three Brothers

Before the Baransons moved to Indiana, they had lived in Philadelphia. There, as a little boy, Danny had taken note that family events were filled with whispers and furtive glances. Many times, when he entered a room, discussions trailed off. He saw clusters of aunts, uncles, and grandparents with lowered heads mulling over uncomfortable puzzlements. It all hinted at a secret that was just too much for a youngster to understand. He thought maybe the subject was too complicated, too scary, or just something for adult ears.

In Philadelphia, Danny would spend time with his Grandpa Isaac, but he never grew close to him. Even when they were in the same room, his grandfather would rarely ask how he was doing in school, what teams he liked, or if he had nice friends; he wouldn't read books to him and his sister, Debbie. Grandpa Isaac was around a lot, but he was always absorbed in a sea of his own thoughts.

Isaac lived with his elegant wife Mina about a thirty-minute drive away in a neighborhood with many other Jewish immigrants. His heavily accented Polish-German English was difficult to understand. It was impossible to recreate without sounding as if you were mocking the man. He dressed mostly in three-piece suits, even on the hottest days. Danny and Debbie imagined Isaac and Mina had once lived in a spired castle, like the one at Disneyland, and they'd had stables filled with well-groomed horses ready for pulling a carriage.

He seemed more interested in talking with his children than with his grandkids. Danny couldn't remember seeing him laugh and, at best, he would acknowledge your presence with a sigh and a slow nod. With a high forehead, cheeks etched with deep creases, and a forceful brow, he was an imposing figure. He'd smile, but it felt forced. His smile only deepened his wrinkles and narrowed his eyes, accentuating his intense glare.

Over the years, Danny noticed his generosity. He was always handing out quarters to the grandchildren and their friends who came over. He was kind; playfulness just wasn't his way.

Danny also noticed that Grandpa Isaac had nervous tics in his head and shoulders and frequently tapped his foot on the floor. When Danny commented to his dad about Grandpa Isaac's austere manner, all he got back was, "It's okay. Let's give Grandpa Ike some time."

David and Shelley had moved from Philadelphia to Dawkins, Indiana, when Danny was fourteen. David established a mid-sized manufacturing plant, similar to what he had once owned in New Jersey. In most regards, the Baransons seemed just like everybody else who lived in Dawkins. Yes, being Jewish in this small Middle American town made them different, but while being involved in church was common, nobody was focused on one another's religion.

Most of the fathers of kids in Danny and Bobby's class had served in World War II. It was common for fathers to reflect on wartime. Danny's own father, David, was drafted in 1943 and served on the USS *Massachusetts* in the Pacific. He had told Danny about massive shore bombardments from the ship's sixteen-inch guns and weathering kamikaze attacks. However, David was waiting for Danny to be old enough to talk about other experiences his family had had in World War II.

Not too long after Danny moved with his family to Dawkins, Danny's dad walked into his bedroom and suggested, "Let's have a chat on the porch." David was carrying a longneck beer and a Coca-Cola between his fingers. Shelley and Debbie were away, so Danny figured his dad wanted to seize the chance for a private father-son talk. He imagined it had something to do with living in the mostly Christian community of Dawkins, and he was ready to bet that the subject of dating and intermarriage was on the agenda.

Instead, at long last, he heard the full story of Grandpa Isaac and Isaac's two brothers.

David sat on a lounge chair, but instead of sliding back in the thick, comfortable cushions, he sat on the edge. He bent forward to put his beer down on the coffee table.

David began, saying, "Danny, we're all settling in here at Dawkins. My business is working out well, and you kids seem fine with the local schools."

After a few bubbly gulps, he began to turn the topic of conversation to their family history. "You know that your family name back in Europe was Borinski, and you know that it was changed to Baranson when we came to America, but there is much more to tell."

Danny asked, "Dad, does this have anything to do with the story Bobby told me about his dad and the concentration camp?"

David didn't feel that Bobby's family story should be his starting point, so he sidestepped the question. He searched for an opening nugget of wisdom instead. "Somebody once told me that if you don't know your history, you're like a leaf that doesn't know it is part of a tree."

David went on. "There is part of your family's history you should know. I think it will serve you well someday. I want to tell you about your grandfather. He's not well now, and I think it would be good for me to tell you more about him."

Danny replied sullenly, "Dad, I'm sorry that Grandpa Ike is not well. I really never got to know him. I tried, but he didn't seem interested in me." Danny paused. "We just couldn't connect."

David ignored the too-familiar observation. "I want to tell you about his life. My father was born in Vienna, Austria. His father, Viktor, was born in Poland and eventually married an Austrian woman. I forget her name. Isaac had two brothers, Leon and Stefan. They would be my uncles. When they were younger, they all lived in Vienna and worked together in a small business. The families were close, and each had a nice home. And you need to learn about all three of them," David stated.

Danny answered, "Dad, I thought he only had one brother."

"No, he had two brothers, and one of them lived in the United States. That was Leon. You met him a few times. The two brothers were a little older than Isaac."

David inhaled and exhaled. "Leon's gone now, but their history, really our history, is worth hearing."

Over the next hour, David told Danny the Borinski family story. He described life in Vienna, and how Isaac's wife's family were citizens of Austria for many generations. The Borinski family had created a successful tool-manufacturing business, and while they weren't wealthy, they were quite comfortable. They even had developed a partnership with an American company located in New Jersey.

Danny was fascinated by his dad's depiction of their family's refined lifestyle in the beautiful city that included attending the opera, winter skiing, and summer travels throughout Europe. Danny imagined the beauty of the Austrian Alps, Sacher torte, gilded opera houses, and an elegant European capital.

David's narrative slowed as he talked about the late 1920s and early 1930s. David was retelling stories that his father had told, but it was as if he had been there. He talked about the growing concerns about the Nazi ascendancy during the Depression. Step by step, David told Danny how the family had watched the growing German menace metastasize into Austria.

He told him how, in 1934, Isaac made the monumental decision to take his family and his aging parents to America. David's tone grew dark as he described Isaac's desperate effort to persuade his brothers to join him. Leon and Stefan argued that the Austrians would resist the boorish ways of the Nazi party and that their family's service during World War I proved their loyalty. It would be appreciated.

David sat there, once again imagining the debates that must have transpired. He was concerned that since Danny had seamlessly relocated with his family from Philadelphia to Indiana, perhaps Danny wouldn't understand the enormity of Isaac's decision.

He elaborated, "In 1934, my parents sold their home and most of their possessions and took my grandparents and siblings to the United States. I was seven at the time, and I spoke some English that I'd learned in school.

"My father worked for the company in southern New Jersey that he had partnered with," David explained. "In fact, the owner of the company, a Christian named Charles Ingram, had sponsored Isaac and his entire family to immigrate. The sponsorship was critical and costly, but Ingram was a good man."

David flashed ahead to the soon-to-be disaster. "Danny, over time, they all saw that Isaac was right to leave Europe."

Almost as if the debate could still take place, David outlined the positions. "Isaac had begged Leon and Stefan to go with him. In 1934, just before Isaac left Austria, there was a Nazi uprising that was put down. He saw the signs both in Germany and Austria of Jew-baiting. It was beyond the level of European Protestant and Catholic anti-Semitism. The sad tale is that the rest of the Borinski family waited too long to leave Austria."

Because David was doing most of the talking, his throat was dry. He excused himself, soon returning with a second beer.

David recited, "On March 12, 1938, the Austrian government chose to forgo a plebiscite during which Austrian independence would have been chosen over a union with Germany. German troops had massed on the frontier, and the Austrian government capitulated to avoid bloodshed. In the Anschluss, Hitler took over Austria.

"Immediately, the streets filled with brown uniforms, and police started to wear swastika pins and arm bands. Nazi flags were everywhere." David described it as if he had seen it unfold in front of him.

Continuing the painful history lesson, David said, "And two days later, when Leon and Stefan opened their tool factory's front door, the first person to enter was a supplier, somebody that they had known for years, and who was now wearing the Nazi armband."

It was clear from the way he recited the details that he had heard that story many times before from his father Isaac.

"Years later, my uncle Leon recalled the icily delivered advice from the supplier. It was for all of the Borinskis to leave Austria – to leave within months."

"Up until the Anschluss, Leon and Stefan were sure the anti-Semitic menace in Germany could be kept from an independent Austria. They thought that the Austrian Nazi Party would be defeated in a national vote," David lamented.

As if reading from a script, David mechanically outlined the rest of the story. "Now, Leon, Stefan, and their families had to quickly escape from Nazi-controlled Austria. Chancellor Hitler himself came into the city on March 14. The cardinal of Vienna ordered the church bells to peel, and hundreds of German planes flew overhead. The atmosphere in Vienna deteriorated rapidly for the Jews, with new anti-Jewish laws, vicious street violence, and escalating theft. Jews were forced to perform humiliating public tasks.

"The Germans now required us to complete official *Verzeichnis über das Vermögen von Juden,* or 'Inventory of the wealth of the Jews.' These documents enumerated all our assets, including property, financial instruments, and even insurance policies. They sold as much as they could over the next six months to accumulate money and to somehow make their way to Venice and then to Geneva to make their way out of Europe."

After pausing to recall the details, David tried to fill in the gaps. "Danny, I understand they applied for visas and immigration to both Australia and the United States under the Polish quota. It turned out that they were Austrian on the mother's side, but Polish on the father's side. I don't know very much about their families, but Isaac and his brothers all had Polish passports.

"But here's where it gets confusing," David stressed. "For the visa application to the United States, again, a sponsor was needed. The sponsor would have to put up a sizable bond to ensure the immigrant wouldn't become a burden on the state."

Even sadder now, David tried to explain what happened. "Apparently, Mr. Ingram could only sponsor one more family. I don't know why. In August 1938, somehow in the confusion Leon was chosen over Stefan. Leon was, in fact, the younger of the two. We don't know how it was decided."

David wanted his son to envision the pressures. He painfully asked, "Try to imagine the tension, the panic, and the agony. It's hard even now to think about the choice and the sacrifice. It haunted your grandfather, and caused terrible trauma to Leon. Stefan and his family would have to find another way."

He pressed on, telling Danny, "We do know that during their stay in Geneva, Leon and his family completed the visas and immigration forms for the United States. They booked passage to Trieste, Yugoslavia, and from there, their plan was to sail to Cuba. They planned that when they got approval, they'd sail to America.

"Once in Havana, they waited for the opening of the 1939 Polish quota. Eventually, they were approved, having Ingram's sponsorship. They entered the United States via Miami sometime in the early fall of 1939."

Danny asked the inevitable question. "Where did Stefan Borinski and his family go?"

David's face grew forlorn. "Danny, I really don't know. I don't think anyone knows for sure. My father has told me that he imagines in the chaos they tried to travel from Geneva to Argentina or Hong Kong."

He knew his son would struggle with the imprecision and lack of closure. "The facts are not known. It seemed that they never left Europe. I don't think their story ever will be revealed. But we believe they died in the Holocaust."

He returned to speaking about what he did know. "Back here, both brothers, Isaac and Leon, struggled the whole duration of the war to uncover information on the whereabouts of Stefan and his family. It was nearly impossible."

Watching Danny's disappointment, he continued, "They worked hard to keep their families together and to earn a living.

"Danny, over time, the full horror of the Holocaust was discovered. The brothers blamed themselves for having abandoned Stefan and his family."

Hoping that Danny would understand the torment this caused his grandfather and great uncle, David added, "The reason you didn't see Leon more often was that he suffered a mental collapse a few years after the war ended, and on several occasions, he had to be hospitalized.

"Over the years, Leon was debilitated by acute depression. The family couldn't help him; nobody could. Until the day he died, he blamed himself for the death of Stefan and his family."

Cautiously, he elaborated, "He had a complex relationship with my father. Maybe Leon thought Isaac could have done more to obtain the second sponsorship. Maybe he was psychologically poisoned, not able to get away from what he imagined happened to his brother and his family. Even though it wasn't true, he was sure everyone blamed him."

David pressed on, "And your grandfather Isaac became responsible for the entire family. He suffered too. He has good reason to be a taciturn, anxious man. This pressure went on for decades. I've read about survivor's guilt, and the experts say that survivors feel they have done wrong by surviving when others did not. I'd guess that's part of it."

Danny watched his dad finish his beer and lean back in the padded lounge chair. David looked out into the dark yard, and then he turned his focus back to Danny.

He said, "I'm sorry if I gave you too much to think about. Just know that our family has had to overcome many obstacles, and we have survived."

Danny heard his dad's encouraging words, and he tried to visualize the story that he had just heard. From books he had read and movies he had seen, he could imagine the desperation of Stefan Borinski and his family as they sought a safe haven while in a life-and-death struggle to evade the Germans. Danny felt trapped just imagining it.

He imagined *film noir* scenes shot at distorted angles, recalling atmospheric, shadowy streets and intrusive facial close-ups. Sequences of letters of transit proffered by deceitful couriers flashed by; dirty hiding places and grim disappointments were spliced together. Knocks on the door, guttural demands, and blaring oscillating sirens flooded over him. However, now it wasn't a Hollywood cast; it was his family struggling to escape the inevitable.

Sitting in their safe screened-in porch in Dawkins, Danny felt his chest tighten. His view of the world was no longer so comfortable or predictable. Playing sports, dating, and college planning were all he had needed to worry about until now. The Baransons weren't religious, but now, Danny saw that his Jewishness had been determining his life all along.

7 The Weekend

Lounging in his second-floor bedroom with his feet propped up on a rickety, messy desk, Danny tossed aside his dog-eared Scholastic Aptitude Test preparatory book. Once again, he had forgotten the meaning of several vocabulary words, including the elusive *effulgent.* But the good news was that nine of the ten math problems he had tried were answered correctly. Preparation for the critical college entry test was coming down to the wire, and he needed the practice. Finishing his homework and SAT prep, he remembered to call Bobby about tomorrow's game.

It had been a few years since the winter toboggan accident, the knee surgery, and the end of Bobby's time playing football. He could have been a star, but he couldn't risk another hard impact to a damaged knee. The doctors had said no, and John and Nancy Langford didn't argue.

Danny needed to talk to Bobby about their weekend plans and work out rides. Maybe they would find dates to take to a movie or go to the Saturday night dance at the amusement park.

Danny jumped out of his desk chair, grabbed the doorway frame, spun to the right across the upstairs landing, and galloped down the staircase two steps at a time. Shelley, had she been home, would have hollered, "Danny Baranson, would you stop the stampede, please?"

The black Bakelite phone hung from the kitchen wall. A coiled cord attached it to its hook, and it was long enough for Danny to lie sprawled on the den's shag carpet floor while he spoke. He dialed. After a few rings, Bobby Langford answered.

Danny began, "Okay, let's figure out the plan. Coach Tallia wants us at the field house by five in the afternoon for the game against Plinkett. It'll be the same routine as the last three years: taping, stretching, the game plan, and his speech."

Bobby responded, "OK, makes sense."

"I'm still third string, but the new sophomore might boot me further down the bench. Could happen. I had a good practice yesterday, but on the last play of the scrimmage, I missed a block, and our QB got leveled. Coach was pissed."

Without waiting for a comment, Danny asked, "Bobby, are you bringing a date to the game? Have you worked up the courage to ask Meg out?"

Bobby sighed. "Nope. Danny, I don't think Meg is interested. She passed me in the cafeteria and didn't even say hello or nod. I'm going to the game by myself. There will be other friends around. Dad said I could take the car. I'll wait for you after."

Bobby joked, "Hopefully the coach will throw you a bone and let you stumble around out there."

Over time, Danny noticed that Bobby didn't need to have every detail of a plan worked out. Whatever happened, happened. He accepted surprises with grace and was amused by little screw-ups and missed opportunities. Bobby and Danny were good friends, and Danny's mediocre football skills were a source of well-deserved, good-humored ridicule.

Danny Baranson was no fleet-of-foot flyer, no knock 'em back powerhouse, but he stuck to football and loved to play. He'd get to play only when the game was a sure win. He loved the Friday night game ritual. He was part of the team. Walking together from the locker room past the fans and hearing the rapid-fire clicking of cleats on linoleum more than justified all the practice and the bruises.

The smell of wintergreen liniment for sore muscles and the sweaty saltiness of his helmet, pads, and uniform were all part of it. He was number thirty-nine; it was his identity for about ten Fridays each fall. The cheering crowd, the marching band, and the cheerleaders were the music; the green field, cut into ten-yard swaths, was the stage. The mere possibility of a heroic moment, the chance to rise to the challenge in front of family and friends, was the coveted prize. It was his senior year, and no doubt, he would not be playing ball in college.

Late in the fourth quarter, Dawkins led the Plinkett team by fourteen points. Coach Tallia came over, grabbed Danny's shoulder pads, and hollered, "You're in on the next set. Get ready. Go get 'em. Jimmy will be calling all runs, so head down and hang on to the rock."

The kickoff was handled by Davey Sherwin, who brought the ball out to the thirty-one-yard line. Danny felt Coach Tallia tap on his shiny purple helmet as he headed onto the gridiron with the offensive team. He must have had a ring on his finger, because Danny heard a staccato click accenting the hollow thwack of hand to helmet. It was his starter pistol; he sprinted from the sidelines to the assembly of ten other players in the middle of the field. They huddled up into a semicircle, facing second-string quarterback Drew Himmel, and Jimmy called, "Swift right – on three!"

It was the play where Danny would run between the guard and the tackle. With Jimmy's clap, they moved to practiced positions. "Seven, seven, three" was barked out. From his two-point stance, Danny lunged forward and saw Drew fake a move to his left and then pivot back. He felt the ball smack into his forearms and stomach. After three steps, he collided with their tackle, and he tried to slip past on the right. He almost did, but he was dragged to the ground. Danny had gained two yards.

On the next play, Drew faked a toss to the fullback and ran around the left end for a six-yard gain. On what would probably be the last play of the game, Drew pulled them into the huddle and called the same play that Danny had just run on first down. "Guys, swift right, on two!"

They gave a single clap in unison, and Drew growled, "Four, four, four, two." This time he broke forward with more power, grabbed the ball, and hit the opening. Danny broke free into their backfield and down the right sideline. He heard the screams and looked up to see an open field. He heard his own breathing. After running about fifteen yards, from his right, he heard footsteps and felt the impact as the other team's safety cut him off, driving him out of bounds and onto the turf. It was a first down, but the whistle sounded. It was the end of the game.

The team gathered back around Coach. Coach smacked the back of Danny's helmet again. He proclaimed, "Good work, kid. You looked real good."

It was all that Danny needed.

After showering and dressing, Danny came out of the main entrance into the clear night air and saw Bobby applauding. Bobby said, "Nice run there, champ. Betting you'll get more time next week. Got the car. Let's get over to Pop's and grab a burger."

It sounded good, and Danny hoped some of his teammates would be there.

Over the past few years since the toboggan accident, Danny and Bobby had spent a lot of time in each other's homes. Slowly but steadily, each boy learned about the other's family and religion. Danny had gladly joined the Langfords for Christmas caroling, and he vicariously enjoyed all the Christmas and Easter festivities. He liked the eggnog and chocolate Easter eggs, but he passed on the Easter ham. When Bobby came over to the Baransons, Danny explained the mezuzahs on the doorposts, the Hanukkah menorah, and the matzo at Passover. Bobby liked kugel and brisket, but he skipped the gefilte fish.

Bobby and Danny would ask each other careful questions about the other's religion, but avoided any topics that might lead to an awkward moment.

Among the boys' group of friends, the subject of religion rarely came up. Bobby noticed, though, that Danny dated Christian girls. Danny explained that it was only dating. He told Bobby, "Mom and Dad are pretty clear that I should marry a Jewish girl. I've gotten the message – I've had the talk. It's not that anything's wrong with girls who aren't Jewish. It's about passing on the heritage and tradition. It's just what they expect."

Bobby eventually shared with Danny the tale about the box in the attic. He edged up to it carefully, not knowing if Danny's family lost anyone in the Holocaust. He wanted to ask, since the attic discovery was so important to his relationship with his dad, but concluded for a while that the subject was off-limits.

When it came to Israel, Bobby mentioned that he'd read one thing or another about topics such as the Six-Day War, the Temple Mount, Palestinians, or the Suez Canal. They didn't focus very much on the Middle East or politics.

At Pop's, Danny received a few claps and hoots. Getting some grass stains on his uniform did wonders for his status. The place was packed, and they slid into a booth with two girls whom they hadn't met before. One of the girls wore several anti–Vietnam War buttons, and the other was a tall brunette who was focused on an art deco Rock-Ola Wallette Selector. After picking a letter and a number, she looked up and introduced herself. "I'm Carrie. Hello. This is Darlene." With a glance back to the Wallette she added, "We've got some good Roberta, Elton, and Carly coming up."

Red plastic baskets lined with waxed paper came loaded with salty fries and hamburgers. Danny and Bobby had to eat them right away to catch up with everyone else.

Carrie and Darlene were from Hilbrand High, and they talked about teachers and gossip that didn't mean anything to the boys. Together, they talked about the new movie *American Graffiti* and tried to match people they knew to the Richard Dreyfuss, Harrison Ford, Cindy Williams, and Ron Howard characters. It didn't work so well, because each didn't know the other's friends and neighbors.

They had fun jammed into the booth. There was a coziness and quick familiarity. Bobby spoke up, "Are you going to the dance at Wambush tomorrow?"

Bobby and Danny had talked about the end-of-season dance at the amusement park. Carrie looked at Darlene, and after a moment's thought, said, "Yes. Sure, we can meet you there. We might come with some other friends, guys and girls. Not one hundred percent sure, but we'll really try."

The scribbled bill came, and they scrambled through blue jean pockets to find the dollar bills and change. The four, single file, worked their way past the counter with the rotating stools to the front door and out of the diner. Danny noticed that the team's printed 1973 Dawkins football schedule had been Scotch-taped to the door, and saw that a *w* had been crayoned over the game against Plinkett. Darlene and Carrie joined up with two other girls in a white Ford Mustang, shouting out, "See you tomorrow!"

Around eight in the evening, Bobby picked up Danny for the ride out to Wambush Amusement Park. Danny appreciated Bobby driving him all the time; he didn't yet have a car, so it was his only option. He was saving up, though, and he was almost there. His mom and dad were all right with him buying a "safe" car.

Bobby brought him a clipping from the local paper's sports page. At the bottom, underlined in pencil, was a surprising mention: "…and the game ended on a nice run by Daniel Baranson."

The amusement park, a vintage classic, was decades old, well kept, and set attractively in a wooded area. The small buildings were neatly painted white, trimmed with dark green and bright yellow carved wood. From the late spring until early autumn, it offered a rumbling wooden roller coaster, haunted house, merry-go-round, bumper cars, and about a dozen other rides. There were little booths selling specialty foods that you couldn't regularly find, like sausage and pepper Italian subs, cotton candy swirling in aluminum tubs, corn on the cob bobbing in buttery boiling water, and corn dogs skewed on wooden sticks pointing skyward. Standards from the American songbook were played throughout the park on well-hidden metal speakers. It was fun for the entire family. The park even had campgrounds alongside a clear-running stream.

The Langfords, when the kids were little, went there at least once a season. Now, Bobby was more interested in it as a place to go with a date. It had a dance pavilion that opened on Saturday nights. It was round with a conical roof of cedar shakes, and it sat about four feet off the pine-needle–covered ground. The walls came about halfway up the sides, and then latticework continued the rest of the way up to the ceiling. It had four wide entryways leading to the dance floor. The pale, smooth wooden slats covered most of the space, except for one side where a raised platform could be used for a small band or a disc jockey. Even in these turbulent times of war, protests, and drugs, it was pastoral, Middle American innocence.

Boyfriends and girlfriends strolled hand in hand through the park's pine trees. The couples would walk together or congregate in small groups, while the unaffiliated rest milled about, trying to be cool and checking each other out.

Bobby was the first to spot Darlene and Carrie. The girls welcomed them, and the four chatted. Soon, more unattached friends emerged and began the delicate process of choosing and joining the active dancers weaving about on the dance floor.

Because unofficial Indiana social protocol called for fast dancing way ahead of slow dancing, you had to choose wisely. You had to predict the song sequence to end up with the "right" girl when the slow song came on. Within a few of these maneuvers, it was obvious that Bobby preferred Darlene, so Danny danced with Carrie. She looked great, she was a better dancer than Danny, and all was right with the world. Nothing between them had particularly clicked, and both knew they weren't the loves of each other's lives. It didn't matter, though. They just wanted to have a good time.

Carrie and Darlene introduced them to several friends from their hometown. They exchanged handshakes. Bobby knew several of them from his church events. The group sat together in some folding chairs in the corner.

Somehow, the conversation turned to the Vietnam War and the protestors. Jessie, one of the fellows Danny didn't know, volunteered, "My older brother finally got drafted and is leaving in a few weeks for induction and training." Jessie asked, "Is anyone looking to buy a nice 1970 Plymouth Duster? It's got the Slant-6 engine. He wants to get rid of it before he leaves."

Bobby jumped in, barking, "Danny, come on over here. This is for you."

Jessie turned his full attention to Bobby and Danny. "It's not perfect; it's got a few dents and dings. It's got a tan exterior, and the seats are black. Think it has nineteen thousand on it. The tires might be shot."

Jessie added, "He needs to sell it quick. I think he's asking nine hundred."

Danny asked Bobby, "Wanna see it with me? Are you around tomorrow? Can you get your dad's car?"

Bobby shrugged and answered, "Sure. You need wheels. I gotta stop being your chauffeur."

Jessie gave them the address, they agreed to meet at four o'clock on Sunday, and he and Danny shook hands.

The last two songs were old slow-dance standards. Bobby danced with Darlene, as he'd hoped. Afterwards, they said good-night and shared routine wishes to "see you soon." Bobby and

Darlene whispered something that sounded to Danny like plans for a date next weekend.

Heading home, Bobby's focus returned to the possible car purchase.

"I'll pick you up at three p.m. Let's hope it's a winner." He went on, "Ask your dad for the name of an auto guy to check it out so, if you like it, you can have it looked at on Monday or Tuesday."

For the rest of the ride back, their conversation turned to Darlene and Carrie and the rest of the football season. Danny thought to himself that Carrie was a little too hyper and a mechanical gum chewer, but totally tolerable. The discussion covered the full range of who was available, who liked whom, who was the hottest prospect, and what would be the right next steps.

The next day, Bobby arrived at Danny's house, and they headed off to meet Jessie's brother. Their destination was in the outskirts of Stellar Hills, a town east of Plinkett, and the ride took almost forty-five minutes. As they drove, they saw more factories and fewer farms.

They pulled into a rutted driveway that led around to a porch and the front door. Before they could knock, Jessie, two friends, and Jessie's brother Don came out. Don, sporting a Pancho Villa mustache, looked a lot like Jessie. They both were ruddy-colored, barrel-chested, and as tall as Bobby.

Jessie introduced Don, saying, "This is Danny and his pal Bobby. They're interested in the Duster. We all met last night at Wambush."

Don gazed at the two and then pointed his finger, directing their attention beyond the house. "The car is in the back."

Danny responded, "Great. Jessie told us about you and the army. All the best of luck."

Wanting to move the process ahead, Don pointed again to the Duster and said, "Take a look. She runs great. There's a dent in the rear fender and a couple of scratches. Go ahead, you take a look. Start her up, take her for a spin."

Circling the car, Danny stepped over a few oily puddles, noted the exterior flaws, and looked inside. It was clean. He slid into the driver's seat. As he rolled down the window, Don handed him the key without saying anything. Danny started her up, nodding his head to confirm that the revving engine sounded peppy.

Don encouraged them. "Go ahead – you and your pal – go take a ride, don't kill anyone."

Bobby jumped into the passenger's side, and they pulled out of the driveway onto the asphalt road. Both were impressed that neither Jessie nor Don joined in, letting them talk it over in private.

After ten minutes, they saw the car ran perfectly, and they circled back to return it to the driveway. Danny complimented Don. "It's a really nice car, and it rides great. As advertised."

Now came the tougher part, the price. Before Danny could say anything, Don volunteered, "It's a bargain at thirteen hundred."

Danny was surprised, because Jessie had said it was nine hundred dollars. Thirteen was more than he could afford. Cautiously, Danny said, "Don, last night Jessie said nine hundred."

Now, Danny was not certain of the true price. He wondered if Don was messing with him.

Don exchanged glances with Jessie and finally shot back, "Okay, how about eleven hundred."

Again, Danny's discomfort over the negotiation was growing. Finally, he said, "How about a thousand."

Don, with pursed lips and a grimace, retorted, "I guess I'm being Jewed down here, Jewed down to a grand."

That phrase, those implications – the words felt like an electrical shock to Danny. It was a thunderclap. The words rang in his ears. Danny's face felt red hot. In a fraction of a second, he asked himself if Don even knew he was Jewish.

It wasn't as if Danny was not aware of anti-Semitic diatribes. His mom and dad had prepared him with enough practical Jewish education to understand slurs like "kyke" and "Heb." He knew they were spoken. He knew about Jewish jokes and stereotyping. But in Indiana, he had found that most people were courteous and respectful.

Before Danny could move, before he could say anything, Bobby exploded. Maybe he felt responsible for dragging Danny into this situation.

He stepped forward, right up against Don, chest to chest. "I don't like that talk at all. Where the hell did you learn that?"

Don stood his ground but moved his head back an inch or two. He barked, "What the hell are you talking about?"

Bobby raising his voice more still, almost screaming, "My friend is Jewish, and we're not going to listen to that cheap, ignorant, hateful crap. Did you learn that talk from your lowlife parents?"

Don, red-faced and under attack, shoved Bobby back with both hands. "I don't need to take that from you and your *Jew-boy* buddy."

Bobby lurched back to Don and both began to throw punches.

Several of Don's punches landed before Bobby could connect with his own. Bobby's athleticism was now on display. He was a blur of motion, moving quickly to gain leverage, to fire off rapid blows, to block punches and get the best of Don. Both Don and Bobby were quickly locked in a wild wrestling match on the ground. In those seconds, Jessie, Don's buddy, and Danny jumped in to the fray. Danny had never been in a knockdown, drag-out fight like this before. A dozen quick punches were exchanged before it all came to a stop.

Bobby and Danny, two against three, fared the worst. They stood there out of breath, with bloody lips and eyebrows. Aligned across from them, the other three were dirty and bloody. Proclamations of "go screw yourselves" and "get the hell out of here" were exchanged. Nobody wanted the mayhem to escalate into anything more serious.

Bobby and Danny turned away and moved slowly and resolutely back to Bobby's car. All five knew that it was a deal gone wrong.

They drove off in shocked silence. Each was breathing hard. Danny could see that Bobby's lower lip was quivering. There was a strong, shared feeling of having done the right thing, the principled thing. The drama and passion of that moment trumped the football game of two days ago.

Bobby's knuckles were raw, and his shirt pocket was gone. Danny's shirt had lost several buttons, and his pants were torn at the knee. The adrenaline passed, replaced by quiet introspection. The only sounds were tires clicking over the road's tarred seams and the hum of the engine. They tried to process what had just happened. The fight itself was an instant gut reaction to offensive words, but its implications would linger with them.

Danny spoke first. He tried to lighten the mood.

"Bobby, am I a better boxer or football player?"

Bobby exhaled and chuckled. The tension melted away. "You were just fine, a tough guy. We were a good tag team." He added with a grin, "I don't know if we would have gone all ten rounds. You know, it was three of them and two of us."

"No chipped teeth, no broken noses, we're going to be okay," Danny assessed.

A few seconds passed. Bobby sighed, "We'll need a good story about the bruises and the shredded clothing to tell our parents."

8 The Pendant

It wasn't her reddish hair, her high cheekbones, or even her sparkling green eyes that caught college junior Danny Baranson's attention. It was the light from one of the many movie marquee's bulbs glinting off a small bronze pendant that made Danny notice her. He was standing in line, waiting to buy movie tickets to see Jack Nicholson in the 1975 comedic drama *One Flew over the Cuckoo's Nest.* It had come out several years before, but this small-town movie theater often showed old movies at discounted prices. When their lines converged in front of the ticket booth, he realized that her shiny pendant displayed an army tank topped with rounded olive branches.

Many weeks later, Danny again crossed paths with the green-eyed girl who had worn the pendant. He was at the Bloomington laundromat with a duffel full of clothes, an orange, and several engineering textbooks. At first, he didn't see her, but then, looking down a row of vibrating stainless steel dryers, he noticed her at the far end sitting on a bench. She was sitting alone, reading a book balanced delicately on her knees.

It was bitter cold outside, and her parka was folded into a pillow that was propped behind her back. Danny, normally quiet and reserved, walked right down the speckled linoleum aisle and said to her, "Hello, did you like the movie?"

She looked up from her reading and pleasantly but coolly answered back, "Okay, you got me. What movie?"

Danny now realized the odd asymmetry of the moment and explained, "Weeks ago, maybe a month ago, you were standing in line to see *One Flew over the Cuckoo's Nest.* It was a Saturday. You were…we were…at the downtown theater."

Danny sensed he was gushing with too much detail. He wondered if he sounded like a stalker. Was he making her feel uncomfortable? He started again. "I happened to notice your pendant, an army tank with some leaves."

This was no better.

"I'm Danny Baranson," he said simply.

It was now the moment when she could roll her eyes and close out the conversation, referencing the need to study for a big exam and wishing him a nice day.

Danny kept going, though. "You have a nice accent. European? German? Austrian?"

Her wet clothes still had twenty more minutes of drying to go, and she thought he was nice enough. He was pleasant-looking, and she decided to save him from himself.

"I'm Maya. I'm not German, not Austrian. I'm Israeli. And, yes, I really liked *One Flew over the Cuckoo's Nest.*"

She added, "Although, it was a very painful movie."

She stood up, straddling the bench, and reached out with a firm handshake. Danny noticed he was just about her height.

She patted the bench next to her. "Have a seat." With a smile, pointing to the round glass door of a revolving dryer, she joked, "Make yourself at home, you can watch my TV."

Now facing her, Danny noted how pale her skin was and how her stare conveyed a blend of intensity, caution, and openness. She faced him without any discomfort, no extra gestures, and maturity that surpassed other girls he knew.

Danny threw his leg over the bench and sat astride. He reached out, nudged her books, and asked, "What are you studying? What's the book you're reading? By the way, isn't Maya the Hebrew word for water?"

She replied with a teacher's precision. "Yes, Maya is related to *mayim*, meaning water."

With that short exchange, they managed to tactfully address the elusive question: are you Jewish? Now, they both knew the other most likely was. There was a realization of something that they had in common, an age-old bond. Both felt more at ease, pleased that they had successfully navigated the tricky social situation. They could both appreciate the delicate dances minorities perform to identify one another.

Maya asked, "Are your clothes ready to dry?"

Danny checked his watch. "Oops, thanks, let me check. I'll be right back."

He was now aware that Maya was very pretty, athletic-looking, and had an intriguing little smile. He was anxious to get back to Maya and her corner of the Bloomington laundromat. He was now less annoyed by the noises and the too-clean scent of soap, bleach, and overheated lint.

Danny returned with his wet clothes piled high in a yellow plastic basket. Danny and Maya were nearly strangers, and washing clothing was more intimate than was comfortable. Neither Danny nor Maya wanted underwear to be casually displayed, so additional care went into bundling and folding.

When Maya and Danny finished loading and dialing in the proper fabric settings, their conversation continued. Maya settled back on the bench and squared up her book. "So, this book. You wanted to know." She spun the book around and said, "It's *Introduction to Sociology*."

She added, "I'm a second-year sociology major. We'll see. I like it so far. How about you?"

Danny didn't answer Maya's standard collegiate "get the basics out there" question. Once again, he was drawn to the pendant. This time, it was affixed to the collar of her white oxford shirt, protruding above a blue cable-knit sweater. "Maya, that's an interesting pin. I never saw one like it. Why the army tank?"

This time, Maya didn't respond as quickly. Her bright green eyes turned slightly downward.

"It was my father's," she factually stated.

Danny sensed from her use of past tense and from her fallen expression that he should respect her privacy and not ask for any more details. It was awkward now, and Danny couldn't think of another question. He wished he'd asked about her professors, sorority affiliation, or summer plans.

Maya gathered herself. Withholding any emotional display, she told him, "My *abba* was in the Israel Defense Forces. He was a commander in the tank corps. In the Yom Kippur War of 1973, he was killed in the Golan, you know, near Syria."

She hesitated. "My *imma* gave it to me."

Danny was stunned hearing her personal revelation. As he sat there, he realized that not an hour ago, he had begun a conversation with a pretty girl about a movie, and now he was hearing a tragic chapter of her life's story from a world so different from his.

His experiences, for the most part, had been stamped out of a Middle American mold. The highlights were a fourth-quarter winning touchdown in high school, acceptance into Indiana University's honors program, and really not much more. Even being Jewish in Indiana had never been a real issue. He knew the pressure of being different, being a minority. But for the most part, he overcame the self-inflicted, self-conscious childhood difficulties of discovery and differences.

Battlefield chaos, the death of a parent, a heartsick mother, foreign travel, and a second spoken language were just the beginning of Maya's bold headlines. He was a little intimidated, but eagerly curious to see where this conversation was heading.

Maya had also been surprised that during a happenstance meeting, at a laundromat of all places, a first chat between two strangers so quickly and casually revealed so much. Was it because of him? Was it something that she wanted – or maybe needed – to talk about?

Following the unemotionally stated facts of the trauma, in her mind she now flashed back to a hillside in Israel, standing in the huge, silent crowd of soldiers and family. Green and tan uniforms were everywhere.

She recalled a haze of older men in white shirts and her grandmother and aunts standing right next to Imma. Maya felt loving hands on her shoulders, on the top of her head. She stared at puffs of dust at her feet stirred up by shuffling mourners. She felt the cool October air on her cheeks and heard the gathering's unified repetition of the Kaddish, the Jewish mourners' prayer.

Her reminiscences traveled back further to Tel Aviv, to her second-floor apartment just off Nachalat Binyamin Street. She imagined looking out from her bedroom, facing a small courtyard laced with droopy clotheslines. She could see metal shutters pinned back against the graying concrete walls. Tattered Israeli flags tied by wire to the wrought iron staircases rustled in the light breeze.

In this reverie, Maya was walking with Abba, holding onto his big hand as they wove their way through the shady covered Shuk Hacarmel heading downward toward the sea. They were going to see Savta Esther on Hayarkon Street. On their way through the *shuk*, Abba stopped dozens of times to buy, taste, and talk to the shop owners. He bought Maya an icy lemonade dotted with mint leaves and let her poke through a stall's collection of silly hats and T-shirts. They tasted morsels of halvah and bought a small bag of assorted olives.

Maya took pride that her *abba* knew so many of the merchants manning the stalls. He was so good at remembering their names and what was going on in their lives: a birth, a marriage, even a new apartment. He was so quick with a *mazal tov*. These were his stomping grounds, and he loved mingling with his friends.

Savta Esther's apartment was the next stop in her daydream. It was as if she was trying to transport herself to past times and to distant places. There she stood with her grandmother, chopping tomatoes, cucumbers, and parsley to toss in a wooden bowl. Maya breathed in the fragrances of all the ingredients. She saw framed photographs on the window's ledge, and from there, just beyond the tiny balcony, she could see small white waves rolling up and disappearing on the beach.

Just then, the first of her two dryers slowed to a stop, and clothes dropped to the bottom of the finned drum. The room's noise grew just a little quieter with one less motor grinding away and with one fewer set of buttons and zippers clicking against glass and stainless steel. The second drum came to a halt a moment later. Both Maya and Danny were now distracted. Maya scooped her dried clothes into a basket and carried them to a table for sorting and folding. Danny stayed seated on the bench, giving her a little space and privacy.

It was Maya who spoke next. "So, let's see your books. What are you studying?"

Danny was thrilled that she was starting up more conversation, but tried to play it cool. "Okay. I've got a bestseller here, *Algorithms*." He added, "This page-turner is *Computer Methodology*. I'm studying computers and electrical engineering, third year."

He opened up the second volume and showed her a page displaying complex graphs and arcane formulas. Looking to minimize the nerdiness of his discipline, he said, "It's a grind, but it's really interesting. Hard to believe, but it is."

Maya nodded. "I can't imagine how difficult all the math and science must be. It wasn't my thing at all."

Danny judged that their serendipitous Bloomington laundromat time together was coming to an end. Maya's laundry was now packed carefully into her flowered fabric tote bag. In a minute, she'd put on her parka and head out the front door. Then she would head home, wherever that was. It was going to be his responsibility, his choice to negotiate the next step. It would be a tricky maneuver. He didn't know if she would be interested, or if she had a boyfriend. He didn't know very much about Maya.

Danny took the initiative and courageously said, "Maya, I'd like to see you again. You know, because I've never spent time with anyone from Israel. Could I call you?"

Maya's answer was, "Of course." The crisp answer was accompanied with an ever so slight affirming nod of her head.

Danny would come to learn that Israelis use the English phrase "of course," or *betach* in Hebrew, as an equivalent to "okay" or "sure."

She brushed back her red hair with a woolen-gloved hand and wrapped her arms around the tote bag. "My number is in the directory. Maya Schein." She spelled it out. Then she headed out the door. Her tone was even, but in the reflection of the glass, Danny caught her smiling to herself.

9 The Concert

At Danny's apartment on Summerlien Street, he looked for the spiral-bound student directory in his roommate Rudy's over-packed, ceiling-high bookshelves. Danny managed to find it on the left end of the second highest shelf, just below a pyramid of empty beer cans. The directory, with Maya Schein's phone number and address in it, had been jammed in with frayed takeout menus, bus schedules, and course catalogs.

His other apartment mate, Gino, worked part-time for the IU Student Association. His real name was Eugene Mulligan, but he preferred the shortened, Italianesque version.

Gino and Rudy were two good guys whom he'd met early on in McNutt Hall, one of the school's freshman dormitories. They were all in engineering programs, and they roomed on the third floor at the far end. Their windows overlooked the tightly mown quadrangle, dotted with frisbee players and crosshatched with pebble pathways. Together, they'd study, play basketball, and share late-night delivered pizzas. For different reasons, they had not joined fraternities and moved to off-campus housing in their sophomore year.

Rudy was from hearty Lithuanian stock and was by far the most prodigious drinker of the three of them. Danny loved to describe how when they were freshmen, on a bet, Rudy chugged half a bottle of cheap vodka and had not *died*. Although to be fair, he was sick for three days.

Rudy prided himself on his collection of imported specialty beers. From European beer meccas such as Germany, England,

Ireland, and Belgium, he had assembled an impressive array of Pilsners, lagers, ales, and porters. Like a museum docent, he'd point out the arcane details of ingredients, alcohol contents, and ages of the brewery. He treasured the empties, treating them respectfully as the heroically deceased.

In spite of several upcoming challenging exams, Danny couldn't stop thinking about Maya. He contemplated where to take her. A first date required careful planning: not too formal, not too casual. In two weeks, the famous Ray Charles would be performing at the Creek Center, and if he could get tickets, it would be perfect. It would be a mellow scene, and Danny envisioned a coffee house afterwards.

After a few days of searching, Gino used his connections at the Student Association and came through with two "VIP holdback" tickets.

Now, it was up to Danny to make the telephone call. On the third ring, Maya picked up. "Hello, Maya Schein."

Danny felt jittery at the sound of her voice. He tried to sound nonchalant. "Hi, Maya, it's Danny Baranson. We met a week ago at Bloomington Laundry."

Maya said, "Sure. I remember. We had a nice talk."

Danny was grateful she didn't mention her pendant. He was still unsettled thinking about her deeply personal admission about losing her father, although he hoped to find out how that might have brought her to study at IU. While Maya didn't appear defeated, lonely, or fragile, he could not avoid thinking her loss left her wounded. He sensed vulnerability, but at the same time recognized a hardened maturity beyond her age.

He went on, concurring, "Yeah, I enjoyed talking with you. I've been dug in prepping for several tough tests, so I didn't have a chance to call until now, but I wanted to ask if you'd like to go out. Would you like to go with me to the Ray Charles concert next Saturday?"

Before Maya could respond, Danny pressed on, "You know about it? The one on the twentieth at eight...the tickets sold out... did you see the flyers?"

He heard himself overselling and worried he was rambling too much. He waited anxiously for her next word, her next sentence.

Maya answered, "Very nice. Yes. Of course."

There was that "of course" again. Was it *of course! I'd love to see you again*, or *okay, I'll attend the Ray Charles concert*?

She added, "I don't know too much about his music, but what I do know, I like."

With a smile that she couldn't see, he closed with, "Great, great, I'll pick you up at your dorm lobby at seven and we can walk to the Creek Center together."

Success. It was a short but friendly interaction.

Danny was glad that he had chosen not to ask any routine questions about her courses, tests, or professors. He liked the way she talked and sensed he'd be better off waiting until they were together for any extended conversation. Her accent, with its speedy tempo, was intriguingly exotic, but interpretation was tough sometimes. Face-to-face would be better, so he could follow her words and her perfectly beautiful lips.

Walking past the faux-leather furniture seating areas in Maya's dormitory lobby, Danny again was struck by her loveliness. Now, unlike when they were at the laundromat, she wore makeup, earrings, and a headband. Danny thought to himself how beautiful she was. She walked lightly, and with her subtle smiles and furtive glances, he was convinced she was happy to see him.

They entered the flow of other couples heading to the concert. Footfalls in the slush and gravel from all the spontaneous marchers created a soothing, syncopated background rhythm. It was late November, and they'd just had their first snow of the season. It was icy in spots, so he guided her elbow to the left or right to ensure she didn't slip.

Walking along the campus streets and under the swaying, clicking branches of leafless trees, he asked her, "How familiar are you with Ray Charles?"

Danny couldn't imagine what music she had heard as a young girl in Israel. He remembered cantorial performances in his small synagogue. At a few bar mitzvahs and weddings, relatives danced the hora to "Hava Nagila." While he was far from an expert in the American music scene, he wanted to be helpful; he wanted her to enjoy the show.

Maya answered simply, "His singing is wonderful and emotional. I've heard many of his recordings."

Maya asked with a knowing smile, "Danny, do you know *any* Israeli music? Besides 'Hatikvah' or 'Hava Nagila'?"

He blushed. She had sized him up very well. Maya went on, "Our music scene is evolving. There were lots of folk songs, some patriotic. Now, there's Tamouz, Uzi and the Styles, The Churchills, and Kaveret. Kaveret's lead singer is Danny Sanderson, maybe you've heard of him. No?"

Danny looked bashful. "Honestly, I never thought about Israel as having a modern music scene."

She chuckled. "We've got nightclubs and tons of concerts. Certainly, as much as a happening place like Indiana," she teased.

Maya wasn't reproaching him for his American-centric view of the music world. She was just making sure he knew that she didn't come from a third-world country obsessed with American music and copycat artists. She was proud of what her young country had accomplished.

Their metal folding chairs on the hardwood floor were not far from the basketball court's foul line. They had a clear view of the stage and its deep purple velvet backdrop curtains. To the left sat a shiny ebony piano and a four-legged stool. Microphones craned at odd angles for the awaited artists, and a platform was there for the backup singers called the Raeletts. Lighting technicians had arranged rigged-up rows of matte black lamps and spotlights.

As the crowd filed in, the small talk and anticipatory buzzing grew louder. Danny and Maya had to lean in closer to hear each other. Danny liked the proximity, the easy touching of shoulders and knees, and the perfume.

The concert began.

It was a fantastic show. Ray Charles, with his strong jaw, captivating smile, signature dark glasses, and rhythmic side-to-side rocking enchanted the audience. His relaxed banter between numbers included little stories about the songs, his family, the Raeletts, and other musicians. Ray seemed to talk directly to you. He giggled at his self-deprecation and inside jokes.

The song selections were perfection. He included all the favorites: "Georgia on My Mind," "Unchain My Heart," "Hit the Road, Jack," "What'd I Say," and "I Can't Stop Loving You." Each received thunderous applause. Maya clapped wildly, and Danny could tell she loved the energy of being at a concert.

Mr. Ray Charles ended the evening with the soulful blues song he made famous, "You Don't Know Me."

Danny, for sure, wanted to know more about Maya.

Roasters Coffee House was downtown, about fifteen minutes away. With the crowds dispersing, they trickled out alongside the herd of students walking toward the bars, restaurants, and shops.

The sensory overload of the concert stoked with the audience's energy, the star's artistry, the amped-up sound, and the dramatic lighting still had them on a high. In spite of Danny's unnecessary and bleak biographical mention of Ray Charles's struggles with heroin, they floated along with the melodies that transported them to Nashville, New Orleans, and Memphis. The rich renditions replayed over and over in their heads.

Danny suggested that they go to a coffee house. The November air had been deceptively warm before the show, and now Maya shivered in her cardigan. Danny draped his coat over her shoulders. On the way there, Maya shared, "When I lived in Israel, I was too young to go by myself to the coffee houses on Dizengoff Street or Rothschild Boulevard. My mother would take me out for an iced coffee or a smoothie. The coffee house could make you anything, but my *imma* would always order instant coffee called Nescafe."

Sounding a little like a teacher, she explained, "You know, *nes* means miracle in Hebrew. You probably know that from the Hanukkah songs. Anyway, it's called that because Israelis are fascinated by how quickly Nescafe is made." Maya got nervous that the Hebrew lesson was too nerdy, so she wrapped up by admitting, "The Nescafe's flavor wasn't as good as real coffee, but Israelis love anything American."

For Maya, remembering the sights and sounds of her beloved city helped to distract her from the dreary, freezing Indiana weather. Danny was beginning to see how, at the flip of a switch, Maya could be conversing in Hebrew and living in the land of her birth.

At Roasters, they settled into green and white wicker chairs next to a small, round wooden table. It was edged up against a wall, so they would have some privacy. With the room's subdued lighting and soft folk classics playing in the background, it was the mellow atmosphere they needed after the high-energy concert.

A waitress walked quietly by their table carrying beverages and desserts. The aromatic smells of coffee, steeping tea, and hot chocolate wafted around them. Maya reviewed the menu wedged between the sugar and the napkin dispenser and suggested, "I'll have an American coffee, and do you want to share a piece of cheesecake?"

Danny agreed, and Maya ordered. She turned back to Danny and smiled. "So tell me a little about yourself. I feel like I keep talking about Israel."

He thought to himself that she really hadn't talked much about her own life and had only hinted about what living in Israel was like. Also, he was unaccustomed to storytelling so early in a relationship. On prior dates, they'd talk more about people they both knew, or movies, music, or teachers. The other girls he had been out with had experienced much of the same old slice of Americana he had, and so there was no need to unpack everyday observations, no need to explore cultural undercurrents of one thing or another. Frankly, it wasn't cool to be too serious or too deep.

While Danny was hoping to hear more about her life in Israel, she had beaten him to the punch. Now he had to craft a way to tell his story that would hopefully be interesting.

He wasn't prepared, and he knew his tale wouldn't feature any heroics or fascinating highlights. While he sat upright delivering his autobiography, Maya thoughtfully sat back in her chair with his coat still draped over her shoulders.

He talked about his mom, dad, and sister, and what it was like to live in a small town like Dawkins. He tried to explain what it was like being Jewish in mostly Christian Indiana. The details of Sunday morning Hebrew school, bar mitzvah preparation, and infrequent visits from East Coast Jewish relatives elicited small nods of interest from Maya. He shared that, with few exceptions, he had not suffered from anti-Semitism. "Most of my friends were Christian."

He shrugged. "Who knows what they said in private or what they really thought, but my experiences were just fine."

To add color to what felt to him like an unremarkable story, he included a description of his car-buying incident with Bobby. He hoped it would also enable him to tell her about his modest football career. But it seemed the football subplot was the topic that interested her the least. Maya was used to all her peers serving in the Israel Defense Forces, so the idea of Danny strapping on a football helmet and pads and running around a stadium for sixty minutes didn't impress her.

Danny described the amusement park dance where he'd learned about the car for sale, the "Jewed down" epithet that had led Bobby to explode, and how they'd brawled in the mud with the three guys. This storyline also allowed him to introduce Bobby, recall the tobogganing accident, and even Bobby's dad's experiences in Dachau.

Now Maya leaned in, as this part of his memoir was more intriguing, more meaningful to her. Her brow creased, and her head tilted just a few degrees to the right. She wanted to hear what came next.

Maya interjected, "So, your Christian friend, Bobby, came to your defense. I guess that he, maybe subconsciously, in an unresolved way, was rescuing you, the only Jew he knew."

She thought for a moment and concluded, "He was trying to rescue you, to save you, like his father couldn't do or did too late for all the murdered Jews at Dachau. He was saving you for his father's sake."

He was impressed at how Maya had made the connections. Danny leaned in toward her. "So, you think Bobby was honoring his dad for sharing painful recollections, maybe for carrying on a family tradition of doing the right thing."

Maya's tone became somber. "Danny, both of my parents lost family in the Holocaust. The difference between survival and slaughter was very small, a matter of a fraction of a second, a blink of an eye, of being in the right or wrong place."

She thought to herself that it was sometimes the difference of whether someone else had the courage to do the right thing. As she squared the napkin on her lap, she went on, "In Israel, the reality of the Holocaust is an everyday thing. It isn't just a stone memorial to visit or a day of remembrance. It isn't even the tattoos we see on our neighbors' forearms or the old photos of lost family members."

She heard herself lecturing, but she went on. "It is a very real part of our national psyche. It is reflected in how we look at the world. It is about our having our backs to the Mediterranean with no other place to go. It's about how few friends we really have."

Danny quietly added, "I have a similar story. My Grandpa Isaac and his two brothers lived in Vienna. Two came to America, and one, with his family, disappeared."

The waitress arrived with their order just as Maya said, "Yes, our families have similar stories. Sadly, not uncommon."

They sat silently for a little while, processing their vastly different lives that somehow held similar threads. Danny suddenly remembered that this was only a first date. Here they were, exploring subjects that he hadn't even really talked about with his own family. With his friends, he'd always avoid subjects that might be awkward or contentious. He felt that there was no good reason to emphasize a difference that could only prove troublesome.

Now though, feeling free to talk about anything, Danny was slowly absorbing how special his experiences with Maya were. He had dated Jewish girls before, but their attitudes, dialogue, and interests weren't much different than those of the non-Jewish girls he knew, maybe because they weren't so connected to being Jewish. Talking with Maya, though, a newly felt poignancy about his religion and Israel began to challenge the way he saw his world. He wasn't sure what would come of it, but he felt very good about it.

10
The Gallery

The county's lumbering orange snowplows had already cleared the main roads from the night's near-blizzard dumping. Now, they worked their way through the smaller back roads. By mid-morning, the Dawkins Christmas shoppers would carefully wind their way into town for last-minute gifts.

Travelers drove cautiously on roads narrowed by the displaced snow, which was piled high onto hidden grass and gravel shoulders. While the shopkeepers did their part in shoveling and salting the sidewalks in front of their stores, parking was difficult, and walkers had to traverse mountains of snow and slippery ice patches.

Bobby and Danny, just back from their fall semester of their junior year of college, had already helped their parents clear drift-covered driveways and footpaths before heading into town for breakfast. Bobby arrived first at the popular Lighter's Luncheonette. The two-decade-old, beloved eatery sat on a corner on the main street. On the cross street side, the windows were covered Mondrian-style with hand-painted posters advertising the specials. One poster had hung there forever, boasting of their "world-famous chili."

Today, with the near-arctic chill outside and all the cooking, dishwashing, and jacked-up heat, the windows fogged over with condensation. Bobby grabbed a booth and waited for Danny. The diner's shiny revolving seats were nearly all filled by cold, damp customers consuming hot coffee and steaming stacks of pancakes.

Once Bobby went off to Purdue and Danny started at IU, they exchanged occasional phone calls and no mail. When they did talk, it was mostly about courses, careers plans, and football scores. They enjoyed playfully bashing each other's schools, which were arch rivals. Some tidbits about girls made the headlines, but nothing really serious had occurred for either of them. Sure, they had dates for the big games, but neither had anyone steady. Neither guy had joined a fraternity, and both were focused on their engineering courses.

In what little correspondence there was, rarely did they address or inquire how parents and siblings were doing. It was the practical, coolly efficient way boys communicated, or more accurately, didn't communicate. They could keep up a good friendship with the bare minimum of personal reflection. As *Dragnet's* Sergeant Joe Friday said, "Just the facts, ma'am." But come the holidays or summer vacation, they'd resume their close friendship, and they'd share much more of what was on their minds.

Today, both guys sensed that unlike prior catch-ups, this would be different. Both had something to announce.

After all, they were now juniors. That was the time many of their friends got more serious about relationships or started to pin down where they would seek employment. A few of their friends had even gotten married and were finishing their college years as husbands and wives.

When Danny pulled open the front door, Bobby grinned widely and hollered, "Hey pal, over here!" Bobby stood up, and they half shook hands, half hugged. Bobby sat back down as Danny pulled off layers of wet, wooly clothing.

"So, buddy, what's new with you?" Danny asked. "Bring me up to date."

Bobby fiddled with the rectangular ceramic sugar packet holder. He leveled all the packets and then blurted out, "Danny, I met a really nice girl about a month ago. She's something special."

Danny playfully asked, "The marrying kind?"

Bobby blushed and answered, "You know, just maybe, just maybe. We've gone out only a couple of times, and I'm just getting to know her, but she's an amazing person, a tough cookie, but so sweet. And she's really pretty." Bobby thought to himself about Andrea's sparkling blue eyes, with little crinkles in the corners.

As Bobby began telling Danny about Andrea, he realized his heightened awareness of her every nuance – the sound of her voice, the curl of her lips, her hand gestures – was greater than with any girl he had previously dated. He had to recalibrate his adjectives for a guy-to-guy conversation. He told himself to hold back, not to go overboard, and not to paint a too-detailed picture of Andrea. She deserved some privacy, and he would respect that.

"Wow, she sounds really great. Unclear why she gave you a chance, though," Danny joked with a smile.

"Ha ha, very funny. And what about you, Danny?" Bobby asked. "Anyone special?"

Danny mused over the similarity of their situations. He had just met Maya, and he thought that his story, on this wintery morning, was going to be the focus of what they'd discuss. He would share her intriguing and transatlantic history later, but for now he answered honestly. "You know, yes, I did meet someone I like."

With a deferential wave of his hand, Danny offered, "But you go first. Tell me more about your girlfriend."

Bobby started by recalling how he saw Andrea Nicholls for the very first time. "She was in a green food services uniform at the student union cafeteria. She was perched on top of one of those tall stainless steel stools manning one of the checkout cash registers."

He admitted, "My first words to her were…corny. I was sliding my food tray, and I said something like, 'You must be new here…I haven't seen you before.'"

Danny joked, "Now, what's a nice girl like you doing in a cafeteria like this?"

"It was almost that bad," Bobby confessed. "But she smiled. Andrea told me that she just transferred from a community college for her junior and senior years."

He thought back to how he got in a few more words here and there, how he had to time it between register transactions. "I was sweating, I was so nervous. Finally, she scribbled her phone number on a napkin and I could exhale again."

A few months earlier, Bobby had considered where to take Andrea on their first date. Instead of sitting in a darkened movie theater or joining the herds tramping out to a football game, he had suggested checking out a traveling exhibition of Andrew Wyeth paintings. It was way out of his comfort zone, but he guessed that a quieter place would be appreciated. His plan included dinner downtown after the exhibit.

Andrea lived in a modest apartment a long way from campus. She'd insisted that they meet halfway and walk together to the campus gallery.

When they met up next to the library, Andrea looked like a different person than the young woman he'd met in the cafeteria. Even in her uniform she was beautiful, but all dressed up, she was a knockout.

They walked together in the late afternoon, talking mostly about her new apartment and the long walk she had every morning. She made a joke about the impressive number of "empties" the male renters threw in the garbage pail each weekend. On the walk to the gallery, they yammered about courses, friends, and plans for summer employment.

At Purdue's one-story contemporary art gallery, just beyond the lobby and coat check was the entryway to the special Andrew Wyeth exhibit. There, they read together on tall, embossed display panels the Wyeth's biographical overview. Both gave the detailed narrative its due attention. Bobby wanted to be sure Andrea appreciated his interest in the art, and he also wanted to have a fighting chance to understand the significance of the artist. As an engineering student, he had taken precious few liberal arts courses and had no meaningful exposure to art history or art appreciation. Standing there, side by side, they learned that his paintings and watercolors of the mid-twentieth century realistic style were noted for conveying a restrained emotional quality.

For both it was hard to gauge the other's reading speed and interest in the subject, so they each shyly considered when to move ahead. Walking slowly, they stopped in front of each work and read the explanatory notes engraved on small, mauve rectangles affixed to the wall.

Bobby was beginning to question choosing the Wyeth show at the gallery for their first date. He had to think out what words of wisdom he'd share with Andrea as they gazed at the paintings. His comments soon became "it's interesting," "it's pretty," "it's different." He felt like an idiot, especially compared to Andrea, who spoke about the artwork so naturally.

Andrea said she had read that Christina Olson, the subject who inspired Wyeth in *Christina's World*, had suffered from polio.

Bobby didn't remember reading any of that at the entryway, or maybe he'd missed it. Probably Andrea just knew more about art history and American painters.

A few minutes later, Andrea casually mentioned that her mom, before she was sick, had looked a little like Christina Olson.

Bobby wasn't sure how to respond. He wondered if she got better or if she died. He cautiously said, "I hope your mom is better now." Bobby could tell from her face that she wasn't.

"When I was young, about eight, my mother, Sofia, was diagnosed with cancer. She died within a year. My dad couldn't handle the responsibility of a little girl, and he...disappeared. There's more to it than that, but basically, he just left."

Other patrons passed them in the tight gallery, juxtaposing oddly with their intense private conversation about Andrea's troubled young life. She told him how the court helped her to link up with Aunt Tina, who'd been like a mom to her ever since.

Bobby listened quietly, his expression forlorn and concerned. Andrea told him, "I didn't intend to tell you a 'poor me' story. You don't have to feel bad for me, I'm okay now."

Andrea reminisced, telling him that her mom's long brown braided hair was just like Helga's. She clarified that although the painting of Helga showed a somber, unsmiling woman, that's not how she remembered her mom, who was cheery and full of fun. She had made the most of the little time that she had left. She always made Andrea feel loved.

Bobby was taken aback by Andrea's story. With the devotion of his parents, he took for granted the security of an intact and comfortable family. Health and enough money were a given, and his life just motored along like a television sitcom.

Andrea stared into space for a minute, lost in her thoughts. She rarely spoke about her parents. Something about Bobby, though, made her feel safe. She looked up at Bobby, smiled, and gently took his arm to continue moving through the exhibit.

Andrea's hand on Bobby's arm was the first physical contact between them. They both felt the electricity. Beyond that, it was a symbolic redirection – a shared decision to move forward.

Over the next few dates, Andrea told him more about her very challenging childhood. Despite the subject matter, their time together was wonderful and not at all depressing. She took great joy in her battles against obstacles and resisted blaming anyone.

Beyond telling him more about her deceased mother and the disappointment of having a father who couldn't handle the difficulty of raising a daughter, she focused most on stories of her Aunt Tina. She described her as a delicate soul, very focused on her church, with an energetic and positive outlook on life. She had lost her husband to an accident and earned a modest living as a teacher at a local school.

With pride, Andrea told Bobby that she'd had a job since she was fourteen and had paid for almost all of her two-year community college education. It was a recent scholarship that enabled her to transfer to Purdue University for her final two years.

Bobby was anxious to get on with telling Danny the exciting part of her biography. "Although Andrea is only nineteen, she has already traveled with her Aunt Tina on two missions with their church, to Central America and East Africa. Maybe it was dangerous, but she didn't say so."

Bobby excitedly told him, "In Kenya, somewhere in a rural area near the Serengeti, she helped build a facility for special needs children."

She told Bobby that most of them were orphans and many had cerebral palsy. She said the team of Americans and some Europeans worked on construction of a new dormitory and educational rooms. The group of about twenty worked with locals to help make bricks, prepare the foundation, and dig a well.

Andrea made sure Bobby knew that they also had fun. She talked about a one-day safari to see lions, elephants, giraffes, herds of zebras, and wildebeests. But mostly, she glowed when describing helping young, impoverished kids who had to sleep many to a bed and spent their days playing in a dusty, litter-strewn street. As she described this foreign scene, she recalled the clearest images of specific children and how much better their lives would be in a clean, safe youth center.

Bobby wrapped up just as the last of the corned beef hash and pancakes were being taken away. "Wow, I was talking for a long time. Sorry I went on so long about Andrea. I'll tell you how it turns out at the spring break." He transitioned, "Okay. You mentioned there's a girl. Who is she? What's the story?"

Danny waited until the waitress finished pouring the third cup of coffee to share his story about the pretty red-haired girl from Israel. He gave Bobby the headlines about the war, her father's death, and her mother's remarriage. He told him about Maya's relocation to Chicago and going to college in Indiana. He confided in Bobby that he was falling fast for this girl.

Bobby listened to Danny's eerily similar story. He felt comfortable enough with Danny to note, "From Israel? I'm sure your mom and dad are happy about her being Jewish."

Danny had talked with Bobby about "the dating thing" before, and while he hadn't ever thought about an Israeli, he knew his parents were hoping their son would eventually marry a Jewish girl.

Danny also resisted sharing too much about Maya Schein. He had been captivated by her combination of good looks, clever mind, and fascinating background, but he was just getting to know her.

He was frank about Maya. "She's very nice. She's easy to be with, but I have no clue if she has real interest in me."

Bobby concurred. "Yes, same here."

"She's spending the holiday with her mom and new step-father in Chicago." He stirred his coffee one more time. "I can't wait to see her when we go back."

11
The Buffet

Danny, twenty-two years old now, sat stiffly in the hotel lobby anxiously awaiting Maya and her family. At any moment he expected to see her, her mother Dahlia, and her step-dad Leonard emerge from the lobby's revolving door. He searched for Maya, wondering what Dahlia and Leonard would look like. Time passed much too slowly.

The five-story red brick hotel abutted the university campus and was the preferred place to stay for visiting parents and prospective students. Danny watched one after another after entering through the revolving door and crossing the cream and crimson checkerboard floor to either the front desk or to the sumptuous Sunday dinner buffet.

Danny thought back to some of the girls that he had dated in high school. He knew their parents and they knew him, and it was all so comfortable. With Maya, it was different; her family would be brand new to him. Her life story was dramatized with Israeli parents, her father's combat death, and a stepfather.

Over the past year, they had dated steadily and grown to be somewhat serious. Maya and Danny overcame many differences and found wonderful similarities. Although they'd been together a while, Danny remembered ever seeing only one picture of Dahlia. It was a dated wallet photo, faded and scored with a dog-eared crease in the lower left. In it, Maya knelt between Dahlia and Yonatan, her late father.

The picture had been taken as they sat on a stone retaining wall near a sloping grove of olive trees, thick with grey tree limbs and covered with dull green leaves. The family loved to hike, and the beautiful scene of a hilltop olive grove was Maya's favorite. Dahlia, looking very pretty with her auburn hair covered mostly by a kerchief, held her arm around Maya. Yonatan, with wavy light brown hair, a white short-sleeve shirt, and khaki shorts leaned in and hugged Maya's shoulders. Maya was maybe ten years old and wore a one-piece yellow and blue jump suit. She smiled the widest of the three.

Maya hadn't yet shared a picture of her new step-dad Leonard, but she described him as a thoughtful, gentle man, considerate of the special challenges she faced during her recent transitions.

They had a heart-to-heart about Maya's family on one of their earliest dates. They had walked off campus to picnic in one of Bloomington's parks. Maya sat up and Danny lay back as she told her story. Maya opened up about her mom and her deceased father, Yonatan.

"Both my parents, Dahlia and Yonatan, were children of Israel's pioneers. They and their families arrived in Palestine in the late 1930s," Maya began. "They were born in Europe, but as young children, they moved by boat, train, and even foot, and I guess by donkeys and wagons through Greece and on to Palestine.

"Both sets of grandparents had lived in Germany in the Grindel and New Town districts of Hamburg. They told me that my father's family, the Scheins, were well off. They lived in a big brick two-story house on a nice tree-lined street."

She went on, "The Scheins were financiers involved in the Hamburg shipping industry. My mother's family, the Marskis, were not as well off but lived a decent life. I think my grandfather on the Marski side was a merchant."

Maya continued with the articulation of her history professors. "Both sets of grandparents were so troubled by the rise of the Nazis and the already escalating, violent anti-Semitism that they made the incredibly hard decision to leave their homes and sizable families.

"Each set of grandparents were newly married and each had only one child at the time, so they were more mobile than their relatives," she added. "With the limited immigration quotas in the United States and England, Palestine was their best choice."

Maya paused for soda and a bite of her Swiss cheese sandwich.

Danny added, "Maya, it's a familiar story. My father David came to America when he was seven. He and his father left Austria in 1934."

Maya asked, "Danny, remember to tell me about the Baransons leaving Austria."

"Sure, but let's get back to your story and the immigrations into Palestine," Danny said. "I guess it was different for immigrants who came before the Holocaust, or were part of the rescues and relocations from around the world."

Maya nodded her head in affirmation and pressed on. Maybe Danny would see her personal story as an adventure. She wanted him to know all about the others who never made it. "There were many aunts and uncles I never knew because almost all of them were murdered in camps."

Maya somberly shared, "Only a very few survived, and they also settled in Israel. For my mother and father and their parents, the Jewish Agency helped them relocate to two different kibbutzim, one not too far from Tel Aviv and one in the north near Lake Kinneret."

Danny was unfamiliar with the history of the Fifth Aliyah, the wave of Jewish immigrants to Palestine from 1929 to 1939. It ended with Neville Chamberlain leading the British government (which controlled Palestine at the time) to issue White Papers that prohibited Jewish immigration. While Maya and her parents experienced economic hardships, they were part of the great rebirth of the Jewish state.

The next parts of Maya's story weren't so much a story as a smattering of details from her life in Israel. She told Danny about how Dahlia and Yonatan, both in the army, met at a Petah Tikvah snack shop during a winter rain. She explained how she herself would have joined the Israel Defense Forces after high school if she hadn't left Israel before she was sixteen. Maya's Israeli Hebrew accent was of course perfect, but her parents still carried the accent of European immigrants. She'd learned English in school, so once she came to Indiana, she became fluent quickly. She described the cold, damp concrete bomb shelter at the corner of their block with its protective steel door.

Maya, now more subdued, added, "My dad was a sweet man. You know, Danny, sometimes too much attention is paid to how somebody dies – what happened on their last day or even their last few minutes – and we forget about all the rest of their time. What they did, who they were, what they stood for."

More cheerfully, she said, "My *abba* and *imma* always seemed so in love, like it was just the beginning of their relationship. They always held hands when they walked together, and my father bought my mother flowers every Shabbat. They covered the walls of our apartment with beautiful pictures of the Israeli landscape."

She went on, "My father was an engineer, just like you want to be. He worked for Israel Aerospace Industries." She ventured, "I think he graduated from the Technion in mechanical engineering, and then worked on the Kfir, a fighter jet Israel was building.

"He went into the armored corps and served as a tank commander," she said. "He fought in both the Six-Day War as an active soldier and the Yom Kippur War as a reservist."

Maya recalled fondly, "He was very close to his tank crew. They would meet up often with their families, and it was always a lot of fun. We celebrated a ton of milestones together between all the births, weddings, and bar mitzvahs, and when someone died, everyone went to the funeral.

"The men in his reserve duty group were like uncles to me. One was a taxi driver, one was a concert violinist, and all loved Israel and proudly served in the army." Maya thought back with a bittersweet smile. "And I loved them."

As their relationship went on, Maya shared more personal recollections about her father Yonatan and her memories of the Yom Kippur War. On a quiet High Holiday morning, she heard the sound of a Phantom jet screaming overhead. She had the growing realization that something awful was happening. Murmurs and whispering filled the synagogue, almost drowning out the prayers.

She could hear vehicles carrying uniformed couriers with mobilization orders. Squealing tires and exhaust noises violated a sacred morning normally bereft of traffic sounds. Soldiers trying to locate Yonatan and other reservists came to their small synagogue to inform them about the Egyptian and Syrian surprise attack. They needed Yonatan to form up for military transportation.

Maya watched the interaction as she swayed with the congregation in her white short-sleeved sundress, singing ancient liturgy that felt all too timely:

> *On Rosh Hashanah it is written and on Yom Kippur it is sealed. Who shall live and who shall die, who in his allotted time and who not, who by water, who by fire, and who by sword.*

Services came to a momentary halt, and Maya and her parents, along with several other families, left the synagogue. Maya described the quick walk back to their apartment and tearfully shared how Dahlia quietly helped Yonatan prepare his personal items and folded them into a canvas backpack. Yonatan gave her and her mother a kiss goodbye, and he was off.

Maya struggled to end the story, even though Danny knew what happened. "Abba was killed on the third day of the war while fighting in the Golani Brigade. His entire tank crew perished trying to halt the advance of Syrian tanks not too far from Nafakh.

"Now the area is called The Valley of Tears," she choked out.

Danny held Maya, and they cried silently.

Danny had been so lost in his daydreams, he was almost startled when he saw Maya finally coming through the revolving door. He jumped up from the leather-covered bench and headed toward her.

Flawlessly, Maya made the introductions, followed by handshakes and cautious greetings. Danny fought the urge to focus on Maya and instead turned to Dahlia and Leonard. "So nice to meet you, it's a pleasure. Welcome to Bloomington!"

Unsurprisingly, Dahlia was a pretty woman. It was clear that Maya's red hair and delicate features came from her. She wore charcoal slacks, an oatmeal-colored sweater, and a simple string of multicolored ceramic beads.

Leonard was a tall man, more than a few years older than Dahlia. Although his hair was thinning, with a prominent chin and an even smile, they made a handsome couple. Danny could see that while Maya and her mother looked alike, Maya also took after the young father who once sat with his small family among the olive trees not too far from Jerusalem.

"Hello, Danny, so nice to meet you," Dahlia chimed in a heavy German-Israeli accent. Her voice evoked in him the rapid-fire chronicling of a child fleeing Nazi Germany, a uniformed soldier, a grieving widow, a single parent. Danny found it hard to comprehend that Dahlia was just a few years younger than his mom. He could not reconcile her complex tale of travel and travail with the *Leave It to Beaver* normalcy he associated with his mom and dad.

"I'm so glad to meet you, too. Let's go get a table, shall we?" Danny tried to sound nonchalant despite his nervousness.

They stepped across the lobby's checkered floor into the large, bustling dining room.

After a plump hostess seated them, a college-aged waiter with a mullet came by for their drink requests. Before retrieving the beverages, he earnestly suggested queuing up for the buffet. "I'd go now if I were you. It's almost seven, and it'll be a madhouse."

The buffet line moved slowly. Danny wondered what these Israelis thought of the display of American dining excess. The buffet began with a warmed plate from a pop-up tower of chinaware bearing the IU logo. Beside the carved melons, ferns, and ice sculpture centerpieces, the four took in the cornucopia before them in bewilderment.

As they went, they chose from salads, vegetables, and dressings. Four different types of pickles, a variety of olives all cured differently, and a clutter of cheeses and cold cuts occupied the appetizer section. A tire-sized, tilted wicker breadbasket overflowed with rolls, croissants, and popovers. There were hot copper chafing dishes of fish, chicken, ham, and beef set at an angle, each introduced with a descriptive place card.

At the very end of the buffet tables was a carving station with roast beef. It had been cooked to perfection, the outer layer crispy, the inside juicy and pink. The carver wore a white starched double-breasted jacket and a small toque pitched to one side.

As each guest passed, the carver asked for preferences for rare, medium, or well done. More often than not, some humorous reference to the Jurassic-sized chunk of meat was attempted.

As Maya's turn came, she asked for a small, thin cut of rare beef. The carver began, but was distracted by a waiter carrying a too-tall stack of freshly cleaned dishes. With one swift but mistaken move, he cut deeply into the palm of his left hand.

Maya, witnessing the carver's pained shock and seeing the geyser of very red blood, yelped, "My God, Danny!"

In a blur, Danny saw Dahlia and Leonard swing around in reaction to Maya's voice. They were across the room already at their table and could only watch.

With quick, precise steps, Danny pushed past Maya and swung around the end of the buffet. He reached down, grabbed the carver's floor-length apron, lifted it up and folded it around the flowing wound. He bent the carver's forearm up against his shoulder to elevate the sliced palm and kept adding pressure. Danny's blue button-down oxford shirt sleeve became smudged with dark red.

In seconds, Danny applied adequate pressure to restrict the bleeding. Now other waiters, a supervisor, and the maître d' arrived and escorted the wounded food services warrior back into the kitchen area. Nearby diners hearing the commotion rubbernecked as they pretended to get more food.

Danny excused himself and headed to the men's room to clean up. He returned a few minutes later, his shirtsleeves rolled up to cover the bloodstains, and he eased himself into his chair. Maya had retrieved his plate, and Dahlia had covered it to keep it warm.

Maya gushed, "Danny, you were amazing. You were so quick and there was no hesitation. I'm proud of you."

Leonard nodded, "Young man, very impressive. Johnny-on-the-spot."

Dahlia hesitated for a moment. Her face was somber, and just before she made eye contact with Danny, she had to refocus. Danny speculated that the situation might have triggered a flashback to her traumas.

Dahlia, sitting to Danny's right, gently placed her hand on top of his. With her thick accent, she said, "That young man was very lucky to have you there as his guardian. You did all the right things. You were very good."

Her knowing, appreciative smile created small wrinkles around her eyes and into the corners of her mouth. After that, Danny was finally able to relax. "So, this is quite a spread here! Tell me, what are buffets like in Israel?"

"Less ham, and more lox," Leonard said with a smile. They all laughed.

12 The Taxi Ride

The cool, clear October day in 1984 was the third occasion when Danny would spend time with Leonard Raskin. As Maya and Dahlia shuffled between the kitchen and dining room preparing dinner, Leonard felt comfortable enough to share family stories with Danny, since he and Maya were now engaged.

As they looked out across shimmering Lake Michigan from their twentieth-floor Chicago apartment, Leonard decided to share with Danny the specifics of his very first interaction with Dahlia Schein. With a wry smile, Leonard told his soon to be son-in-law that it was Dahlia who had introduced herself to him, and not the other way around. The notion that it was the beautiful Dahlia who spoke to him first was an amusing anecdote he loved to repeat. He paused for just a moment, organizing in his mind all of the important details about the events he loved to describe. He wanted to be sure he didn't miss anything.

It was the year 1975 when Leonard had just finished up a business dinner that followed his formal presentation at the pharmacology conference at Tel Aviv University. Dahlia, in order to talk to him, had wedged herself into the small circle of Israeli professionals asking Leonard about his talk. The *Pharmacology Trends* lecture attendees wanted to know about his update on the medicinal advances in post-combat trauma and stress management. Leonard, the only one wearing a tie, stood out as the obvious token American. He comfortably fielded their inquiries.

Waiting for the right moment, Dahlia shook his hand and breezily introduced herself. "Dahlia Schein, I'm a nurse in a village hospital. Great lecture." She added that she had served in the IDF medical unit and was now a psychiatric nurse. Dahlia first carefully described her work with severely disabled patients, including Holocaust survivors. She thoughtfully inquired, "Do you think your pharmacological work to help Vietnam War Veterans – those suffering from post-traumatic stress disorder – could be helpful for Holocaust survivors?"

Leonard noticed how eagerly she waited for his response. Her question was heartfelt and very perceptive. It was downright clever. It opened up a whole new line of study and possible application for the advanced drugs.

Eventually, he would retell how he was immediately attracted to her, proving it by recalling in detail how she had been dressed in a dark blue skirt and an eyelet blouse, and even pointing out that she'd held a cup of tea in her left hand.

At the mental health village, nestled in the low wooded hills just north of Herzliya, many of her patients were deeply affected by the Holocaust. They essentially lived in two different worlds: one of the present, and one of the past. Dahlia was keenly aware that each of her hospitalized survivors was severely distressed by remembrances of the unimaginable. She did her best to quietly improve their lives and provide them with some semblance of dignity. She worked to help them find small moments of sunshine to brighten their perpetually fearful darkness.

Dahlia felt that some of the village's practices were failing these patients. As she watched the patients walk about the hallways in their pajamas and robes, she wondered if their baggy uniforms were too close to the striped garments issued by the Nazis. Did the whitewashed walls and guards of the village that confined the residents keep them from experiencing a quality Israeli life? Did the boundaries resemble the camps' barbed-wire fences, guard towers, and helmeted soldiers? Were the open shower rooms too reminiscent of the gas chambers and the horrors that followed? What did they see when they looked at the steam and the soap? Hoarding food was also common, and she thought that if the patients were assigned cubbyholes, they would be less likely to hide perishables in their clothing.

She submitted recommendations to remedy the problems, but few of her ideas were accepted.

During her tenure at the village, she focused her attention on this distressed population of Israelis. Impressively, most survivors fared very well in their lives in Israel. Many literally stepped ashore in British Mandate Palestine and instantly transitioned from victims to fighters in the War of Independence. The majority of the nascent Israeli Air Force pilots were Holocaust refugees, and over two-thirds of all the soldiers in the War of Independence were survivors. Holocaust survivors also created forty of the most successful community cooperatives. Some of these survivors worked their way to become wildly successful businessmen, influential politicians, or international prizewinners in the arts and sciences. But some just could not move beyond the horror and loss.

In Dahlia's mind, they received inadequate attention. Whether they came to the asylums directly from the camps or arrived after a few years of relative normalcy and then fell prey to schizophrenia, manic depression, or other mental illnesses, they, like most mental patients, largely disappeared from Israeli society.

Mental institutions were simply underfunded. The early years for the new state brought severe economic hardships, driven by demands to absorb the influx of immigrants and defend against continuing threats from Israel's neighbors. Postwar rebuilding and the influence of the oil-rich Arab nations complicated alliances with the United States and other countries.

On a typical day up until the Yom Kippur War happened, Dahlia would eat her breakfast of yogurt and vegetables, say goodbye to Yonatan, drop off little Maya at school, and take a northbound bus from her Tel Aviv apartment to the village. After sitting for a quick Turkish coffee, Dahlia would begin her morning rounds.

She would quietly and efficiently dole out the medications and dutifully record vital signs. Wherever possible, she engaged her patients in conversation and encouraged them to take part in activities and socialize. For the most part, she found the Holocaust survivors didn't build relationships with each other, but her easy manner comforted them. At the end of the day, she traveled home, and the survivors returned to their small rooms.

Over the years, Dahlia came to appreciate the individual lives lived by her patients. To the newcomer, they were all mental patients weighed down with unmanageable baskets of plagued memories, anger, and guilt. Dahlia made sure to learn about their former happier times. She admired her patients' gradual improvements, their subtle physical and psychological victories, and their displays of courage, humanity, and resilience.

There was a particular patient that Dahlia often thought about. This woman, with uncanny consistency, obsessively retold a memory from the concentration camp. She was caught reaching into a garbage barrel. She had seen a scrap of bread and tried to hurriedly retrieve it. The Nazi guard raced over, jabbed her with a stick, and told her to roll up her sleeve. He wanted her identification for punishment. At that moment, the guard lost his footing in the muddy yard and almost fell. She tried to steady him, but she got another sharp poke in the ribs for her effort. He awkwardly righted himself. She showed him her arm as she had been told, and he noted her tattooed number in a little book.

The next day, when the prisoners assembled for work duty, another German guard called out a prisoner number and another woman stepped forward. She was taken away and never seen again. Weeks later, Dahlia's patient came upon the other woman's sister. Somehow, the story of her getting caught at the garbage barrel came up. When she showed her arm to the victim's sister, they realized that the digits 66188 had been viewed upside down by the Nazi guard as 88199, the tattooed number of her sister.

Ever since, Dahlia's patient was plagued with reliving this guilt-filled memory over and over. Second guessing dominated her world.

In the evenings, Dahlia would often share her interactions with her patients with Yonatan. She recounted bits and pieces of their lives before the war. She felt the need to bear testament to the horrors that her patients bravely retold. She would validate their feelings of loss, anger, and fear. Yonatan listened to Dahlia, both because it helped her decompress from her difficult job and because the stories were often interesting.

Over the course of their lives, Yonatan and Dahlia had seen the construction and dedication of the Yad Vashem Holocaust Memorial. It was first opened in 1953. In 1959, Israel declared a day of remembrance of the Holocaust: Yom Hashoah. Even as a little girl, Maya knew that at ten in the morning every Yom Hashoah, the siren would blare to mark a moment of remembrance. All traffic and movement would come to a complete halt. If you were on a highway, you stopped, got out of your vehicle, and stood silently for two minutes. It always looked like a movie that someone had paused.

Dahlia shared selected stories with her young and inquisitive daughter Maya. Maya came to understand the Holocaust through individual experiences, rather than through incomprehensible statistics. The survivors in Dahlia's village were people with first and last names, people with blue eyes and brown eyes and green eyes, people who, with great difficulty or great courage, stumbled forward. She became somewhat cynical toward stone monuments, well-attended ceremonies, and screaming sirens. These were reminders of the darkest of statistics, but they also obscured the individuality of the human beings they represented.

After the death of her beloved husband Yonatan, Dahlia suffered through the wrenching months of late 1973 and into the next year. Finally, to try to break through the mourning, she returned from her hiatus to the job at the village. There, she was able to focus on the patients' problems and begin helping herself return to a version of normalcy. Their problems replaced hers.

When she wasn't working, her anger, shock, grief, and disappointment over the failures of the Israeli government during and before the war consumed her. The National Commission of Inquiry investigated the failures of the Yom Kippur War, and IDF Chief of Staff David Elazar and others resigned. Still, she and others who'd lost loved ones wanted to vent their extreme anger and point and shout at the bureaucratic "murderers." But over time, slowly, Dahlia healed.

Leonard, still standing with Danny, considered for a moment if he would share the second part of his romantic story. He decided not to. Danny hadn't asked questions, probably thinking Leonard's recounting was already a bit too personal for their budding in-law relationship. He nodded along and respectfully listened.

In the brief silence that followed, both watched the slow-motion sailboats tacking the lake's wind as Leonard gathered his thoughts to continue his recollection. He thought back to the first encounter with Dahlia.

After the circle of colleagues dispersed, Leonard found himself at the edge of the room alone, gazing down at the cookies and fruit assortment. It was then that he saw an older, tall, dark-haired woman engage Dahlia in a brief conversation. He saw her place both hands on Dahlia's shoulders, give her a hug, and say, "I was very sorry to hear about your husband's death. It is all so terrible. I hope your daughter is coping with the loss. So many. So many." She gave a sad smile. "We pray for your peace of mind, for consolation."

Dahlia nodded her head silently, acknowledging the well wishes, and managed, "Thank you. We're doing our best."

Minutes later, Leonard gathered together his briefcase and his notes from the lecture and walked out to the street to find a taxi back to his hotel. It was now dark, and he saw Dahlia walking several steps ahead of him.

Leonard caught up to her and asked, "Can I offer you a ride? Or do you have a car?"

Dahlia replied, "The buses come by regularly, I'll be fine."

Leonard persisted, "Mrs. Schein, please let me assist. There are lots of taxis, and I can at least get you closer to your destination."

Dahlia's answer came slowly, as if the question required contemplation. "All right. I need to head back downtown. My daughter is waiting. A taxi ride would be very nice."

They were only a few sentences into their cab ride chat before she alluded to Yonatan in the past tense. "My husband was associated with the university. He worked in the aerospace industry before he was killed. He was a reservist."

She still cringed at the awful words. She pressed on. "He went to school here and had business connections with several of the professors."

Leonard nodded and let her words hang in the air for a minute. He decided that readdressing the issue of stress disorders and mentally scarred survivors would be an easier topic. "Mrs. Schein, once again I want to thank you for your question. Most of my research has focused on wounded warriors. The trade-off of quality of life for soldiers and their impairments makes me think about the possibility of longitudinal research."

He added, "It is easier to segment the tens of thousands of our wounded into homogeneous cohorts..." Leonard paused, realizing that his professional jargon conveyed coldness. Wanting to again redirect the conversation, he said, "I know that Israel lost..."

Dahlia interrupted, "We lost about three thousand soldiers, including my husband, and I don't know how many were wounded."

She apologetically added, "I should know how many were wounded, but I don't." Dahlia contemplated for a minute all the wounded. No matter how sensitive to others you are, or you think you are, you are inclined to dwell only in your own misery. But grieving was both a personal and a national experience for Israelis.

As the taxi wound its way through the narrow streets navigating southwest toward the sea, Leonard said, "I'm sorry for your loss. I have no words that can help." He added, "My wife passed away two years ago, and I still struggle knowing I cannot call her, that she is not back home waiting for me."

"Dr. Raskin, I'm sorry to hear about your wife." She went on, "For me, it's like living on a chess board. Sometimes I'm standing on a light square, sometimes on a dark one." She explained, "It's a silly metaphor, but that's how I feel."

"That's a good description. It is so unpredictable. If my kids call, I feel better. If I wake up alone in the middle of the night, then not so good," Leonard mused, looking at her in the dark of the taxi's back seat. "And by the way, you can call me Leonard."

"Please do call me Dahlia."

They talked quietly for the rest of the ride, sharing small glimpses into each other's lives. Some of the chatter was about the light squares, and some about the dark ones.

Leonard had been able to convince Dahlia to allow the driver to go directly to her apartment near Nachalat Binyamin Street.

Just as the cab slowed down, Leonard told Dahlia, "I'm going to be here in Tel Aviv for the next three days."

Cautiously, he added, "It would be my great pleasure to see you again."

Dahlia at first didn't respond. It was as if these English words didn't make sense. She instead looked out through the taxi's streaked windows at the familiar shop fronts and electric signs. There was the fabric store with its window sills stacked with tightly wound bolts of cloth and cascading displays of fancy buttons and trim. She studied the closed butcher shop, a dingy mini-market, and a small restaurant with a couple of tables and chairs occupied by two older men.

She stared down at the curb and the smooth cobblestones lit by the streetlights. It was where she and Maya, and once upon a time, Yonatan, had so often walked.

She then looked directly into Leonard's eyes. "Yes. That would be very nice."

13 Leonard's Gift

The happy crowd gathered in Maya and Danny Baranson's living room to celebrate the *brit milah* of their brand-new baby boy, Yonatan. Danny and Maya called him Yoni. With the rabbi, the *mohel*, and their friends and family jammed in, there was almost no room to move. As a special treat, Danny's childhood friend Bobby Langford had flown in to be with them.

Eight days after Yoni's birth on June 29, 1985, as per the commandment in Genesis 17:10–14 and Leviticus 12:3, the rabbi led the traditional service with a mix of tutelage, piety, and humor. Chanting the beautiful prayers, the rabbi drew the loving crowd into the spirituality the event signified.

Just before the service ended and everyone dispersed for refreshments and conversation, Danny and Maya stepped forward arm in arm. Dahlia and Leonard stood to their right, and to the left were Danny's parents, David and Shelley. The new father, drained by the last eight days that included Maya's labor, the wonderment of the birth, and bringing a baby home, gathered himself for a few prepared remarks.

Maya couldn't take her eyes away from the bundled baby boy she held. Danny graciously thanked all present, thanked God for the miracle of his new son, and joked about what chance meetings at laundromats can lead to. Danny concluded by explaining, "The name Yonatan means 'God has given,' and it was chosen in honor of the baby's grandfather Yonatan, who was an Israeli hero and my wife's beloved *abba*."

A few years later, a smaller group came to the birthday party for four-year-old Yoni. He sat on a tiny chair next to a pile of wrapped presents. Fidgeting and running his hands through his chestnut hair, he was anxious to tear into the goodies to see what was there.

Before any of the other presents were opened, Leonard wove around the other guests, stooped down on one knee in front of Yoni, and handed him a small, flat box. Leonard, with his easy, gentle manner, explained, "Young man, I have something very special for you and your mommy."

Leonard continued, "I know you like guessing games, but I don't think you're going to guess this one. It's not a toy or candy, but it's very, very special."

With theatric seriousness he added, "It is my extreme pleasure to share this with you." He spoke just loudly enough for all to hear, but softly enough that it would seem like a personal one-on-one with Yoni.

Dahlia knew what was in the box, and she was already tearing up. Maya and Danny wondered what Leonard had brought, but their gaze was on Yoni, not on the box.

About six months before Yoni's fourth birthday party, Leonard traveled to Israel to complete his three-part lecture series at Tel Aviv University. Normally, he'd fly over with Dahlia, and they'd spend time with her few remaining family members. But this time, he was on his own, and Dahlia wasn't there to help with the language and the customs. There were many meals where he ate alone and took a stroll by himself.

As Shabbat neared, one of the professors, Dr. Emile Weisbrod, asked him to join his extended family for Friday night dinner. Emile was Leonard's primary contact for the lecture series. He had helped him sharpen his focus on the subjects of most interest to the doctoral students.

Their home was in Ra'anana, and the travel time from the downtown hotel by taxi was just under forty minutes. The city sat on the Sharon Plain and was home to many European and American émigrés.

Leonard rang the front bell and was soon greeted by Emile's wife. After a few pleasantries, he was escorted through the house and out the back to the large backyard. Several long tables with seating for the almost two dozen guests had been prepared. A stream of ceramic platters and bowls piled high with food made its way from the kitchen to the center of the tables. Pitchers filled with juices and six uncorked wine bottles stood on a square table standing off to the side.

Emile welcomed him and began the introductions of neighbors, family, and colleagues. It was a clear night, and even though it was December, outdoor dining was delightful. White electric lights dangled among the thick-limbed mango trees. Five lanterns burned warmly around the perimeter of the yard. Emile and his wife circulated, encouraging the guests to find a seat.

Leonard was seated near but not next to Emile. He and his wife weren't particularly religious, but every Friday they lit candles and made blessings over the wine and challah bread. Just before the meal officially began, their two children scampered out of the house and the Weisbrods covered their children's heads with their hands and raced through the Priestly Blessing. A few kisses, and the children returned to their home.

The guests at Leonard's table spoke English in order to allow him to join the conversation. However, they mainly discussed Israeli politics, so Leonard listened and asked just a few questions. The Israelis did their best to explain the situations in terms of equivalent American events, although some didn't have clear parallels.

Leonard was well into the meal when a woman to his left asked him to share a little about his family. Leonard complied, starting with his late first wife, then sharing how he met Dahlia Schein. He nostalgically recounted their chance encounter at a pharmacology lecture series.

The folks near Leonard began to overhear and took interest in his romantic story. They subtly toned down their voices and listened.

He recounted that Dahlia had been married to a wonderful man, Yonatan Schein, who was killed in the Yom Kippur War, and she had a beautiful daughter named Maya. He added that Maya was now married to a Jewish man from the American Midwest, and they had a three-year-old son named Yonatan.

The guests who were listening to the story were all too familiar with the reality of war, death, and the need for the survivors to move on. They empathized that his life was complex and that he, too, had experienced tragedy.

On this perfect evening in Ra'anana, he was no longer a stranger. He wasn't just the American professor whom Emile invited over.

As fruit platters replaced the main courses of fish, chicken, and salads, a woman came over to Leonard. She introduced herself. "I'm Rebecca Melman. I think we knew of your wife and her deceased husband. Was his name Yonatan? Did he die fighting in the Golan?"

Leonard raised his eyebrows and replied, "Yes, that was his name. He was killed in the Golan. My grandson, Yoni, is named after him."

Rebecca clarified, "We didn't actually know the Scheins, but we did know a family called the Shapiras. Eli Shapira also died in the Golan along with his entire tank crew, including Commander Yonatan Schein." Shaking her head, she said, "So many died, but this I remember."

Rebecca thought carefully and added, "We were at Eli's wedding, and it would have been likely, very likely, that Dahlia and Yonatan were there too."

Leonard was familiar with Israeli weddings. Often attended by about five hundred guests, they were very casual and notoriously ran behind schedule.

Rebecca continued, "We have kept in touch with the Shapiras. We knew that Eli's reserve duty team members were all so close, like family. The loss was terrible. Like a healthy tree being wrenched from the ground."

Rebecca finished, her voice just a notch quieter, saying, "Someone mentioned that the commander's wife did eventually remarry an American. And she moved to the US with him and her daughter."

Leonard had been quiet, taken aback by how he and this stranger shared all these connections. "It sounds like Dahlia and Maya. I'm sure it is. Thank you for the story. I will tell my wife."

The evening in Ra'anana wound down, and after many thank-yous and Shabbat shaloms, one of Emile's friends drove Leonard back to his hotel in Tel Aviv. Having eaten and drunk so much, there was little talk in the car. Leonard just stared out the window, the skyline of Tel Aviv silhouetted against a full moon and millions of stars.

In his hotel room, Leonard turned on the television, but he was soon bored by the meager entertainment offerings. He walked out onto the balcony, and staring down ten floors below at the thin rims of breaking waves washing onto the broad beach, a question occurred to him. He thought to himself, *wouldn't it be fantastic if little Yoni could someday see a movie of his namesake, Yonatan, to see him alive, in action, maybe even with Dahlia or Maya?*

And he wondered whether anyone had any videos of the Shapira wedding. And he wondered whether maybe, just maybe, Eli Shapira's tank crew and their commander would be in the amateur's film. Even a brief look at a once-upon-a-time grandpa would be a great gift for Yoni.

On Sunday – a business day in Israel – Leonard walked into Emile's office, described his plan, and asked for help. Emile recognized the good-hearted generosity of his colleague's interest. This kind of thoughtfulness from a stepfather on behalf of his stepdaughter's child was uncommon. Emile was moved. He promised to speak to his wife, who he knew was friendly with Rebecca Melman.

Later that afternoon, after the lecture, Leonard returned to his hotel room and found the telephone's message light blinking. Emile had left the phone number of Rachelle Shapira, wife of the late Eli Shapira. He added that she now lived in Herzliya, not far from Tel Aviv.

Leonard called Rachelle. After a few minutes of trying to explain despite the language barrier, he learned that she, in fact, did have a fifteen-minute, 8-millimeter film from their wedding in 1962. An American uncle had brought a hand-held home movie camera and half a dozen boxes of three-minute black and white film.

Rachelle invited him to come to Herzliya and take a look at the film.

Two days later, Leonard found himself ringing the doorbell on the third floor of a Herzliya apartment building located about ten streets away from the beach. It was a warm day, and even climbing three flights made him work up a sweat.

Rachelle opened the door and welcomed Leonard. "*Shalom, shalom*, please come in."

Leonard responded, "Mrs. Shapira, thank you for taking the time to see me. I greatly appreciate it."

She was approximately the same age as Dahlia, maybe a bit more weathered and her attire more matronly, but he was charmed to hear the very same accented English that his beloved Dahlia spoke.

Inside the apartment, Rachelle offered Leonard a choice of hot tea or a cold soft drink before they sat down at the dinette. Alongside a plate of pastries were a photo album and a yellow Kodak box. Leonard resisted the urge to flip through the album and first introduced himself, explaining the reason for his visit.

Mrs. Shapira said, "First, please call me Rachelle. Americans are too formal."

Leonard chuckled, "Yes, of course. Thank you, Rachelle."

Leonard sipped the cool drink and nibbled on a pastry. After a brief reference to the Shabbat dinner in Ra'anana, Rachelle broached the topic of the long-ago wedding and the handiwork of the American photographer.

"Leonard, before we look at a photo album and try to view the home movie, let me share a bit about my husband Eli and the tank crew." As she spoke, she stood up and walked to a bookshelf, then to an end table, and finally to a window ledge, collecting five framed pictures.

She returned to the dinette. First, she handed him a picture of the tank crew standing in front of their behemoth M60 Patton. Leonard held it at arm's length, looked into Rachelle's eyes, and said, "I have seen this exact picture before." He explained, "My wife Dahlia has a copy, and she keeps it in a small leather pouch. I know the man on the far left is Yonatan. Please, which man is Eli?"

Biting her lip, she pointed to the man second from the right, and said, "That is Eli." Both Leonard and Rachelle were pleased they had used the present tense.

Rachelle continued, "You know that they fought together in 1967? In the Golan then, too. They were called up for reserve duty. The rest of the reserve crew came from other units. In 1973, they were part of the reserves called up on Yom Kippur."

She sighed and described, "Every few months, we'd get together for one event or another –a wedding, a birth, even just a barbecue on the beach."

Rachelle wondered how she should talk about Yonatan and Dahlia. She spoke more slowly, saying, "I hope you won't mind, but Dahlia and Yonatan were a wonderful couple. Everybody liked them."

She went on, "Dahlia was a nurse or a social worker of some kind. I think she helped Holocaust survivors who struggled to get along. I think Yonatan was an engineer. Their daughter Maya was spirited and smart and lovely." She paused. "I suppose it's odd to tell you what you already know."

Leonard felt uncomfortable with the asymmetry of the recounting. He plaintively asked, "Please, Rachelle, would you tell me about Eli and your family?"

Rachelle handed Leonard three more of the photographs she had retrieved and sighed, "I've gotten along. I didn't remarry. Almost, but I didn't. Maybe someday. Our three children live nearby, and I have already five grandchildren. I'm all right."

Leonard looked at one of the photographs. Rachelle was in the center, and all around her was the family that she and Eli had created. Leonard studied the pictures as she shared the names and relationships of all the bright, tanned Israeli faces.

The last framed photo was the largest, and it featured a large, posed group at Rachelle and Eli's wedding. The men of Yonatan's tank crew stood alongside their wives or girlfriends. The men were in simple dark pants and white shirts. The women wore light summer dresses, while Rachelle was dressed in a classic, modest wedding gown. There were Yonatan and Dahlia, just to the left of Rachelle and Eli.

Rachelle said wistfully, "We were all young, all so poor. Remember that the State of Israel was only thirteen years old, and everything was in turmoil. But it was a fun-filled, beautiful evening, and I loved the man I married."

She stopped to gather herself from her reminiscence. She sat up straight and remarked, "It was very unusual to have home movies. We didn't even have television in Israel until 1969, and even then, only two hours a day."

Rachelle reassured, "Even if the movie isn't any good, you know, maybe it's ruined from the heat and humidity, at least your grandson can see his namesake with his very best friends."

Leonard saw that Rachelle had found the Kodak projector with its built-in protective holding case and had brought it into the dining room. Without too much trouble, he was able to thread the brittle film through the docks and sprockets and adjust the lens for viewing. With a flick of the power toggle, the machine hummed to life. After several moments of scratchy, milky, abstract images, the wedding's scenes began to dance across Rachelle's dining room wall.

The pictures, in black and white, had deteriorated little over almost thirty years, and the silent apparitions encouraged the observer to conjure up the music and voices. Leonard was transfixed by the jumpy images of once-young people gliding by at a wedding, now recreated decades later in a dining room in Herzliya. In spite of crude splicing, the sequence of the ceremony and the party revealed the flow of the evening's festivities.

He heard Rachelle's breathing deepen as the ghostly, bittersweet tableau flickered by at the end of a dust-filled throw of light. The machine whirred away with the sprockets nosily pulling the thin, brown film from reel to reel and past the bright projector bulb.

They saw the rabbi facing Rachelle and Eli, the three of them and the couple's parents gathered under a four-cornered wedding *chuppah*, the canopy symbolizing their first home. The bride and groom were all smiles, and they moved effortlessly among guests and onto the dance floor.

Leonard's eyes glistened when he caught a sight of Dahlia walking arm in arm with Yonatan. They, too, danced to silent music and soundlessly mouthed what must have been words of congratulations and best wishes. Leonard thought to himself how they, in this celluloid world, would forever be joined. Moments later, the last of the film fed through the projector, and the trailing end's repeated slapping in its reel signaled the end of the time travel experience.

It was a rude reminder for them to return to the present. Leonard saw that Rachelle's face was wet with tears. He placed his hand on her forearm and said, "I hope this wasn't too painful." He confessed, "When I see a photo of my first wife, I am dazed by the madness of irreversible time."

Moments passed, and each strained to return to the present and to regain their composure.

"Thank you for sharing all this," Leonard said. "I know Dahlia will be very moved, and I'm sure that both Maya and Yoni will be very grateful."

Over the next few days, Leonard arranged with a local photography store to copy the old film onto two new VHS cassettes. He returned one to Rachelle along with the original eight-millimeter film, and the other he carried back to the United States. He would wait for the right time to share these memories and images with his family.

Yoni unwrapped the small, flat package. He saw the VHS cassette and imagined it was a funny cartoon movie. Maybe it was a numbers and letters show, or maybe it featured his favorite jungle animals.

Leonard chose not to prolong the suspense. As Yoni's little fingers undid the scotch tape and ripped open the paper, Leonard told the highlights of the story of his remarkable discovery.

Leonard paused and made tender eye contact with Dahlia. The two of them shared a trusting nod, and he asked Maya directly, "Honey, Dahlia and I want this to be a special, meaningful moment for you as well. Would you rather watch it later, maybe by yourself?"

Maya thought for a few seconds and answered, "Leonard, this is so wonderful of you." She stopped again for a moment, not wanting to lose control of her emotions.

She finally managed, "You are such a wonderful step-dad. I love you."

She placed one hand on Leonard's shoulder and one hand on Yoni's head, "Yes, let's watch it together. Let's introduce Yoni to Yonatan."

14 The Class Project

Mr. Brenner's Hebrew High classroom was replete with evidence that he firmly believed neatness was not a virtue. The bulletin boards were plastered thick with news articles push-pinned into the cork, and maps of Israel dangled haphazardly, shingled with curled yellow sticky notes. His teacher's desk and even his bent plywood chair were covered with books, pamphlets, and newspapers. His six-foot-two, filled-out figure wouldn't have fit at that desk anyway.

All the parents loved Mr. Brenner because nobody kept the kids interested like he did, especially given that their Hebrew High School class was right after their regular public school day ended. He was special.

For Yoni, now in ninth grade, Mr. Brenner's scholarship added to all that his Israeli-born mother had taught him. It was obvious that Mr. Brenner was very well versed in contemporary Israeli history. He often toted around the most recent publication on the subject, and he'd scan through Israeli newspapers. Yoni, thanks to Maya, was the class's Hebrew-speaking superstar. For the most part, his classmates were interested in and supportive of Israel. Since Jews were a tiny minority in Indiana, the class was one of the only Jewish parts of the students' lives. Their class of nine, with four boys and five girls, had been together since preschool. They used to feel like brothers and sisters, but now that they were in high school, they started to have crushes on each other.

Mr. Brenner often applied the Socratic method of asking questions to his students to frame the lesson. Bits of the Bible, current events, and Hebrew language were embedded in the brainteasers he'd use to challenge his pupils. When the answer wasn't soon found, he'd dole out enticing hints. Sometimes, he'd give them challenging codes to crack based on *gematria*, the numerical values of Hebrew letters.

Legend had it that before Mr. Brenner started teaching at the Plains Hebrew High School, he was a senior partner managing an advertising agency on Madison Avenue. The rumor was that he had been very successful launching big-time marketing and communications campaigns. His catchy tag lines, smart strategies, and targeted ads made him a millionaire many times over, and he supposedly sold the company and chose a simpler life back in Indiana.

Mr. Brenner minimized classroom competition and instead fostered a love of shared effort. He'd often quote Helen Keller: "Alone we can do so little; together we can do so much." The kids would nod in agreement, even though they couldn't envision the corporate dysfunction that helped him reach that conclusion.

He promoted individual thought, and at the same time finessed a collegiality searching for a shared, improved intellectual product. He'd traffic-cop a rapid-fire debate, adding and subtracting ideas while lurching forward toward a climactic consensus the class could claim as its own.

Yoni had settled into his seat just as Mr. Brenner spun around, gathering energy and using his pointer finger like a magician's wand, proclaiming, "I just hired this class – you creative geniuses – to take on a new marketing campaign."

With a stern expression, he warned, "Don't be too happy, it is a very tough assignment. You'll be marketing a product that has been kicked around for a while and has many critics."

He shared with the kids, "Once upon a time, I worked in the advertising business. I helped companies sell all kinds of goodies, from toilet paper to hotel rooms to cars."

They listened intently, fascinated by their teacher's past life. "Believe it or not, you can make a living convincing the public they want what they don't need..." His voice trailed off.

With flexing knees and outstretched arms, he announced, "Okay, here we go. Our firm of Kugel and Kreplach, LLP, has been hired by the State of Israel to launch a public relations campaign."

The kids giggled.

He paused and then added with mock gravitas, "They need a series of posters that help tell the story of the rebirth of the Jewish state and increase tourism."

He prodded dramatically, "Are you up for it?"

Together, the class voiced its approval.

Yoni Baranson was enjoying the buildup and was fully on board. He nudged Samantha, who was sitting to his right. He excitedly commented, "This should be fun." Yoni had a thing for Samantha, but she rarely showed him any interest. Today was no different as he received only the faintest, dismissive smile in response.

Mr. Brenner reached into his shirt pocket and pulled out a folded page. "It's from the deputy prime minister's External Affairs Committee."

He continued adlibbing as he read the fictional memo, "Dear Sir, please ensure that your posters include reference to the legal basis for our Jewish state. We greatly look forward to seeing what you create. Best, Yogi Bearstein."

He folded the fake page and tucked it back into his pocket.

The class laughed, appreciating his attempt to entertain.

Mr. Brenner wondered out loud, "Can we come up with something that is visually exciting? How about something that details Israel's geopolitical reality? Something that describes and illustrates her legal basis?"

He added, "Gang, you should consider historically accurate references about the rebirth of Israel."

With five quick steps, Mr. Brenner moved to the flip chart easel. He turned over the top pages and smoothed out the next unused sheet. "Staff, what do you think are some important historic, pivotal statements or agreements that lead to Israel's rebirth? Let's start there."

The class was at first slow to respond. But soon, Mike Rabinovitz answered, "How about the November 29, 1947, UN vote for Israel's statehood?"

Mr. Brenner corrected, "Actually, Mikey, the 1947 vote was for UN Resolution 181, which would partition Palestine into two states, one Jewish and one Arab. But you are right, it was a very special date." In all caps, Mr. Brenner wrote RESOLUTION 181 on the blank page.

He reminded them: "And the vote was thirty-three in favor and thirteen opposed. Ten abstained."

Jabbing her hand in the air, Shelley Lester got his attention and spouted out, "May 14, 1948, Declaration of Independence, Tel Aviv."

She received a thumbs-up from Mr. Brenner. He affirmed, "Yup. It was an electric moment." He quickly followed up with a question. "Where did it happen? Anybody know?"

Marty Specter cautiously said, "Independence Hall."

Mr. Brenner shook his head with a half-smile, looking to see who would get the answer. Sheryl Miller raised her hand and volunteered, "I think it was at Mayor Dizengoff's home."

Again, Mr. Brenner shook his head. He asked, "Do you have another guess?"

Yoni spoke up, "It was at an art gallery. No, it was at an art museum."

Mr. Brenner smiled and concluded, "Close enough. It was, at the time, the Tel Aviv Museum, at 16 Rothschild Boulevard." He wrote DECLARATION OF INDEPENDENCE on the oversized page. "Remember, Tel Aviv was barely thirty-nine years old," Mr. Brenner added. "The city was created outside of ancient Jaffa with a lottery of sixty-six parcels of land."

Yoni raised his hand and suggested, "What about the Balfour Declaration?"

Mr. Brenner retorted, "Yes, what about it Yoni?"

Yoni told the class, "It was the first formal recognition of Jewish sovereign rights in the Middle East for two thousand years." He remembered reading how it was the British who wrote it. It came about twenty years after Herzl and the First Zionist Congress in Basel called for the creation of a Jewish state. The earlier Sykes-Picot Agreement influenced it.

Mr. Brenner nodded. "Mr. Baranson makes good points." He added BALFOUR DECLARATION to the easel's page.

"Okay. These three are enough," he announced. "Over the next twenty minutes, use the history books right here in the room or in the school library and find what you think are the key words for each of the documents. I will divide you into teams." With his index finger, he instructed, "You, you, and you" until there were three groups of three.

While the class scrambled, rustling through books and scribbling notes, Mr. Brenner taped three blank pages to the battleship-grey cinder-blocked wall. In bold block letters, he added onto each of the sheets one of the three critical events. He pronounced, "Ten minutes to go, write your headline at the top, and then we'll talk it over."

Yoni, Samantha, and Gary were done first. Samantha volunteered to write out their extraction from the Balfour Declaration: "His Majesty's government view with favor the establishment in Palestine of a national home for the Jewish people." Her handwriting was neat, and the words covered just the top sixth of the page. Also, her willingness to be the team's scribe, plus a few more relaxed interactions, were all that Yoni needed to feel a little more positive about his chances with Samantha.

The second group huddled around their blank page, and Mike wrote a quotation from UN Resolution 181: "and the establishment of the independence of the Arab and Jewish States."

Finishing last was Marty. He wrote in script a few key words from the Israeli Declaration of Independence: "hereby declare the establishment of a Jewish state in Eretz-Israel, to be known as the State of Israel." He placed his black marker in the tray and sat down.

Mr. Brenner eyed their work, rubbing his chin and considering what to do next. He told them, "You did a great job. These are the important words from three important documents. Together, let's look at each one, and let's see if we can somehow bridge between these legalistic phrases and today's Israeli reality."

As Mr. Brenner went on, Yoni couldn't help but daydream about traveling to Israel with his friends. Maybe he'd go on a program with his camp or youth group. He had gone several times with his parents, but now, he wanted a little independence, some adventure, and to meet Israelis. Maybe he'd even end up on the same trip as Samantha.

Wouldn't it be fun to walk on top of the ramparts of the Old City or to float in the Dead Sea? He could taste the dust from a climb up the rocky path to Masada. He'd done some of these things before with his family, but going with friends would be a whole different experience.

He would stroll along the beach next to the skyline of Tel Aviv that was once just barren sand dunes, not far from Rothschild Boulevard and Independence Hall, which Mr. Brenner described so well.

15 The Church

The pastor, silver-haired and bespectacled, paused and looked out across the overflowing Bethany Baptist Church. It was the year 2001, and the late-morning light filtered through the stained-glass windows, cutting diagonally across the room and brightening the varnished wood that accented the largely unadorned sanctuary. He had paused before finishing his eulogy for John Langford. As he spoke, he kept asking himself if he had done right by the deceased. Had any of John's fine qualities been overlooked? Was anyone forgotten when he listed all who loved John or had received his love?

The pastor concluded the eulogy with a parable. "Isn't it odd that when a great cruise ship begins its journey – when it is pulling away from the dock – that there is a joyous, noisy celebration, replete with a brass band, streamers, and champagne?

"Doesn't it make more sense that the hurrahs be reserved for after the passage has been successfully completed? Shouldn't the cheers be postponed until the challenges have been met, after crossing the roiled waters and plowing through dark storms?

"John Langford has successfully completed his life's journey, navigating through its difficulties. He completed it with flying colors, carrying all his passengers safely to the other side. And he did all this with a wonderful reputation in place, and with the love of his family and friends. Now, that's a journey worth celebrating."

With a comforting smile, the pastor gazed out across the crowd, his eyes finding and settling on Bobby. With a subtle nod, he stepped away from the pulpit and sat down.

Bobby rose slowly from the front row of seats. He had been sitting next to his mother, Nancy. Next to him were his wife Andrea and their two children, Susanne and Meredith. His two older sisters and their families sat next to them. His longtime friend, Danny Baranson, and Danny's wife Maya sat just two rows back.

Bobby walked to the pulpit past the honey-colored coffin, which was draped in an American flag to honor his father's military service. He was prepared to share his public goodbye to his father.

John Langford had lived to be seventy-four in spite of smoking two packs of cigarettes a day. Even after becoming a born-again Christian, he couldn't break the habit. He had been an active member of his church, a trusted business associate, and an ever-willing helper in his neighborhood.

His passing marked the last of his church's veterans who'd returned home to Dawkins to raise a family and live out their lives. He and his wife Nancy had never moved away and had settled into a tranquil lifestyle.

Bobby, standing tall at the pulpit, looked down at his prepared outline. He had fastened to his notes the picture of his dad standing by a jeep with his army buddies. The grainy, yellowing photo had hung in his father's home ever since Bobby found the box in the attic. His intention wasn't to use it as a prop, but rather, to keep himself centered on what he had come to think of as a defining moment in their early relationship. John's experiences in the war, as best as Bobby could determine, were the ones that shaped his life.

Bobby shared his discovery as a little boy in the attic some fifty years before with the congregation. He revealed how his father had hidden away mementoes from his time as a soldier until he explained to his family the painfully poignant events he experienced. Bobby shared pieces of his father's story of fighting in Germany, where he participated in liberating Dachau in 1945 and saved Jews and other victims from certain death. As for so many others of the Greatest Generation, the war constituted the most dramatic episodes of his life. Bobby expressed how the values of comradeship, dedication, and courage had guided his father's professional and family life.

Bobby went on to recall his father's principles and achievements. He remembered how attentive and affectionate John had been with his children and his grandchildren. He referred to John's virtues as a supportive and involved father and a sensitive and loyal husband. Although John's business partner had passed away a few years before, he recalled their collaboration and steadfastness through good times and tough ones.

"Dad, this is my last thank-you," Bobby somberly pronounced, his eyes shining with tears he refused to let fall. "I have come to appreciate a man's passing with his reputation intact and having walked humbly with God."

Stepping cautiously down from the pulpit, Bobby again passed the flag-covered casket. He squared his shoulders and brushed his left hand over the crisp, neatly stitched stripes.

Three months later, in a different church and in a different town, a different pastor was waiting in his office for Bobby's sixteen-year-old daughter, Susanne. Although Bobby loved growing up in Dawkins, after he graduated from college, he'd gotten a job in Petersville. He and Andrea really enjoyed the community there.

The pastor had taken a few minutes to prepare for the surprise he had to share with her. It was going to be a fun, gratifying meeting.

Swinging back away from his desk, he looked out of a partially opened window to the nearby pasture. He reflected on his life's journey. In college, he had majored in English literature and minored in biblical studies. Over the next few years, he'd taught English at Mast High School and become the coach for their baseball team. In these same years, Ed had begun to feel a calling to the church and a deepening of his Christian beliefs. He and his wife Patti had decided to plan out a life that would include ordination and eventual ministry.

While Ed's father and mother were devout Christians, they hadn't pressed him to pursue the clergy as a career. Relying on the money he had saved and his wife's income, he enrolled in a nearby seminary to become a Christian pastor. He was a very good student of the Bible, having studied it since he was a little boy.

As an ordained Christian pastor, he taught life's lessons and shared religious doctrine. He had thoroughly learned the Old Testament, so he was knowledgeable about the history of ancient Israelites and the Lord's covenant that gave them the land of Israel. The New Testament, with its narratives of Jesus and the Apostles, various letters, and the Book of Revelations provided the basis for his faith.

But Pastor Ed would readily say that it was his six-month study program in Israel where he experienced a revelation. He loved to say that seeing Israel made the Holy Scriptures come alive. Walking on the land where Jesus preached heightened the spiritual significance of those passages for him. Walking the streets of Jerusalem, Nazareth, and Bethlehem or swimming in the waters of the Jordan River and the Sea of Galilee, the Bible was his roadmap. He felt a visceral, practical connection to his Savior, and he returned to the United States ready to advance the word of the Lord.

In addition to the Bible coming alive for him in the Holy Land, Pastor Ed had come to seriously value God's eternal covenant with the Jewish people and His faithfulness to return them to their ancient homeland after centuries of exile. He came to understand better the Hebraic context of Jesus's ministry as well as the Jewish roots of Christianity. Jesus and the Apostles were Jewish and had observed the prescribed customs and festivals. They had led Jewish lives in a land that is today the modern State of Israel.

Susanne's light footfalls on the wooden staircase alerted Pastor Ed to her arrival. He quickly straightened his chaotic desk. The unruly stacks of books, notes, and magazines covering the entire surface embarrassed him. His door was already open, so she knocked on the doorframe. "Hello, Pastor Ed."

He gave Susanne a hearty handshake and a shoulder thump. Even in threadbare jeans and a dated sweatshirt, her fresh, glowing persona added energy to the room.

He offered her a Dr. Pepper from his mini-refrigerator, and she happily accepted.

These meetings were pretty usual for the two of them, because Susanne was so involved in the church. The pastor and Susanne had a great relationship, and he counted her among the most devoted of the high school kids. She worked with him on the Christmas show and the Easter pageant, and she was a workhorse on the multi-church food drive. She liaised between Saint Vincent's Catholic Church and the Jewish Temple Beth David to coordinate interfaith youth events.

Over the previous two years, she had been a spark plug in the Israel Study Group. She was fascinated by how her spiritual learning related to physical places in Israel. She had several Jewish friends from her interfaith events whom she would always ask about it. Some of her friends even had family there. She came to understand the country's modern struggles. She yearned to go there someday.

Pastor Ed wanted to believe that Susanne's deeper interest in Israel began with a sermon he had given a little over two years before. On that rainy Sunday morning, he recounted, "When I was in Jerusalem last fall, I talked with the archivists at Yad Vashem." Pastor Ed clarified, although he was sure most of his congregants knew, "Yad Vashem is Israel's national memorial for all those murdered in the Holocaust."

He had struggled through all of the exhibits, including the Holocaust History Museum and the Children's Memorial. He had emerged feeling depressed and ashamed. "Somehow, being a man of the cloth, I felt a personal guilt for Christianity's role in anti-Semitism over the centuries. In spite of the fact that I cannot think of a member of my family who has ever uttered a vile word of hate, I still felt a deep, nauseating guilt.

"To process my thoughts, I took a walk on the grounds. I found myself on the Avenue of the Righteous among the Nations. It's where Christians and others are recognized for saving Jewish lives. There, I read many plaques noting their names and nationalities. I read also that when Yad Vashem was opened in May 1962, in Prime Minister Golda Meir's speech, she referred to the non-Jewish heroes as 'drops of love in an ocean of poison.'"

Pastor Ed let the words sink in. Then he asked, "Can anyone guess how many Righteous among the Nations heroes have been identified? How many Christians stepped forward and risked their own lives to save Jews from the Holocaust?"

He leaned in closer to his flock. "Think about the dangers they faced, the banging on their doors in the middle of the night. Think about the Nazi brutality and what would happen if you were caught hiding a Jew. We all know about Oskar Schindler and Raoul Wallenberg and Archbishop Damaskinos. But who were the other brave souls who saved Jewish victims? Yad Vashem has kept records. Their archivists know."

The parishioners were trying to picture the terrifying scenes, trying to imagine what was at stake. Hands went up and voices blurted out, "Fifty."

"Five hundred."

"One thousand."

Ed pointed skyward. "More."

Someone shouted out, "Okay, three thousand."

Pastor Ed's solemn face brightened. "My dear friends, there have been over twenty-four thousand recognized cases, and there are certain to be more that were never recorded. Twenty-four thousand."

Eyes widened.

Pastor Ed nodded. "It was sadly a small number in proportion to the six million Jews killed. But I know you have heard the phrase, 'If you save one life, it is as if you have saved the whole world.' It's from the Jewish Talmud."

His tone changed from somber to matter-of-fact. "We, as good Christians and as Christian Zionists, must recognize today's threats from all over the Middle East and around the world too. We must help protect the Jewish state."

The pastor opened the Bible that sat before him and read, "Genesis 12:2–3, regarding the Jews and the land of Israel: 'I will make you into a great nation, and I will bless you; I will make your name great, and you will be a blessing. I will bless those who bless you, and whoever curses you I will curse; and all peoples on earth will be blessed through you.'"

He turned to another page. "Have you carefully read Isaiah 62:6? It says: 'I have posted watchmen on your walls, Jerusalem; they will never be silent day or night.'

"The phrase 'never be silent, day or night' says that we are here, proactive, for the long term, prepared to address crises or have the resilience and the persistence. The word 'watchmen' implies steadfastness. It's plural, thereby embracing all of our many constituencies. The verse means that we Christians all stand together upon broad, defensible 'walls' that are ours and have been there for millennia."

He wished everyone the chance to visit Israel. He prayed that members of his congregational family would find their places on the wall.

Dr. Pepper in hand, he asked Susanne specifically about her mother, Andrea. "Please tell me, how's your mother doing? I haven't spoken with her in a while."

Susanne had told Pastor Ed about her mother's difficult early life. After her mother passed away and her father abandoned her,

Andrea's new life with her Aunt Tina had healed so much pain and had introduced her to the church and humanitarian service missions. Pastor Ed saw that Susanne's altruism and interest in the church stemmed directly from Tina's guidance and strength.

"She's good. Nothing new, really," Susanne reported.

"Okay, well, send her and your father my regards."

Although he was sure he knew the answer, he asked, "Susanne, do you remember the sermon I gave a while back about Yad Vashem?"

She affirmed, "Yes, I definitely do."

He said, "Your dad once told me about your Grandpa John's experiences in the war liberating Dachau. I'm sure he's told you as well."

Susanne nodded. "My dad has told me the story many times."

He took a sip of Dr. Pepper. "Well, that's why I bring up the Righteous among the Nations. Your grandfather, in a way, is a part of that. Your family holds a very special legacy."

He cut the intensity with a wide smile. "Susanne, our church wants you to go Israel next summer for a two-week learning program. Now, unfortunately you'll have to raise the money to cover the flight, but I already reserved a place for you. I hope that's okay," he winked.

"Of course it's okay! I can't believe I finally get to go to Israel!" Beaming, she sprung out of her seat to grab her notebook. "Tell me the dates!"

16 The Parade

It was the fourth of July, and the Dawkins high school band marched down the street past Scuitto's Hardware. From the Langford family's vantage point, all they could hear were the muffled thumps of the base drum. The band stopped every hundred feet or so to play, slowly approaching where the Langford family stood.

Three gleaming fire trucks motored by. Local Boy Scout and Girl Scout troops clumped past, carrying wide banners. Following them was a mixed contingent of veterans with chins held high, wearing angled caps affixed with World War II, Korean War, or Vietnam War badges.

The band churned forward, led by flag bearers and pom-pom-shaking cheerleaders, until the drum major whistled them to a halt. On the crowded sidewalk, Bobby held onto Susanne and Meredith's shoulders, edging them forward just a bit. "Perfect spot. Look girls, they're playing just for you." Even though his daughters were both in high school now, Bobby couldn't help but treat them like his little girls.

Bobby and Andrea stood behind them, not wanting to block the view of the Dawkins Independence Day extravaganza.

The drum major wore a tall, white, fuzzy hat, decorated with braids and buttons and with a small shiny black brim. Thrusting up his long baton, he signaled for the beginning of John Phillip Sousa's magnum opus, "Stars and Stripes Forever."

The sidewalk audience was enveloped for three and a half minutes by the stirring strains of the famously identifiable 1896 march music. It featured the recognizable piccolo obbligato playing against, and eventually with, the powerful brass trumpets, trombones, and tubas. It was pure small-town Fourth of July American patriotic majesty, and the Langfords loved every minute of it.

As the band moved past, Bobby was drawn back to a parade of thirty years before. His father wore his best suit, dark blue with a fine pin stripe, along with a blue button-down and a red herringbone tie. John's spiffy parade attire contrasted with Bobby's casual ironed blue jeans and short-sleeved shirt. Soon after the parade finished, John Langford would stand on the speaker's platform with the mayor and the town councilmen. The celebration committee had asked him to read Abraham Lincoln's Gettysburg Address. It was an honor reserved each year for a veteran who had served his country. The entire Langford family was honored.

The Memorial Park centerpiece was a four-sided grey marble obelisk to honor those who died in the Civil War, the Spanish-American War, and the First World War. On the sides of the obelisk's base were the carved names of the honored dead.

With a little American flag in hand, Bobby had listened to each of the 273 words that his dad had spoken with poise to the crowd. John had not mimicked the elaborate, dramatic oratorical style of Lincoln's day; instead, with reverence, he smoothly enunciated each word.

Today, Bobby especially missed his veteran father.

Last year, the Baransons had joined the Langfords for the parade. Bobby and Danny had reminisced about their school days and recalled their shared experiences and common friends. Their families had gotten to know each other very well over the years. This year, though, the Baransons hadn't been able to make it.

Bobby watched the parade and all the people in attendance. He thought about how their town was made up of steadfast, multigenerational locals, not the upwardly mobile transients from big cities. They had no high-paid sports teams or garish, expensive stadiums. People in Dawkins loved their local high school and college teams, who played before parents and friends all sitting on backless bleacher seats.

People slept well knowing that American soldiers would always defend them. Patriotism was authentic and not just felt one or two days a year; it was rooted in the ground that cradled their dear departed defenders.

When the band finished playing and continued marching down Main Street, the Langfords waited for the crowd to clear. They meandered over to Memorial Park to hear another townsperson honored with reciting the Gettysburg Address.

On the way, Meredith spied Pappy's Diner with its red and yellow awning and suggested, "Let's stop for a hot dog and a soda. It will be a while until the ceremony finishes. By the time we get to Pastor Ed's barbecue, we'll be starving."

Bobby knew she was right because of the knotted-up parking lot and the traffic on the back roads to the church.

Andrea piped up, "Sure, Meredith, that's a good idea."

They grabbed four franks and four cans of soda to go and ate them on the way to the park. Soon after the ceremony, they found themselves maneuvering to escape from the chaotic downtown parking lot. They eventually reached the back roads for the hour-long drive back home. Their route took them past a tapestry of pastoral scenes. Bobby quietly drove on.

As Bobby drove, he thought about Dawkins – his parents' hometown, the locale of his childhood, and how he always enjoyed sharing it with his wife and daughters. It was hard to describe why he felt so deeply connected to it. Was it a statement of solidarity with his mom and dad's past, a prayer that his kids would value their pathways? Having them there with him was a sort of promise kept, a check mark in a mythical ledger.

Recently, Bobby had been sensing the slippages and uncertainties of aging. What used to be a muscular abdomen suddenly became a pot-belly. Energy never used to be an issue, but now, fatigue set in after only a little exercise. His smooth runner's glide was now jerky, and jogging jarred his knees and hips. Susanne and Meredith would soon lead their own lives. He wondered if they would bring their families back to Dawkins. There was a nagging urgency to grab something permanent.

Finally, after nearly a two-hour ride with all the holiday traffic, the Langfords arrived at the Bethany Baptist Church. Bobby pulled off the road and onto an adjoining grassy field. When he stopped the car, his wife and daughters woke up.

Bobby announced, "Here at last! Thank God Almighty, here at last."

All four took their time stretching before opening car doors and stepping out into the late afternoon sun. Bobby was the last to emerge from the car. He sighed, "I'm beat. Maybe the dinner will pep me up."

They all could see smoke rising from the fire pit, square pop-up tents, white-aproned cooks, and rows of tables.

Bobby scanned the crowd, looking for familiar faces. He focused on Pastor Ed and watched him drift from table to table, talking easily with his parishioners and saying hello to the newcomers. Getting closer, he heard the pastor juxtapose Jesus's miraculous loaves and fish "menu" with the roasting chickens, side dishes, and desserts. He enjoyed innocent riffing on the simple feeding of the five thousand, two millennia before that was recorded in all four canonical Gospels.

Pastor Ed was in his element, joyously entertaining and feeding the masses on the nation's birthday. Everyone was mellow, sated, and appreciative.

After dinner and after bits and pieces of chattering with fellow congregants, the Langfords headed home. Like everyone else, they'd had fun, and the chicken hadn't disappointed. Only Bobby seemed out of sorts.

On the drive back, Andrea inquired, "Honey, you didn't even polish off your plate, and normally you go after part of mine. Wasn't it up to snuff?"

Bobby speculated, "Maybe it was the hot dog back in Dawkins. I just feel…well, not one hundred percent. Maybe it was the long drive."

After covering a few more miles, Bobby suggested hopefully to Andrea, "I'm sure I'll feel better tomorrow."

17 Treatment

Off to the right of the Palm Grove Cancer Center's chemotherapy waiting room, a dozen tropical fish swam in their cubic world. With a soothing slow motion and synchronized pace, they easily avoided colliding with each other or sideswiping the three steep coral mountains. It was 2008, and while the rest of the country listened to Alicia Keys and Chris Brown, soft oldies tunes washed over the Florida hospital's older patients.

In the center of the waiting room, sitting behind an oval island desk was the tall young woman who reviewed the sign-in sheet. She'd watch the patients autograph the lined page, and with a soft voice she identically told each patient, "Please take a seat until you are called."

Comfortable bucket chairs and sofas were arranged in groups of two, three, and four, and side tables offered neat stacks of up-to-date magazines.

As a result of Bobby's diagnosis, even though he and Andrea were in their forties, they had decided to retire early and rent a home in Florida half the year. The cancer made it very difficult for Bobby to continue working. Thankfully, he'd done very well for himself as an engineer, so retiring early was an option. He and Andrea had always dreamed of retiring to an area with warm weather and a beach. With Bobby's declining health, they decided to live there part-time as Meredith went off to college.

Bobby was already sitting alone in the middle of a three-chair grouping when Arnie Krakow walked in. Arnie sat down and began shuffling through a manila folder stuffed with newspaper clippings. His head was tilted up and his eyes focused down as he looked though the lower half of his eyeglasses, trying to read each piece's headline.

Recognizing each other from prior visits, Bobby and Arnie nodded. They had seen each other three or four times and shared simple pleasantries. Bobby imagined that this kind of modern medicine camaraderie, shaped by common misfortune, must be similar to combat buddies in a shared foxhole. They silently acknowledged each other's courage, understanding the other's pains and fears.

Bobby sat down near Arnie and asked reflexively, "How are you doing?"

Arnie responded, "You know what they say. What's a little cancer so long as you've got your health?"

Bobby burst out laughing. "Perfect."

"It's a favorite of mine."

"That really sums up it up. Half full, half empty, " Bobby added.

Arnie continued, "More like *quarter* full, half empty."

Arnie had always liked non sequiturs with their clever use of the absurd and clear disrespect for the conventional, the convenient, and the cliché.

Minutes later, a nurse, carrying a thick folder, stepped partway through the double doors at the back of the waiting room and called out Arnie's name. "Arnold...Krakow, Arnold."

Arnie thought to himself about the sonorous, hopeful tone that doctor's office nurses used when they announced your name. It never seemed to fit the situation. He wondered if maybe they thought they were announcing your winning selection by the lottery commissioner and didn't realize that what you hear is the warden's unsympathetic voice echoing down the concrete corridors of death row.

When Bobby's name was called, like Arnie's before him, he passed through the double doors and was led to a cozy, square room designed not to feel like a hospital. Instead of stainless steel, white Formica, and glass, there was wooden furniture and comfortable seating.

Exiting the pre-treatment room, Bobby was then escorted through another set of double doors and around a corner to the infusion room, where a plaid lounge chair waited. There, magic elixirs would be introduced into his body through his previously installed chest port.

The infusion room's chemo delivery chairs were nicely spaced and separated by privacy curtains that were drawn back. The chairs looked much like La-Z-Boy loungers, but with extended armrests. Different combinations of electronic monitors, rolling infusion poles, two-tier utility carts, and visitors' chairs stood by each patient. As Bobby walked by, Arnie looked up, happy to see that he was to be docked right next to him.

Bobby was soon seated, wired, and connected. His specially prepared cancer-fighting cocktail dripped through a tube downstream from a saline pouch that hung limply from a pole. Arnie thought to himself that he'd give Bobby time for the nurses to complete their routine before he began a conversation.

About fifteen minutes later, Arnie looked to his left and saw Bobby was awake and looking passively at the tiled ceiling. Quietly, he asked Bobby, "Are you comfortable? Would you like to chat?"

Bobby turned his head and then his shoulders toward Arnie. "Sure, it's a good way to make the time pass. Let me introduce myself."

Bobby felt the loneliness of battling cancer. His wife Andrea had been so kind and supportive. But the impossible-to-suppress fears for himself ping-ponged around in his mind.

Sometimes, Bobby thought back to his father and mother and their clear-eyed view of right and wrong. He faced the battle with cancer knowing he was his father's son. Recalling the Indiana home where he was raised and the events that had shaped his life, Bobby thought to himself, *Dad fought his way across Europe and survived to tell about it, and now I have to tough it out with radiation and chemo and whatever else is in store for me.*

Bobby rearranged his blanket and began, "I'm Bobby Langford. I'm originally from a small town in Indiana, and my wife Andrea and I still live near there. We have a small winter home here in sunny Florida near Stuart."

Brightening, he added, "I told my wife I could handle this one by myself. She'll be here to pick me up afterwards. How about you?"

Pausing for a moment, Arnie had to organize his thoughts so he could give an equally succinct response. "I was born and raised in New York City, and we lived in New Jersey before retiring to Florida," he said. "We have a place near Boynton Beach."

Bobby nodded. Arnie continued, "Yeah, Fran will retrieve me later, too. She's off duty right now."

They sat in silence for a moment. Arnie noted, "Congratulations to us. Neither of us chose to identify our cancers."

"Great. I don't know about you, but I resent being tagged as the 'fill-in-the-blank malignant organ guy,'" he said.

Gathering steam, Arnie added, "We both led full lives and there was no damn reason why some misanthrope's 'glad it's not me' pity should define me as one diagnosis, one flawed body part, and skip over the full measure of my life, and not acknowledge all the good stuff."

Bobby smiled back and agreed, "Absolutely right. It's the same as when somebody dies and all the chatter is about what in his last days or minutes he said or did. It's all out of proportion."

As Arnie repositioned himself in his lounge chair, a manila folder stuffed with news clippings slid off his blanket and onto the floor.

The clippings cascaded out. An auburn-haired nurse happened to see the minor accident and glided over. She scooped up the newspaper fragments and tucked them back into the folder. With a smile, she handed them back to Arnie.

Bobby casually asked Arnie, "Whatcha got there? Working on something interesting?" Arnie was now faced with a dilemma. He thought to himself that Bobby, who was a total stranger, seemed like a bright, affable fellow. They had exchanged only a few dozen unremarkable words, but Bobby did appreciate his gallows humor.

The real reason for the clippings was to help Arnie craft a letter to the editor of a national paper concerning a sensitive subject. Arnie was unsure of how to answer Bobby or how candid he should be.

Arnie cautiously inched forward with his explanation. "Well, I don't know your politics, but here goes." Deliberately avoiding the big reveal about his touchy subject and his point of view, Arnie stalled, "I'm writing a letter to the editor to a national paper. It probably won't be published, but it makes me feel better."

Bobby listened carefully, waiting for the specifics. He showed no reaction and simply inhaled and exhaled a little more deeply. The tubes, the funky colored liquids with the little bubbles, the antiseptic smells, and the unnatural quiet of the facility had slowed down his reality.

It had occurred to Bobby that he had surrendered some big chunk of himself to the science that was keeping him alive; instead of the flowing medicine becoming part of him, he had become a part of the invasive, hygienic, therapeutic plumbing. He was just one stage, one human component, in a chemotherapy filtering and absorption process. Where did he end and the chemistry begin?

When first forming relationships with people, Arnie knew you should proceed slowly, ducking and weaving around any potentially sensitive subjects. Certainly, his wife Fran appreciated when he chose to "just let it go." Fran was just as committed to his causes, but she thoughtfully selected who was worthy to discuss them with.

Robert Langford – he's a Christian, he's gotta be, Arnie thought to himself. *Therefore, especially when it comes to Israel, you should step cautiously forward into the dark waters of political or religious discourse. First dip in your opinionated big toe; check how cold the water is.*

Being Jewish himself, Arnie saw Christians as a people for whom things came more easily and more naturally. After all, America was largely a Christian country. He figured Christians could feel at home, comfortable in their own skins.

When it came to how Christians, in general, felt about Jews and Israel, Arnie assumed a genuinely benign indifference. He guessed they viewed Jewish stereotypes with some amusement.

"I want to refute the false, uninformed, and probably malign claims made by a bone-headed, biased reporter. He is the typical hack that the paper employs. The paper has a bad reputation for its..." Arnie decided to slow down as he verbally ran to the end of the proverbial dock.

As he lay there essentially motionless, Bobby waited for the specifics. Bobby's mind was pleasantly still, and he watched Arnie struggle to articulate his issue.

Arnie revealed, "This biased columnist is impugning the sincerity of Israel's desire for peace with the Palestinians. He's accusing Israeli leadership of hypocrisy, delay, and dishonesty. This self-appointed genius wrote that Israel's settlement policy was singularly ruining the Israeli-Palestinian peace process, and he didn't once mention the generous offers Israel has made that were rejected."

Well, I guess I'll find out now if we'll be friends or not, Arnie thought. Once again, he had opted for bluntness. Arnie pondered whether his chemotherapy mate knew or cared about the subject and whether he would respond with interest. Hey, he might take the absolute opposite point of view.

Over the years, Arnie had struggled to accept the reality that not everybody was predisposed positively to Israel and to the Jews. He was painfully aware that many Jews and non-Jews were simply indifferent to the festering geopolitical Middle East Gordian knot. It was an old story for Arnie. It *was* Arnie's story.

Today Arnie hadn't wanted to litigate Israel's or the Jewish people's many trials and conflicts. Yes, he could vigorously argue the case; he could, with legal exactitude, trot out the evidence. He could cite the millennia-old archeological and biblical proof. He could refute the oldest and most cleverly masked anti-Semitic or anti-Israel canards. He could face down the Holocaust deniers, the biased, the haters, the self-loathers, and the ill-informed.

Today, Arnie was worn down. He would have preferred talking about movies, travel, favorite foods, or family. Even over the few seconds describing the letter to the editor, Arnie regretted revealing his deeply held beliefs. It was too much.

With the cancer and all the associated uncertainty, Arnie had softened. His passionate, hair-trigger combativeness was being replaced by self-pity. The stress of juggling doctors, medicines, and medical discoveries weighed down on him.

Bobby simply told him in a low, even voice, "My best friend is Jewish, and his wife was born in Israel. Over the years, we've kept up with all the fighting, terrorism, and efforts to make peace."

Confidently, Bobby professed, "The initiatives of Barak in 2000 and Olmert in 2008 would have given the Palestinians almost all of what they want today. Even the 1947 UN Resolution 181...it offered the Arabs a lion's share of British-controlled Palestine. Arafat and Abbas, they're two guys who just can't get beyond the victimization story line."

He looked to Arnie, asking, "Wasn't it Abba Eban who said, 'They never miss an opportunity to miss an opportunity'?"

Arnie just lay silently in his medical lounge chair and didn't move a muscle. He wondered if all this was real. He was stunned.

Bobby had even more to say, but for now, he closed his eyes and tried to relax until his treatment was completed.

Arnie sat quietly, alone with his thoughts. His mind wandered back to memories from before he knew he had cancer.

18 The Book Club

In the late winter of 2002, the members of the Oak Creek men's book club gathered in Neil Freidman's home. It was Neil's turn to be the host. Skinny and slightly stooped over, wearing a collared madras shirt and pressed linen pants, Neil waited for the other members.

Some of the men drove cars, some came over in their golf carts; all brought their copies of the assigned book. The twenty beyond-middle-aged men trickled into Neil's two-story faux-Moorish Florida home and maneuvered through the disarray of folding chairs into the dining room to get to the eats before the discussion began.

The book to be discussed, *The Prime Ministers,* was Israeli ambassador Yehuda Avner's celebrated recollection of five early leaders. Looking back across the previous choices, the selection was unusual; it was non-fiction. It seemed the guys gravitated toward the Grisham or Ludlum page-turner adventures, or to avoid the cost of buying a new book, they borrowed selections from their wives' book clubs.

Last month, when the time came to select a new book, Arnie Krakow piped up, "I've found a terrific book. It's fascinating. You'll love it."

He petitioned hard for *The Prime Ministers* to be selected. Nobody was surprised, as it was on a pro-Israel subject and fit Arnie's intense focus on the Jewish state, political activism, philanthropy, and the Middle East.

To close the deal, Arnie eagerly volunteered to lead the one-hour discussion.

Fran and Arnie Krakow had moved to Oak Creek Country Club from an upscale neighborhood in northern New Jersey a few years before. Their kids had settled across the East Coast, and Florida was their logical retirement choice. They had traveled to Israel six times for bar mitzvahs, family gatherings, and Jewish programs.

More recently, in reaction to mounting pressures on Israel, they had focused on political activism. Their large circle of friends extended to nearby communities and many others at Oak Creek, and they were bound together by their philanthropy for Israel. Jews and Christians alike, they and their friends shared an abiding concern for the safety of Israel and its important relationship with the United States. Arnie and Fran took great pleasure working with these similarly committed folks. They pulled together to lobby Congress and to raise money to support Israel's soldiers.

At the book club meetings, Arnie would always talk up the importance of pro-Israel political activism and philanthropy. He would make a compelling case that support for Israel affected Jewish life in America. Though it was a Jewish book club, the guys showed little interest and just barely tolerated Arnie's advocacy.

Just give Arnie an opportunity, and he'd pour forth a torrent of praise for the Israelis, or he would detail their accomplishments, the continuing challenges in the Jewish Diaspora, and the struggles for peace with the Palestinians. He could go deep or he could go wide.

Nonetheless, nothing seemed to dent the book club members' apathy. The indifference of his fellow readers drove him nuts. He saw fellow book club members' expenditures on new golf clubs that wouldn't improve their pathetic games or even a fifteen-dollar martini as provocative. They were wastes of money that could've been put toward helping their fellow Jews.

He saw their trips to the Galapagos, Southeast Asia, Antarctica, or Africa as a reason to ask if they had ever been to Israel. One guy said he wouldn't go to Israel because he didn't like the food, and Arnie never spoke to him again.

Any comment about Israel being "dangerous" would be sure to trigger a counterpunching regurgitation of South Florida's Route 95 or turnpike traffic accident statistics. Arnie would recite, "If you're too damn afraid to go to Israel, then don't drive on our roads."

Fran tolerated Arnie's intensity, but she warned him about his growing hostility. She was every bit up to date on Middle East politics, and she was way more knowledgeable about Judaism and Hebrew than her husband. Fran had been better able to overlook their contemporaries' apathy and played cards and golf with the wives of members of Arnie's book club. The women themselves had their own book club, and they all got along very well.

Arnie's binary good-guy-bad-guy view of the world worried her.

The first to arrive at Neil's home was Arnie. With his salt-and-pepper, balding buzz cut and furrowed brow, he showed the wear and tear of his years. He was anxious to get on with the review and couldn't help but be unfashionably early. In fact, he rang the doorbell before Neil had finished setting up the room and putting out all the snacks and drinks. He carried a dog-eared copy of *The Prime Ministers* with several extra pages filled with notes and comments, and he had a folder with brochures from his favorite organizations.

Arnie had observed that every time a book discussion invoked a Jewish theme, the other guys would wax on about Israel's rights, her unfair treatment on the international stage, and what Israel should do about the Palestinians, the Iranians, Hezbollah, and so on. Arnie would respond, "Guys, if you feel strongly about supporting Israel, then, like me, give to Israel Bonds, Hillel, Friends of the IDF, and the American Israel Public Affairs Committee. There's also the Jewish Federation that helps out over there. How about American Friends of Magen David Adom, you know, the Israeli ambulances? Or besides giving money, you can lobby your congressmen."

Over the years, the book club gang remained all talk and no action. Only one guy joined AIPAC, and only a couple bought bonds or sent a check to the FIDF. Contributions to the Jewish Federation were puny. His frustration with their apathy grew more bitter every time they mentioned Israel or the plight of the Jews, as if they cared, when they never followed up with action. For Arnie, it cast a shadow over the entire book club experience.

Phil Okowitz was the next to arrive. He wore a black exercise shirt that pulled tight across his oversized belly. His basketball shorts were emblazoned with a Knicks logo.

Neil greeted him, "Welcome to my humble *chapeau*."

It was a malapropism stolen from Lainie Kazan, playing the part of Belle Carroca, who welcomed Peter O'Toole in the 1982 movie *My Favorite Year*.

Phil responded with a brief nod and mumbled, "Sure, you bet, glad to be here."

"Don't ya get it, *Phil*?" Neil probed. There was a hint of an accusatory tone. Arnie just sat back and watched the interplay.

"Get what?" Phil responded, wondering why the French vocabulary quiz came before he got to his favorite snack, the peanut M&Ms.

"*Phil*, it's *chateau*, not *chapeau*...that's the joke. *Chapeau* means hat, not house," Neil pedantically lectured.

"Not your best joke, my friend," Phil replied with a sarcastically sympathetic clap on Neil's shoulder.

Only a week ago, Arnie had heard Phil and Neil argue publicly – and viciously – about whose financial portfolio was best tuned for the current low interest rate environment, although they used the phrase "dear, dear friend" to describe each other. Each prided himself on his stock-picking prowess. Each had the better financial advisors. Each read more insightfully the financial reports. And, like Las Vegas gamblers, each talked more about the wins than the losses.

It was okay, because everyone quietly enjoyed watching the two pretend to be best buddies while their contests awkwardly played out. Arnie's granddaughter taught him that nowadays, kids would call them "frenemies." He found the term delightful.

But right now, Phil let his desire for the peanut M&Ms, with their buffed sugary veneers, trump his not-so-slow boil. He knew Neil's weaknesses, and he'd wait until later to stick a shiv in the back of his "dear, dear friend."

In walked Harold Silvers. Again, Neil cranked up the same *My Favorite Year* greeting, but this time, Harold got it. Harold brightly answered, "Wasn't it Lainie Kazan who said it, and wasn't her husband a Cuban fighter?"

Neil swung around with a jarring quiz-show buzzer imitation. "Errrk. Wrong. He was a Filipino," Neil proudly corrected. He stridently added, "Carroca! That was his name." It was a Trivial Pursuit victory.

Arnie leaned over to Harold and noted, "Good old Neil – he does not award points easily."

Harold shrugged and made himself a plate of chips, dips, pretzels, nuts, and M&Ms. He settled in for the book club discussion. More of the guys trickled in.

As they chatted before the discussion of the book started, Marty Zabitz happened to mention that he grew up in Kew Gardens. Arnie jumped at the chance to give an impassioned lecture about the infamous 1964 Kew Gardens stabbing of Kitty Genovese. He detailed the well-documented apathy shown by over three dozen of her neighbors. "They heard her screams, but they did nothing."

Arnie painfully drew the parallel of Kew Garden indifference to today's uninvolved American Jews. He pressed, "Do you get the point I'm making, do you?"

The silence suggested that they did not want another beating from Arnie.

Lou Krause had also been asking for it. Two weeks before, Arnie had found himself a target of yet another email burst from the self-proclaimed, trophy-winning, open-ocean-sailing marvel the guys called "Captain Lou." Everyone had been regaled with his weathered tales of sailing with Mosbacher. All forty email recipients got to read about Moe Berg, the one-time Jewish baseball player and World War II spy. Prior missives from Lou addressed what he thought were curiosities of the Hebrews, like Jewish American fighter pilots who pitched in during Israel's War of Independence. He recalled the 1936 Berlin Olympics with Avery Brundage maliciously excluding two Jewish sprinters, including the future announcer Marty Glickman, from the four-hundred-meter relay. He offered up the lopsided comparison of Nobel Prizes awarded to Israelis compared to citizens of the Arab states. The story of Sandy Koufax missing the first game of the 1965 World Series meant a lot to seafaring Lou. But it frustrated Arnie that all Lou ever seemed to care about was the past when there was so much to focus on in the present.

Lou loved to share historical tidbits with his friends, and he always included an assumptive note that he "knew you'd be interested."

The last time Lou bumped into Arnie and delivered one of his fun facts, Arnie jabbed back, "Hey, Lou, that's all ancient history. Why not focus on what's going on today, don't you read the papers?" Arnie didn't disagree with what Lou was saying, but he felt strongly that everyone's attention should be turned to current events, advocacy, and philanthropy to help Israel in the here and now.

The last to arrive was Les Hirsch. Over the past few weeks, Les had contacted Ambassador Avner's office and arranged for a telephonic book discussion with the author. He had learned from other book club leaders that writers, including politicians and novelists, were often open to chatting with groups of readers. He was often pleasantly surprised with their cooperation.

Arnie liked Les. They had connected easily and frequently played golf together. Arnie and Les were a few years younger than the rest, and both had similar family and travel experiences. So Arnie was hopeful that of all the guys in the book club, it was Les who was most likely to take to heart the arguments for supporting Israel.

The chitchat wrapped up, and folks settled into their chairs for the discussion. Snack plates were in easy reach.

Neil began with a discussion of possible selections for next month. Arnie was tuned out as he mentally reviewed his discussion outline. In a few minutes, Les would make the prearranged overseas call to Ambassador Avner. Arnie allowed his optimistic side to believe that the book's compelling story and the celebrity author's personal words would be the secret weapon in this stand against callous disregard for his favorite cause. He was determined to sell the case for action.

Arnie wanted these neighbors to find their souls. He also wanted to stop being so critical of them and to simply enjoy their company.

High Noon

Israel's ambassador Yehuda Avner, the book's distinguished author and the patriot who was a prime ministerial advisor, diplomat, speechwriter, and secretary, had agreed to call in from his home in Jerusalem to talk with the Oak Creek book club. Over his fascinating and productive lifetime, he had been the consummate insider to Israeli politics, a fighter in the 1948 War of Independence, a founder of a kibbutz, and a witness to decision making about rescues, peace treaties, and wars.

At his home just off tree-lined Marcus Street, sitting in his book-lined study, eighty-year-old Avner was about to be connected across thousands of miles to Neil Friedman's Florida home.

The scene in Neil's living room was, in Arnie's mind, right out of Hollywood's 1952 western classic *High Noon*. It was a gunfight showdown. Arnie was the stand-in for Gary Cooper's squinty-eyed, dedicated Sheriff Will Kane, and the dead-from-the-neck-up book club members were the townspeople so cravenly fearful of the Miller Gang. He knew the moment was coming, and he was anxious to get on with it.

He recalled in the Stanley Kramer production that about two minutes before twelve o'clock, Will's deputy Herb was shocked to learn that nobody else had volunteered to defend the town. He, too, chickened out, saying, "I got no stake in it."

To Arnie, it was the simplest truth about his fellow book club members' relationship to Israel. He had come to think that, for the most part, these guys didn't have a stake in it. Or if they did, they couldn't recognize it.

The phone line snaked all the way from the outlet in the dining room and plugged into the back of a GE handset. Les dialed, and everyone listened for a response. After the two-ring sequence, the ambassador answered, "Shalom, Yehuda Avner here."

Les replied cheerily, "Hello, Ambassador Avner, we are so pleased that you can speak with us. We are – all twenty of us – honored."

He answered, "It is my honor. I'm so pleased you took the time to read my book. It was my great fortune to have been associated with so many amazing people who lived such important lives, and I will enjoy telling you more about what I have written."

There was a small delay on the line. He offered, "Please, share with me your questions or comments, and I will try to be helpful."

He was born in Manchester, England, in 1929 and didn't move to British Mandate Palestine until 1947. His well-schooled, elegantly precise voice flowed over the sixty-five hundred miles.

Arnie spoke up, "Hello, Mr. Ambassador, I'm Arnie Krakow, and it is my great pleasure to be the leader of the book discussion. Some of my friends have prepared a few questions, so first we will read those. Then, I will open it up for others to speak."

Arnie asked Ambassador Avner the three questions submitted from other members. He thought that they were fair questions, but not very interesting. The chance to explore the behind-the-scenes workings and impacts of Israeli politics and international diplomacy was being missed. Nonetheless, the ambassador answered each question by adding context and not just providing the simple facts. He prefaced each response by complimenting, "That's a fine question."

One question concerned the rocky relationship between David Ben-Gurion and Menachem Begin, and he explained how both were outstanding leaders and came from two different political parties.

Begin had a deep connection with Jewish tradition and respected the details of the Bible. Ben-Gurion would claim that the Bible was the Jewish mandate to the State of Israel, but he was less interested in religious and philosophic avenues developed by Diaspora Jews. Diaspora Jews tended to be more attracted to Begin and less to the secular prime ministers.

Avner asked if there were any more questions, and at first, none were posed.

Arnie then asked the fourth question, "On page 288 of *The Prime Ministers*, in the chapter about Prime Minister Yitzhak Rabin, you referenced the critical importance of American pro-Israel support. Please expand on that point and share with us your perspective on the current situation. How important is pro-Israel lobbying?"

This was going to solicit irrefutable proof from an expert witness that political action was critical to Israel's survival. As Arnie anticipated, the ambassador began by quoting Menachem Begin, "Whenever a fellow Jew is in danger, you must do all in your power to come to his aid."

He described how Begin would often reference Leviticus 19:16: "You should not stand idly by the blood of your neighbors."

Avner elaborated, "In one of the later chapters, I describe a meeting in 1981 that Begin had with several dozen young Americans visiting his office. One of the young men asked how his memory of the Holocaust impacts his attitude toward Germany today."

He recounted, "Prime Minister Begin described in graphic detail the murder of his parents, brother, and cousins. He did not spare them the manner of their execution. And he ended by saying, 'it colors everything I do. I shall live with it to my dying day. Now, thank God, we Jews have the means to defend ourselves. We have our courageous Israel Defense Forces.'"

Avner continued methodically quoting Begin, "'Never pause to wonder what the world will think or say. The world will never pity slaughtered Jews. The world may not necessarily like the fighting Jew, but the world will have to take account of him.'"

Arnie was sure these scholarly words, describing pivotal events in the first person, would be heard by the townspeople hiding behind shut windows and closed doors. Arnie imagined – no, he prayed for – his group's moment of clarity. Arnie so desperately hoped the attendees would hear Avner's words about pro-Israel activism, constructed on the bedrock principle that personal responsibility must be converted into just action.

Israel is the sovereign homeland of all Jews. Israel is in danger, and Jews around the world must come to her aid. It was all so clear to Arnie. This was the case, and it had now been proven beyond a shadow of a doubt.

The clock on the wall ticked to noon.

On cue, the ambassador gave a resounding, robust endorsement for pro-Israel political action. He carefully enumerated the many achievements pro-Israel lobbying had accomplished and its importance going forward.

He checked off influence with the UN, funding for weapon systems, and anti-terrorism cooperation. Avner expressed his gratitude for the many American citizens, Jews and non-Jews alike, who from the time of President Truman had come forward to help.

Arnie's case had been made, and you could see his relief and deep pride.

About twenty minutes later, the overseas call ended, and the book club meeting began to wrap up. The group buzzed with appreciation for the experience and the rush of having been connected with someone of importance.

On the coffee table, Arnie had fanned out brochures and membership applications for several pro-Israel organizations. He pointed and directed, "Here they are. If you have any questions, please give me a call. Our next event is in about five weeks."

Some grabbed the brochures, but most did not. Neil noisily announced to all, "I'll see you at happy hour." The book club members quickly filed out for half-priced drinks.

Lou and the others never did join any of the organizations, and ever since, Arnie could only handle short, meaningless social exchanges with the guys.

Soon thereafter, Arnie dropped out of the book club.

Neil did join one of Arnie's pro-Israel political action organizations and participated for a few years. But one day at the driving range, he walked over to Arnie and confessed, "it's just not our thing. I know you're really into it, but it's not for us."

The book club members continued to rarely be seen at Jewish charity or pro-Israel events. They remained a tight, insular clan, socializing with each other in permutations of smaller groupings of their broader, disinterested constituency.

To Arnie, their apathy remained a true mystery.

20 Vodka

After their first full day docked in St. Petersburg, Russia, the tour group returned to the cruise ship's official entry control booth set tight to the English Embankment. Instead of reboarding their glistening white ship, Arnie and Fran deviously ducked away from their fellow passengers and headed back to the city streets.

The low, dirty clouds that had been spitting raindrops in the morning were mostly gone. Also, the almost twenty-four-hour daylight in the northern latitudes kept the late July temperature very comfortable.

Arnie had felt bridled at the group's touring constraints and wanted a little unfettered strolling with Fran in the beautiful "palace city." He knew their tourist group visa was limited to travel with an officially approved tour guide, and they were taking a chance.

Walking along the street, keeping the murky Bolshaya Neva River to their left, they headed toward Senate Square and the Bronze Horseman statue. Arnie assured Fran, "We'll be fine. I checked it out, and we'll be gone for no more than two hours."

He teased, "What could go wrong with a couple of Jews sneaking around mother Russia?"

Feeling more daring, they crossed the street at the corner, walking back to the quay's waterside. Arnie first, then Fran, saw the police officer stationed at the next block, but they kept up their pace and their chatter. They made no eye contact. He was a tall young man with an angelic face and was focused more on traffic movement than on pedestrians. No issue.

Arriving at Senate Square, they maneuvered respectfully around the other strollers. Still a little self-conscious, they paused for photographs near the Bronze Horseman statue that dominated the square. Arnie stood back, admiring the dramatic positioning of a bold military officer astride a muscular horse riding up a cantilevered thrust of granite.

Fran said to Arnie, "It's Peter the Great. He's pointing to the Neva River."

Fran, concerned about their limited strolling time, checked her watch and gently reminded Arnie, "Time to move on." They pressed ahead toward their second and last stop, the onion-domed St. Isaac's Cathedral.

The wooded park between the square and the cathedral was darker, muddier, and less crowded, and the people were more casually dressed. Heavyset women, each managing a two-wheeled wire mesh shopping cart, wore kerchiefs, drab coats, and thick-soled shoes. They sat in twos and threes on benches positioned a few feet back from the graveled walkways. These women, in spite of their tired, matronly clothes, conveyed a subtle dignity. You could reasonably guess that they had lived challenging lives affected by harsh wars and political turmoil. They had survived. Today, they enjoyed a warm afternoon and some familiar surroundings, and they accepted that their tomorrows were sure to be constrained by meager pensions and frail health.

Further along, a small group of children huddled to one side of the pathway. A weathered, bearded man, indifferent to their presence, walked with a small, woolly, drooling brown bear. Holding a thick leather leash, the man had the glassy stare and the too-wet mouth of someone who had been drinking heavily.

Walking on to the golden onion-domed cathedral, treasuring their photographic "find," Arnie and Fran looked at each other thinking the same thing: *a Russian bear in a park. Too perfect.*

Strolling back to the ship along a commercial street that paralleled the quay, Arnie noticed a liquor store. The building's ornate imperial Russian-styled corner doorway suggested that at one time it was the entrance to a residence of a high-ranking person.

The two wide front windows, rococo ceiling, and elegant support columns contrasted with the shabby tables and cheap shelving. In addition to the Stolichnaya that Arnie recognized, there were dozens of vodka brands he had never seen in America.

It suddenly occurred to Arnie that photographs of the worn liquor store with the rows of vodkas would make clever, eye-grabbing pictures for his vacation's coffee table photo album. *What a great idea,* Arnie thought as he visualized close-ups and fish-eye shots of the exotic bottles and their labels. Arnie had now become Alfred Stieglitz angling for just the right images.

A middle-aged store clerk edged over toward Arnie. He was a large, barrel-chested man with a round, shaved head one size too big for his body. His pale, puffy face featured a pouty mouth and sleepy eyes set just a bit too close together with thick lids. His clear plastic glasses, defying laws of physics, sat securely atop his bald, slanted head, barely touching temples or ears.

He stared carefully at Arnie and asked in broken English, "Hello. Anything interesting? What are you looking for?"

Arnie turned to face him. Since he didn't have any intention to buy, he immediately felt ill at ease. He answered simply, "Nope. Just looking."

With growing annoyance, the clerk watched as the merchandise and his employer's store were treated as a curiosity. To him, the souvenir hunter was disrespectfully trampling over his place of business.

Again, he spoke to Arnie, "So you like to take pictures. Please, what's so interesting? Do you not have vodka in the United States of America? Do you not have liquor stores?"

He continued with rapid fire. "How are our prices? What vodka do you prefer? How about Five Stars, it's made very close to here."

Arnie's discomfort grew.

Finally, the shopkeeper burst, "Are you here to buy, or to take *free* pictures?"

Before Arnie could respond with answers, the clerk pressed ahead on a different tack. "My name is Gregor. What's yours?"

He had to respond. He timidly shared, "Arnie."

"And where are you from, Mr. Arnie? Where in the *United States of America*?"

Arnie responded, "From Florida."

Gregor uttered a stream of disconnected Florida word associations. "Miami…Disney…oranges…Orlando…crocodiles."

Swiftly, Gregor grabbed a bottle with a silver label sporting raised red Cyrillic letters and featuring a small cabin in a snowy forest. Gregor stepped forward just a fraction of an inch. He invited, "Come, you try my favorite. Very good, very smooth. A sample. It won't cost you *nothing*."

Gregor, with a forced smile, asked, "Are you sure you're not from New York? From New York City? You look to me like you are from New York City. I hear you people from New York City like things that are *free*."

Gregor offered a wooden tray holding flimsy plastic shot glasses filled with Gregor's apparent favorite.

Gregor drank down a shot.

Arnie quickly followed suit.

Arnie wondered what the hell he meant. *I look like I'm from New York City? Was this Russian liquor salesman telling me that he knew there is a large Jewish population in New York? Is he telling me he's sure I'm Jewish?*

Arnie thought about how the man referred to people who like things that are free. The unsettling recognition of this man's anti-Semitic comment sank in.

Gregor was distracted for a few moments by a telephone call.

Arnie used the time to clear his head.

He leaned over close to Fran and whispered, "Did you catch his comment? I wonder, who were his grandparents? Do you think it's just him, or were his ancestors the ones carrying out pogroms?"

With a slow, dignified motion, Arnie set down the flimsy plastic shot glass. Guiding Fran's elbow and with a direct stare at Gregor, he stated, "I much prefer Tito's. It's way smoother. It's more refined. It's American. You know, from Austin, Texas. And it is kosher." Together, they walked to the store's exit and hurried down the stone steps.

When Fran and Arnie gained some distance from the store, they breathed a sigh of relief. Sadly, neither were entirely surprised by the anti-Semitic encounter. They were both well aware of the history of rampant anti-Semitism in Russia. It wasn't nearly as bad now as it used to be, but there were certainly remnants left over. Fran's relatives had actually fled Russia for the United States as a result of pogrom attacks on her grandparents' village.

Fran noted to Arnie in a sarcastic tone, "I'll bet Gregor's grandparents didn't exactly attend my relatives' going away party."

Arnie chuckled. They walked after that in silence. They were somberly aware that even in the twenty-first century, anywhere they traveled in the world, being Jewish had the potential to get them into trouble.

Arnie and Fran quietly returned from their bizarre ad hoc tour of St. Petersburg, cleared Russian shipside security, and labored up the ship's angled gangway. It reached up from the stone and brick pathway bordering the Neva River quay dangling just feet away from the riveted, gleaming white ship's hull and terminated next to the entry door landing.

The ramp was still slick from the light mist that had just fallen. The top handrail of the gangway was highly varnished nautical wood. Although it sloped upward, the rainwater still beaded into nickel-sized droplets.

Arnie lugged his bag stuffed with a *Best of the Hermitage* art book and two sets of nested, lacquered Russian dolls that he had bought earlier at the museum's gift shop. The vodka's effect hadn't dissipated, and halfway up the sloped gangplank, his foot slipped out from under him. In his awkward attempt to protect the bag, he reached out with his left arm for the gangway's railing as gravity pulled the bulk of him downwards.

It was a Flying Wallenda Brothers moment, and with a cartoonish display of flailing arms and legs, he mostly righted himself. But he badly strained his left shoulder in the process.

21 Piccolo Venezia

Dinner in Piccolo Venezia, the cruise ship's Italian specialty restaurant, was a treat. All the little details were there, from tall, twisty bread sticks to the overly complex olive oil and vinegar mini-menu. Fran and Arnie enjoyed a modicum of privacy in the starboard side's most aft corner table for two.

Looking outward through a large window, they saw the ship's churned wake, white and fluorescent green, trailing behind for half a mile. Ahead of them, the restaurant sparkled with milky glass chandeliers and mirrored walls interlaced with painted scenes of the soft rolling Italian landscape. The truffled veal chop and crispy branzino were excellent.

The only issue was Arnie's sore left shoulder, which ached even when he reached for his wine glass. He wanted to ignore it, but he couldn't.

The chef made the rounds and appreciatively accepted praise for his masterful preparations. With two slices of opera cake and good coffee, the meal was complete.

Arnie chose not to visit the ship's medical officer as he self-diagnosed the painful shoulder as simply twisted; only aspirin and a hot shower would be needed. The next day, Arnie did avail himself of a heating pad, and he was extra careful as he wove his way down passageways or sat wrapped in a blanket laid out on the teak-framed couch on the swimming pool deck. His shoulder felt a little better.

Over the remaining days of the cruise, Arnie endured the discomfort and managed not to miss any of the land tours or shipboard pleasures. Following the docking and de-boarding in Copenhagen and the twenty-mile van ride to the Kastrup Airport, the flight home was long, boring, and provided no comfortable position for Arnie's shoulder.

Back in New York, Arnie used the two-hour transfer time to call his Florida orthopedist, and an appointment was arranged for the afternoon of the following day. The change of planes in New York, the flight to Ft. Lauderdale, and the hefting of their luggage back into the house was barely tolerable.

Arnie toughed it out. He looked forward to tomorrow's appointment, anticipating the doctor's prescription of painkillers, maybe a cortisone shot, and physical therapy.

Dr. Sessions puzzled over the three x-rays for a longer time than Arnie would have expected. He alternated between looking at them close up and at arm's length.

In their short time home, Arnie hadn't bothered to go onto the internet to explore the range of shoulder joint damage possibilities. All that Arnie could hope for was that it was a soft tissue tear and hopefully not something worse that would delay his return to tennis and golf.

Dr. Sessions began, "Arnie, it is a ligament strain from hyperextension, and we can help it along with some steroidal creams and maybe injections. Nothing's broken."

Arnie felt relieved.

The doctor then sat down on the black plastic rotating chair, scribbled a few notes in a file, and swung around to Arnie. "As luck would have it, the x-ray technician took three images, and one was a broader view than was needed for your shoulder trauma. The image included a portion of your left lung's upper lobe. Arnie, something is not quite right there. I'm seeing a spot. I'm not an expert in that area, and I don't want to alarm you, but I want you to have it checked out."

Arnie looked straight ahead.

The words *lung* and *lobe* ricocheted off the walls.

"When you leave here, my nurse will give you the name of a good pulmonologist who'll get to the bottom of it."

The word *spot* hung in the air.

Arnie was always amazed how his power of speech and reasoning evaporated when visiting a doctor's office. He regressed to become a child. He always returned home wishing he had asked this question or that. He knew he should bring a list of afflicting dents and dings to address at an annual checkup but never did, and he never wrote down what the doctor said.

He attributed his muteness to a realization that doctors did their business in the mortal domain. He inexplicably felt that if you annoyed the all-powerful doctors, especially with a stupid question, they could inflict a terrible disease upon you. If they merely scribbled the affliction on their white prescription pads, you were doomed. "John was a jerk today, let's give him some hemorrhoids. Mary was uncooperative, she needs a sinus headache."

These were the modern medicine men; they had the power of life and death. Even when they socialized with doctors, Arnie and Fran felt there was something different. They questioned whether doctors saw them as pre-something, time bombs of a cellular roulette wheel.

Stunned, Arnie sat there realizing his sore shoulder had become a lung problem, a *spotted* lung problem to boot. He had, in a split second, seen himself transition from a runner of simple errands to a diseased victim wrestling with something unknown and very concerning. Before, he was attending to shopping lists and complaining about traffic; now, he was fighting for his life.

He was immobilized, and he was nearly mute. With all his concentration and courage, he forced out an infantile question, "Okay, what do you think it is?"

Dr. Sessions, in sotto voce said, "Arnie, it could be a lot of things. Let Dr. Kessler look at you." The doctor's attempt to calm his anxiety was unsuccessful.

Arnie tried another approach. He begged, "Should I be worried?"

Dr. Sessions answered nearly identically, "Arnie, it could be a lot of things. It's very hard to tell. Let Dr. Kessler look at you."

Aliyah

In 2006, in a modest apartment near Petah Tikvah, Yoni lay back in a room that tripled as a bomb shelter, bedroom, and storage space. His eyes gazed around at the mix of boxes, camping gear, bicycle wheels, and playpen parts. The Israeli government mandated that all new residential construction include a room that can be sealed against a conventional or chemical weapons attack. Gas masks and supplies were packed in there, too, and would have to be found if an emergency arose. Besides those moments when there were warnings of threats, these shelters were used just like any other room in a home.

Yoni was glad to have a few quiet hours alone. After flying overnight from New York and reuniting with his friends in Israel, he needed to decompress. He listened to Israeli songs coming from a television or radio several rooms away. The lyrics were a challenge for Yoni, since his Hebrew skills still had a long way to go. Identifying a few key words, Yoni surmised that the tune lamented a boy's loss of a beautiful girlfriend, and he enjoyed the lilting female voice supported by an instrumental combination of guitar and violin.

Earlier in the day, his Israeli friends Arieh, Doron, and Dov stood together in the arrival room just outside the immigration control and baggage claim area. They carried a handmade sign announcing "Israel is safe, Yoni is here." The backslapping, high fives, and hugging left little doubt that the "lone" part of his soon-to-be lone soldier status would be only partially true.

Yoni fired off a joking critique of Doron's reddish facial stubble. "Is that all you grew in six months?"

Doron quipped back, "Aww, how sweet that you don't even know about shaving yet. Don't worry, Arieh here will teach you when you're older."

The pseudo-insults were drowned out by Dov's less acidic sentiments. "Yoni, we're so glad to have you here. We missed you. Welcome back."

Wordlessly, Arieh grabbed the baggage cart advertising Bank Hapoalim and hoisted Yoni's stuffed backpack onto it. Doron piled on Yoni's suitcases, and Dov took Yoni's jacket for him. Yoni was left with only his New York Mets cap tilted back on his head.

On the lower level of Ben-Gurion Airport, the four guys headed for the exit doors leading to the parking lot and Arieh's dust-caked Subaru.

Yoni's trip to Israel was different from those he had made before. He wasn't accompanied by his parents or grandparents, and he wasn't on a summer program with camp friends. On earlier trips, as he walked through the Tel Aviv airport he looked forward to the thrill of exploring Israel. Sure, he always had an itinerary, but all of his past trips had been filled with pleasant surprises. It seemed there were always new friends, magical venues, and discoveries about his religion, his homeland, and himself.

This time, he was going to become an Israeli citizen and a soldier in the Israel Defense Forces. This time, he was focused on a long to-do list that included the immigration process, immersive Hebrew language classes, IDF enrollment paperwork, and finding a cheap apartment.

As a lone soldier, he would serve in the Israeli army without the comfort and convenience of having family nearby. After all, because of Israel's size – comparable to New Jersey – soldiers could travel home by bus for most weekends and holidays. Because of the challenges involved, lone soldiers received government benefits such as housing stipends and time off from the army to visit their families overseas.

For Yoni, no parents would greet him for Shabbat, and no leftovers would be sent back to base with him. Laundry would be a problem, and he'd have to solve the puzzle of where to go for holidays. But Yoni hoped that his good friends would pitch in, and he was confident that other lone soldiers would be assigned to his unit. He was comforted by the existence of organizations that had sprung up to support lone soldiers like him, of which there were thousands every year.

The little contingent pushed the squeaking baggage cart forward. On the other side of the double doors, he'd be in the fresh Israeli air of the late afternoon. He'd be home as a citizen of a land he had grown to love.

He noted the mezuzah affixed to the doorway, a small white case with a scroll containing verses from Deuteronomy inside it. Some travelers ahead of him reached up to touch it on their way out and kiss their hands, the ritual symbolizing recognition of the divine presence in every space one enters. Yoni was used to encountering these in Jewish homes, but something about seeing them in an airport made him feel like the doorway was personally telling him, "Welcome home."

Arieh reflected on his own immigration to Israel. His family had come from Ethiopia when he was a young child. The Ethiopian Jews were isolated for twenty-five hundred years in northeast Africa in near stone-age conditions. Their faithful retention of Judaism and their recent redemptive exodus was an inspiring miracle.

The secret missions, Operation Moses in the 1980s and Operation Solomon in the 1990s, were followed by the hard work necessary to absorb them productively into mainstream Israeli society. Many had come to Israel trekking across the harsh desert to Sudan, losing thousands to every kind of terror and hardship.

Arieh's family had made it through, though. Now, having lived in Israel for nearly all his life, he thought back to how new everything used to feel. His friend Yoni would have an easier transition than he had, but it would be challenging at first. Arieh felt determined to be there for him.

Ever since Yoni first traveled to Israel as a little boy with Danny, Maya, Dahlia, and Leonard, he had been fascinated with Israeli soldiers. Even then, he intently watched them as they walked by in their thick, laced-up boots.

At the Western Wall on Shabbat, during prayers that were so spirited everyone danced, Yoni was delighted every time a group of olive-green-clad soldiers joined in. He'd stare at them in wonder as they sang and danced with their enormous guns strapped over their shoulders. Their voices added to the rhythmic prayers of all assembled in front of the wall.

Little Yoni saw that many of them were women and that many of the men wore yarmulkes. He watched them standing on the bus, lugging home groceries in stretched plastic bags, and even sometimes walking with spouses and infants. Yoni came to appreciate the quiet pride of these mostly young soldiers.

Maya had told Yoni about his grandfather Yonatan – his namesake – and how he had died fighting in the Yom Kippur War. He treasured the picture of Yonatan standing next to his mud-caked tank with his crew. Yoni knew how his grandmother needed extra thoughtfulness during Yom Hazikaron, Israel's day of remembrance for more than twenty thousand soldiers who had fallen. Leonard knew her thoughts were elsewhere, and with a quiet kindness, he took his cues from Dahlia.

When Yoni was ten, he was on a trip to Israel with his parents, sitting on a bench in the Old City near the Hurva Synagogue. Yoni had asked Maya, "Mom, were you a soldier when you lived in Israel? Did you fight to protect Israel?"

Maya responded, "I left Israel when I was twelve, and you only begin your service after high school when you're eighteen. But if my *abba* had not died, I wouldn't have left, so like all of my classmates, I would have. To be honest with you, sometimes I feel ashamed that I didn't serve like everyone else. I think serving in the IDF is one of the most meaningful things a Jewish person can do."

"But would you have met Dad then? Would you have come to America at all?"

Maya had learned to appreciate her son's endless curiosity, but these hypotheticals were a challenge. It seemed that no explanation would allow Yoni to understand the happenstance of his very existence.

Maya answered, "Yoni, life is full of twists and turns, full of serendipity, full of good news and bad news. You, young man, are very good news."

They sat quietly people watching for a little while. Maya quizzed Yoni, "When you see Israeli soldiers, they have three Hebrew letters stenciled above their shirt pocket. What are they and what do they stand for?"

Yoni proudly answered, "*Tzadi*, *heh*, *lamed* are the Hebrew letters that stand for *Tzeva Haganah l'Yisrael*. It means army for the defense of Israel, or the Israel Defense Forces."

Maya replied, "Very good. We can all choose to be defenders of Israel. If you live in Israel, you do that by serving in the army."

Watching his shiny brown eyes, she said, "If you lived in Israel, you would be part of the first Jewish army in almost two thousand years. You would feel it is a privilege to defend your country."

Maya paused, placing a hand on Yoni's shoulder. "But as an American, you can do other things. That's what Daddy and I do."

Danny latched onto the chance to promote alternatives for American Jews. He talked to Yoni about political activism and philanthropy. On the one hand, he was impressed with Yoni's seriousness and interest at such a young age. On the other, though, he knew of families in which the children became so enamored with Israel that the kids grew up and moved there.

For many Diaspora Jews, aliyah was widely encouraged. The word itself came from Hebrew and meant "going up," due to the spiritual elevation associated with being in the Land of Israel. Many felt the Jews "wandering in the wilderness" should return and join the Israeli population.

Danny was hesitant to draw a line in the sand, but that didn't keep him from harboring a fear of losing Yoni to a faraway place. He dreaded his son having to face the dangers of the Middle East, especially as a soldier. *He's only ten, now, though*, Danny reminded himself. *It might only be a phase.* Danny would wait, he wouldn't show his hand too early, and he would try to think it all through with Maya.

Yoni sat quietly watching the stray cats sneak around the camera-toting tourists.

He didn't react the whole time his parents spoke about what Americans can do. He waited politely for them to finish and declared, "When I'm older, I want to be an Israeli soldier."

Back home, Yoni's room evolved into a mini-museum for his Israeli experiences. On top of his dresser was a Coca-Cola bottle embossed with flowing white Hebrew letters, stylized and transliterated to match the American original.

He had also brought back a bottle of *schug*, a fiery Middle Eastern condiment not for the faint of heart. A huge fabric Israeli flag hung on the wall next to a torn but repaired travel poster featuring the Tel Aviv coastline. Group pictures were taped to a large mirror and showed a smiling Yoni clustered with classmates, teammates, and Jewish youth group members.

On Yoni's nightstand was a ceramic ritual hand-washing cup Leonard had bought for him in an Armenian pottery shop in Jerusalem when he was nine. The cup was ornately detailed with vibrant colored flowers, birds, leaves, and fruits. Inside were about a hundred small buttons.

Yoni had been collecting buttons since he was eleven years old. It began when he attended a bar mitzvah of the son of one of his dad's associates. The service was held in Bloomington. When they arrived, before going into the sanctuary, Yoni and Danny explored the new, large synagogue. Down one hallway, they discovered a library. In the library's window, they found a display that made them both pause and reflect.

At the base of the display case, there was a neatly inked mauve sign that read "HOLOCAUST BUTTON PROJECT." The plaque went on to explain that it engaged the synagogue's school as a hands-on way for members to memorialize and visualize the enormity of the loss of one and a half million innocent children murdered during the Holocaust. One button would be collected for each lost child. Small random buttons of every color and shape were piled almost to the top of ten clear glass cylindrical vases, each column about eight inches wide and nearly three feet high.

Yoni's eyes darted from one button to another to another, from one glass tower to another. He tried to estimate how many there were, but in the end, he simply concluded that there were a *lot* of buttons. He then looked at the thermometer-styled image colored in only thirteen percent of the way up. They were still collecting buttons. The poster said that, to date, the enormous collection in front of him contained only two hundred thousand buttons.

Danny saw that Yoni was hypnotized by the imagery and almost paralyzed by the realization of the dimension of the horror. The relevance to yet another Jewish child hit home. Yoni's eyes were wet with tears.

Danny turned Yoni to face him. "Yoni, we've talked about the Holocaust and how our people swear *never again*."

Danny, struggling with his own emotions, managed, "It's all right to cry because we are mourning for the loss of our people. On our next trip to Israel, if you want, we will visit Yad Vashem, and together we can learn more."

Danny coaxed Yoni away from the library window, back in the direction of the sanctuary and the celebration.

Just as they rounded the corner, Danny stopped and shared another idea. He said, "Yoni, at Yad Vashem, there is a place where people who were not Jewish and saved Jews are recognized for their valor. They're called the Righteous among the Nations. We can walk in the Garden of the Righteous."

Danny pressed on, "And there's another story I want to tell you on our drive home. It's about my good friend Bobby's father, Sergeant John Langford. During World War II, he helped liberate a German concentration camp. He saved Jewish lives. You remember the Langfords, of course. It's important to remember that good people are around us. It's an important story."

On their drive back home, Danny told Yoni the full story of his friend's father liberating Dachau, and how he met Bobby when their lives came together on a snowy hillside. Yoni listened to every word, and it made him feel proud that his dad had a friend like Bobby Langford.

Danny also reminded Yoni about the Baranson family losses and of the Borinski brothers and their tragedy.

Just before they arrived back home, Yoni proposed, "Dad, I want to collect buttons. And once in a while, will you drive me back to the synagogue's library so I can help with the memorial?"

The pain and complexity of Jewish history was becoming clearer to Yoni. Danny swelled with pride.

Flashing forward seven years, Yoni was traveling to Israel for the first time without parents and without being on a structured program. He and his friend Steve had just graduated high school, and they went for the summer to take Hebrew classes at the Hebrew University. They were mostly excited, though, to explore the country on their own in their free time.

The last time he and Steven were in Israel, they were sixteen. It was a six-week trip through their summer camp to learn about Israeli history and tour from the very north at Rosh Hanikra down through the Negev to Eilat. It was an amazing trip, but he and Steve were eager to experience the country independently.

One evening, they stood at the entrance of a Jerusalem bar on Yoel Salomon Street, just off Zion Square and near Ben Yehuda Street. They breathed in air laced with the telltale smell of stale beer, fried food, disinfectant, and cigarette smoke. The bar, Yaakov's Tavern, was a misguided composite German beer hall, Irish pub, and British public house. Plastic vines dangled from Germanic beer steins, and faux-timbered walls were covered with an incongruous array of rugby shirts, American university pendants, and Israeli basketball posters. While the bar advertised a large menu of foreign beers, the featured brews were the local, cheap Goldstar and Maccabee.

They grabbed a table and waited to be served. Almost immediately, a pretty, dark-haired waitress came up and asked in English, "So, guys, what do you want?" The boys felt butterflies in their stomachs, even though in Israel they were legally allowed to drink at the age of eighteen.

Steve, the slightly older and more enthusiastic of the two, asked, "Can we have two Goldstars and two orders of chips?"

Steve felt his use of the word *chips* instead of *fries* elevated his worldliness.

She jotted down the order. "Of course. Glasses?"

Steve tried to finish the deal boldly. "How about icy mugs?" He got, in return, an eye roll and an are-you-kidding tilt of the head just before she disappeared behind the bar.

With beers in hand and first gulps down, they began a conversation about the beaches and how to travel from Jerusalem to the beaches in Herzliya for surfing. At the next table, three Israelis, about their ages, overheard the conversation. One of them came over and asked, "Want help?"

Yoni and Steve responded almost in unison, "Yeah, that would be great."

In an instant, the Israelis jammed around the table, and in their best English began showering them with bus numbers, schedules, and tips on surfboard rentals.

Somebody began a bottle-clinking combination of "cheers" and "*l'chaim*," and a round of introductions followed. When it came to Yoni, he gave his back story. "I was born in America, in Indiana. My mother was, I guess still is, an Israeli, and she lived for twelve years in Tel Aviv, on Nachalat Binyamin Street."

Yoni sensed more detail was needed. "Her father was killed in the Yom Kippur War. Her mother remarried an American and moved to Indiana, and here I am drinking lukewarm Goldstars with you all."

Yoni's story brought down the cheerful, frivolous conversation. The three Israelis, Doron, Dov, and Arieh, were immediately drawn to Yoni. They listened respectfully to Steve's highlights, but something had clicked with them and Yoni.

Doron, whose English was the best, told the Americans about preparation for entering the army in less than two years. "We all want placement into the elite combat units, like Sayeret Matkal, which is kind of like your Marines, or special forces, or maybe strategic intelligence."

He explained how their schooling, test taking, interviews, and even their youth group experiences converged to influence the all-important unit assignment. He described a draft letter and the *tzav rishon*, a daylong physical examination and interview. After careful assessment of the *tzav rishon* results, the army calls them to enlist when they turn eighteen. The army processing and basic training would begin after high school.

Doron acknowledged, "Parents worry, but they all served and know what goes on. It's still a tough time for them."

The Americans wrestled with the obvious contrast in thinking about military service versus college. Doron alluded to a year of travel after the army. After that, he'd figure out college and a job. He said he'd hopefully get a job in high tech someday because that's where the money was, but picking a major was far off his radar. He had already targeted India and the Himalayas for his jaunt.

Yoni shared, "I'll be spending the next four years at Indiana University."

The Americans listened intently to the Israelis about futures that were so different from theirs. The Americans deeply respected their peers for their impending service to defend the country. They'd always supported the IDF through camp and youth group activities to send care packages and the like, but now, it felt so much more real.

For the rest of the summer, the Israeli boys shepherded the Americans, ensuring they made the most of their free time. In addition to directing them to the best bars and beaches, the Israelis helped them understand the realities of living in Israel in a way their Hebrew school teachers never could. They explored the polemics of peace with the Palestinians, the wild threats of annihilation from Islamic leaders, bus bombings, suicide vests, and border incidents. Over the course of the summer, they began to see that many of the locations they visited that felt so carefree to them had actually seen terror not long before.

On the drive back from the airport, Yoni and his friends had a lot to catch up about. Doron, Dov, and Arieh had finished high school and completed their service in the IDF. All three had seen combat in Gaza or on the borders. Meanwhile, Yoni had been busy at Indiana University with his involvement in Hillel and Israel advocacy on campus. On two occasions, Yoni had visited Israel during school vacation to spend quality time with them. Hundreds of instant messages kept them all connected and up to date on assignments, girls, and family. While college life offered many distractions, Yoni remained focused on fulfilling his boyhood Zionist dream of serving in the IDF as part of the lone soldier program. He had just graduated before he made aliyah.

He knew his dad was worried. He didn't hide it well, either, constantly talking up graduate programs to try to keep Yoni in America longer. Yoni had taken on the challenge of convincing Danny that serving in the IDF was not a hobby, whim, or ill-conceived pipe dream. It was, in fact, central to his sense of self; it was his life's purpose.

For almost as long as he could remember, Yoni had yearned for the moment when he'd step off a plane, and his friends would greet him as a fellow protector of Israel. Looking out the car's window as the Israeli landscape whizzed by, he could hardly wipe the smile off his face.

23
Bible and Gun

Yoni still had thirty tough kilometers to go before finishing the exhausting *sof maslul*, the march that marked the end of his platoon's army training. For the next fifteen minutes, it was his turn to carry the heavily loaded medics' stretcher along with three other Givati trainees.

Their sixty-five-kilometer march in full battle gear began in the foothills on the coastal plain and wound along near Route 1 to Jerusalem. When they finished the trek, they would receive the fighter's pin, the mark of a combat soldier in an active IDF company.

Yoni's immediate attention was focused on the rock-strewn ground in front of him and trying to ignore toe and ankle blisters that burned with every step. All around him were the cumulative sounds of crunching from hundreds of thick boots hitting the ground, labored breathing in the dusty air, and leaders barking out orders in Hebrew.

Many of the soldiers were suffering from red, raw chafing where the equipment wore heaviest on the body. The guys called the wounds *shawarma,* like the grilled, shaved meat served throughout the Middle East. Yoni wrapped medical tape on his back, sides, and shoulders before the trek to prevent it.

At the end of the march, his proud parents waited. His father still wasn't entirely comfortable with him being a soldier, but ultimately, he was impressed by Yoni's persistence and ideals. Maya, on the other hand, felt overwhelmingly emotional at the thought of her son protecting the Jewish state as she herself never did.

Yoni trudged on, motivating himself by reflecting on the journey it had taken him to get to this point. He had sacrificed, he had dealt with self-doubt, and he would succeed.

Being on this final march as a trainee was what he had so badly wanted and what he had worked so hard for. As difficult as the *sof maslul* march was, he saw it as just one of a set of challenges in pursuit of what some lone soldiers jokingly call "the biggest mistake you'll never regret."

As he pressed forward, he thought back over the past months in dogged pursuit of becoming a combat soldier.

It had only been eighteen months ago that he had come to Israel. Basic training was behind him, and now advanced training was almost complete.

Transitioning from Diaspora Jew to Israeli citizen was a puzzle, but he had managed with the help of an organization called Garin Tzabar. They guided him through the Israeli bureaucracy of the drafting process. Being a lone soldier through this organization meant that he and his group were "adopted" by a kibbutz, giving them a place to rest and do laundry on their time off. The friendships that he had made through this program with peers who were going through the same experiences as him were invaluable to his transition.

Garin Tzabar also provided a framework for Yoni to improve his Hebrew. He had a basis from his mother, but living way up north on a kibbutz near the Lebanese border meant being able to use it regularly. He took a pre-army immersive Hebrew program called an ulpan. Once he was in the army with no choice but to speak Hebrew constantly, he became fluent quickly.

Ultimately, serving in the army was the key to successful immigration in Israel. Your circle of friends, your career, and your station in Israeli society depended on getting into the best units.

Yoni had wanted for a long time to become a combat soldier. He knew that he needed a good overall evaluation score. The critical evaluation included his health profile, his intelligence score, and Hebrew proficiency.

Running on the roads near the kibbutz, Yoni improved his endurance and aerobic capacity, which would be so important at the IDF tryouts. With others in his *garin,* he did push-ups and sit-ups and carried stretchers.

When it came time for the first round of try-outs, Yoni was better prepared than many, but he still struggled. Jerome Serlstein from Australia, Gabe Sussman from Los Angeles, and Yaacov Brill from Russia outperformed all others. Carrying full jerrycans of water up and down sand dunes and having too little to eat or drink, the candidates were evaluated carefully for stamina and willpower.

Yoni had played linebacker in high school, and easily concluded that even with twice-a-day practices, wind sprints, and blocking sleds, the IDF would be far more demanding.

With sand everywhere and the fury of others laboring around him to do well on the test, Yoni bore down, ignoring burning muscles and strained joints. His sweaty T-shirt crusted with sand drooped from his shoulders as he bent forward trying to get better leverage on the sloshing jerrycan's weight.

At the swearing-in ceremony three months into his service, neither Danny nor Maya were present. They could not afford to fly out for every ceremony. They were not there to witness the drama of the nighttime gathering in Latrun where he received his Tanakh and a ceremonial M4 carbine. A few of the soldiers were non-Jewish Israelis, and he was interested to notice that the Christian ones received the Bible and the Muslims received the Koran.

When his turn came, he stepped forward, received his gun and Tanakh, saluted his platoon commander, pivoted, and walked back into formation. Then, the Givati trainees, standing in blocks of uniformed, proud men, yelled out in unison at the top of their voices, "I swear." They would now uphold the expectations of country and army, to give unconditionally to the protection of the State of Israel.

The bugles sounded, the military music filled the air, and the diagonally split purple and white Givati flags danced by. He backslapped and hugged his soldier brothers. His closest army friends, Ori, Moshe, Itai, and Yosef, did their best to make it fun by dragging him over to their families for praise and snacks, and his friends Doron, Dov, and Arieh even came to celebrate. He wished his parents could have been there, but with his Israeli family, he was not alone.

Already at the swearing-in ceremony, he had a sense of accomplishment. The first weeks of basic training had been tough, especially with his sub-par Hebrew language skills. He had background coming in, but it was hard to understand his fast-speaking peers, and articulating a response took so long that by the time he could get it out, it was too late. With his commander firing orders at him, he was often at a loss. He often ended up just watching where everyone else went and following the pack.

Lone soldiers from overseas, at a very basic level, wanted to be a homogenized part of the IDF. Their goal was to blend in with the native-born defenders. Yoni had a leg up because of his Israeli mother. Maya had tried to make Hebrew a second language in their home.

The Israeli music, movies, jokes, idioms, and sensibilities were a barrier crossed only with patience and good humor. When the day was through, there was a brief hour of free time. He often hung out with his fellow "Americans." In fact, they weren't all from the United

States. Some were from Britain, Australia, or South Africa. However, the Israelis referred to all native-English speakers as Americans.

The Israelis generally saw America through Hollywood's lens; they knew about big-time sports and a gaudy two-party political system. Through their army experiences, the Israelis and "Americans" shared enough in common to forge close friendships. Still, sometimes Yoni needed the comfort of being able to reference a movie like *The Godfather* and be understood. Only a few Israelis got the "leave the gun, take the cannoli" wisdom.

Yoni had come to accept that he'd be out of the loop on many conversations. He just couldn't keep up with the rapid-fire Hebrew, and even when he could, many references and slang words went over his head.

Once, he labored to tell his platoon a joke about how the world tends to criticize Israel. Yoni began hopefully by asking, "Did you hear the one about the unlucky Jew walking in the desert who was set upon by a dozen vicious bandits?"

He regaled, "They beat him mercilessly and then buried him up to his neck in sand. They hit him even more and threw rocks at him. When one bandit ran by him too closely, the Jew quickly moved his head and managed to trip him. The other bandits yelled out in outrage, 'Fight fair, Jew, fight fair.'"

Yoni thought everyone would be intimately aware of the world's double standards for Jews the way he was. All the guys from the Diaspora sighed and laughed, but the Israelis were confused. Itai asked Yoni what all the other Israelis in his platoon were wondering: "Why the hell did the Jew allow himself to get buried in the sand?"

The commitment of the lone solder was, for the greatest part, very sincere. Rarely did you find war-happy guys interested in prancing around with guns. They'd wash out from the grueling training. Almost half of lone soldiers made aliyah, and many signed up for combat units.

The Israelis treated them with praise tempered with incredulity. Israeli soldiers often called a lone soldier a *freier*. At first, Yoni was totally confused by the term until someone explained that it meant "sucker." Israelis grew up knowing they would be *required* to serve, but they didn't necessarily want to. Especially during the toughest parts of training, they couldn't help but make fun of their friends who chose to get themselves into this.

"Why are you here, crawling in the mud and not barbecuing on a beach with a beautiful girl?"

"Just think, if you were back in America, instead of washing these disgusting toilets, you would probably be polishing your Corvette. But good choice, bro."

Hours later, the sun came up over the eroded limestone cliffs. Now with only ten kilometers to go, the mood of the exhausted company lightened. The end would soon be in sight. In a merciful stupor, the soldiers struggled to a higher plateau and to a wooded overlook. Through foggy eyes, Yoni could see a profusion of trucks, chairs, and tables with drinks and food, and he could see that a platform had been erected. Music played from speakers, and officers were congratulating the filthy soldiers as they came to a halt and waited for orders. There were none.

The officers' congratulatory back thumping was a much-appreciated reward. Water flowed in abundance. In short order, the company formed up into platoons. The commander offered his heartfelt congratulations on earning the purple berets that the platoon leaders handed them.

As the soldiers approached Ammunition Hill in urban Jerusalem, sweat soaked and exhausted, cars honked their horns in applause as they drove by. The drivers instantly recognized that the soldiers were completing their *sof maslul*. Many of the men in the cars had been through it themselves. The cars' sounds reminded Yoni of the Rosh Hashanah *shofar* blasts.

Over the last few months, Yoni's thoughts had been a jumble of pride and uncertainty. He wasn't sure, but he had a good idea where he would be assigned; he guessed which region would be his to defend, and he thought about taking on a specialty. But at this moment, finally crossing the finish line of his ruthless training, Yoni was overwhelmed with feelings of brotherhood and loyalty for his fellow IDF soldiers and pride in their accomplishments. Just being with them at this moment, it was almost too much to hold back the emotion.

Yoni spotted his beaming parents in the crowd. It meant so much to him that they had made the trip. They could not afford to fly out for all his ceremonies, so Yoni had to pick which one meant the most to him for them to attend. This one felt to him to be the biggest milestone, as he had to endure the most challenges to reach it.

The presentation of the fighters' pins had begun. The fatigued soldiers limped into rectangular platoon formations, and the commander handed the pins to the platoon leader, Corporal Davidoff. He walked down the rows and, with care, attached the pins to the soldiers' shirt collars. With each pin exchange, Davidoff shook hands and heartily said "*mazal tov.*"

When the last pin was given and the platoon leader returned to the front of his team, the commander rejoiced with the full company. He proclaimed, "You are now, and always will be, part of the army that defends the Jewish state." He said, "For thousands of years, we were weak. Now we are strong, and we can defend ourselves."

The troops were dismissed, and the celebration began.

Yoni turned to Adam Restoff, a fellow lone soldier, and they hugged. The other guys were fist bumping and high fiving, but Adam and Yoni both shared another level of this experience, because they had chosen it for themselves.

Out of nowhere, Yoni heard familiar voices. It was Arieh, Doron, and Dov. Each of them had skipped class to travel to Jerusalem's Ammunition Hill.

Dov began, "Nu, you didn't tell us that your parents were coming this time! What did you need us here for?" Yoni knew he was joking. His friends would never miss one of these ceremonies.

Arieh interrupted, "Congratulations and *mazal tov*, Private Baranson. More than that pin, you need a shower."

Doron chimed in, "Whew, I agree. You smell even worse than Dov here did after his *sof maslul*."

Yoni tried to think of a good comeback for his sarcastic friends. Their humor did not mask their deep admiration for his commitment to Israel. He had known them since they were teenagers, and even then, they treated Yoni with respect for wanting to protect Israel without having grown up there.

Yoni gave up on thinking of a comeback. Beneath his brand-new purple beret and his dirt-encrusted uniform, Yoni choked back tears.

24 The Outrigger

Over the months of Arnie's chemotherapy, he had remained positive and had done well handling the uncomfortable side effects. At his last checkup, Dr. May was pleased with his healing from the surgery to remove the lung lobe containing the large nodule. A year before, the highly recommended, considerate doctor hadn't declared his situation as serious, but he also candidly told Arnie his battle would be a long one. He never used the word *terminal.*

Regarding the prescribed chemotherapy, Arnie had studied the literature and understood the treatment's benefits as well as the likely side effects. Besides the hair loss, nausea, dry mouth, and fatigue, he was familiar with what is commonly called "chemo brain." It's described as a fog-like confusion that reduces concentration and memory and affects your multitasking. Arnie had experienced the fuzziness and some of these diminutions, but felt that he still had a firm grasp on reality and his emotions.

Now, hearing Bobby Langford's surprisingly informed, sophisticated, and supportive statement on Israel and how the Palestinians politically bungled opportunities for their own sovereign state, Arnie drifted in an air of unreality. His head was swimming. Just before Bobby's exposition, all his radar signals about Bobby added up to a nice guy, an unaware fellow, someone indifferent to the history and current events threatening the State of Israel and the Jewish people.

Arnie now admitted to himself his initial assessment of Bobby had been wildly incorrect. In his lifetime, Arnie had more often committed errors of overestimating people than underestimating them: for example, assuming his Jewish peers would actively support Israel. He was pleasantly surprised to be wrong in the other direction this time.

From an over-the-shoulder glance at the dangling plastic pouches of liquid, it was obvious that the chemotherapy infusions for both Arnie and Bobby would soon be completed. Only half an inch of Arnie's amber liquid remained in the bottom of the collapsing bag. He knew the routine; the nurses would arrive, remove the port connections, and complete the paperwork. Somewhere in the wrap-up process, the patients would be served a paper cup or two of their requested fruit juice and some bland cookies.

Only a moment later, Bobby sat up and swung his legs over the side of the lounge chair. He closed the top two buttons of his oversized Tommy Bahama shirt. It was the one with the rows of cocktail glasses, as opposed to with the typical oversized tropical leaves. Because he had loosened his belt before lying back, he now fished the end through the loop, pulling as he searched for the right hole to cinch up the buckle.

Bobby was fully aware of Arnie's astonished reaction to his opinion about Israeli-Palestinian issues, and he guessed he would want to know more. Both men were quiet as they tried to transition from medical patients to decently functioning human beings. A bit of privacy would have been appreciated in this process.

Arnie wanted to be sure he could find a time and a place where they could talk. He needed to know more about Bobby and how he had acquired his knowledge base and a perspective that he so deeply appreciated and that was so unexpected.

As he and Bobby were shuffling around, removing the blankets and searching below for their shoes, Arnie thought through the options.

Over the last few decades, Bobby had surprised many of his friends, acquaintances, and family members with his special feelings for Israel, Jews, and their millennia-long struggles. Almost nobody knew about his dad's war stories and his friendship with Danny Baranson. In addition, the Langfords were devout Christians, and their daughter Susanne had already traveled to Israel on a church summer program.

He was prepared to quote the Scriptures about blessing Israel, and then explain how Judaism and Christianity share common roots. Bobby's interactions with the world of Indiana Christianity over the years had brought him face-to-face with prejudice, misunderstanding, and ignorance. On the other hand, many people such as those at his church felt the same as he did. He had lots to say.

The tiring routine of his treatments was grinding Bobby down. He felt a touch of social isolation. Sure, friends attempted to keep in touch and include him in their regular games and evening events. He was welcomed back into the golfing foursome, but he was so fatigued he often couldn't finish a full round. Bobby could sense the averted eyes and people walking on eggshells to avoid upsetting him. One golfing buddy cringed at his own faux pas when he shouted out, "Dead in the hole!" as Bobby's ball flew straight at the cup.

He could tell how friends would tiptoe around what was okay and what wasn't okay to ask. It was as if he had become a member of the Malignancy Club of South Florida, and nobody wanted an invitation. He had become an outsider, or at least he felt that way.

Arnie spoke first. "Bobby, I'm scheduled to return here in three weeks for another dose. What about you?"

With a hand swipe over his balding head, Bobby brightened and said, "Why don't we give ourselves a week or so to rebound from the poisoning, and then let's meet somewhere? Somewhere where *normal* people hang out. West Palm Beach is about halfway,"

Bobby proposed. "There's a restaurant called the Outrigger. Do you know it? It's right on the Intracoastal Waterway. We can grab a sandwich and a beer."

Arnie nodded his head in agreement. "Great idea. Palm Grove Cancer Center is just fine for cutting edge chemistry. For fried fish sandwiches and beer, though, gotta look elsewhere. Besides, we might not get matching appointments again."

Bobby concurred. "We've got rocky roads coming up for a few days, then some clear sailing."

As they walked through the double doors into the waiting room, sitting not too far apart were Arnie's wife Fran and Bobby's wife Andrea. Hearing the doors thump open, each looked up and saw her husband and a stranger walking together. The women rose, and the four met just past the humming aquarium. Both wives were buoyed seeing their husbands and mentally checking off that another of the required treatments was now behind them.

Arnie made introductions. "Fran, please say hello to a new friend of mine, Bobby Langford. He's from Stuart, originally from Indiana."

Bobby jumped in. "Andrea, this is Arnie Krakow. They live in Boynton Beach. Arnie was born in New York City."

The wives and husbands shook hands, and the four walked out to the parking lot together.

Ten days later, Bobby and Arnie met at the Outrigger restaurant. The hostess sat them down at a round table with a thatched umbrella on the restaurant's pier, poking into the busy Intracoastal Waterway.

From their white, molded seats they could see one of the hundreds of drawbridges that spanned the north-south inland passageway. This one would go up and down every half hour, allowing the tall-masted sailboats and mega-yachts to pass by.

They could watch every means of navigable transportation propelled by rowing, sailing, or motoring. A few of the boats would eventually dock, and sandaled passengers would climb up slatted ladders to the Outrigger restaurant. It was a delightful spot, and even the waiter stopped to watch the acrobatic pelicans glide about, fishing for their lunch.

Unlike at the cancer center, where they didn't talk at all about their illnesses, it was the first subject they discussed. Bobby, looking gaunt and grey, asked, "Arnie, was your week as bad as mine?"

Arnie, also droopy, nodded affirmatively.

Bobby continued, "I'm getting better at managing the nausea, and the lethargy, and the…well, you know the drill. It's very hard. My family is so committed to helping me through this, and I want to be positive and *will* these chemicals and surgeries to work. My friends, almost all the neighbors, and my church community are praying for me."

Bobby paused for a moment to frame his next comments. "Arnie, I'll shut up in a minute, but sometimes I wish I could be left alone to deal with my fears, anxiety, and depression. I don't care what anyone says…it's a drag being the focal point for all this psychic energy."

Bobby breathed deeply and went on. "Andrea has been wonderful. She hides her personal concerns, although I know she's talked to our pastor. I hear her praying and crying at night. She's so devoted to my getting better and for us to return to our normal routine, but I feel like she's asking for something that I just can't deliver."

Arnie also paused before he spoke. He looked down at the glistening water and watched two small boys and their dad tie up their eighteen-foot Boston Whaler. He listened to their playful back-and-forth over who was responsible for scuffing the prow as they fought the three-knot current and the ten-knot side breeze. He was happy to hear that the dad didn't assign blame, but he instead rhetorically asked what his little crew might have to think about when they left the dock later.

Then Arnie reconnected. "Bobby, I know that Fran, my kids, and my friends are worried about me. They're hovering all around trying to help out, trying to be my cheerleaders. But in a crazy way, I'm emotionally drained thinking about their disappointments. When the doctor doesn't pronounce me miraculously cured, I feel like I failed them. I'm the bum. It's confusing figuring out what to say honestly and what to spin into a more upbeat storyline."

Bobby followed quickly. "I'm sure we've both read all the glossy pamphlets and self-help books and perused the web for wisdom about handling the fear and anxiety. It's helped. It makes sense."

Arnie sighed. "I don't know about you, but I come away with a feeling that my cancer is a battle as much for my dignity as it is for my survival. Bobby, you and me, we've lived reasonably long lives. We're not kids. What we face isn't a tragedy. It's a trauma, it's disruptive, it ain't good, but it's not really a tragedy.

"One more thought and then let's order our lunch," Arnie suggested. "I've come to the point where I've reconciled with several facts. First, I've led an interesting life, and I've done my best to stay focused on what's important."

Bobby agreed, "Yeah, I've always joked that nobody lives forever. It's helped me justify a diet loaded with fatty steaks."

Arnie chuckled. "I haven't been perfect, or even easy to handle, but I take some pride in what Fran and I have achieved. Second, over the course of my life, I've seen some wonderful changes. I've come to the realization that my family and the world will march on after I'm gone. It isn't like the Hollywood movie that ends when I end. We get to see just a blink of an eye's worth of the movie, not the beginning and not the end. Smart money is on the grim reaper."

Bobby looked away from the water and straight at Arnie. He reached out and gave him a friendly little poke to the shoulder. Grabbing the printed lunch menu, Bobby confided to Arnie, "I'm so glad we met. You know what they say, 'timing is everything,' and I'll confess, this is just the conversation I needed to have."

Arnie replied, "I feel the same way. It's our own support group of two."

Peering down at the menu, he noted, "I'll bet the grouper sandwich is good here."

Over plates loaded with crispy fried fillets in toasted buns, coleslaw, and fries, Arnie and Bobby continued commiserating over the full range of non-medical, but cancer-related experiences they had encountered. They related stories of dropping the bad news bomb on their children. Both could relate that what were once easy decisions about vacations and family events suddenly became complicated. Now, they had to carefully address treatment impacts and future plans.

Arnie and Bobby had heard the siren call of cures and miracles, but office visits were never conclusive, and you never heard exactly what you or your family wanted to hear. It was sometimes a blue-sky patchwork of improvements, and maybe, just maybe, remissions. They knew that at too many visits, the doctor's tight-jawed face gave away the news that not all was positive, and more high-tech options were to be considered. For the two of them, the "cancer free" end of the rainbow proclamation was out there, but not just yet.

Two wedges of key lime pie crisscrossed with squiggles of whipped cream arrived at the table along with two cups of black coffee. As good as the fish sandwiches were, the dessert got their attention. It also signaled that the end of the lunch was nearing and redirected them to get back to their unexpected exchange at the last chemotherapy.

Arnie reminded him, "Bobby, about ten days ago we stumbled onto a topic that is of great interest to me. I have to admit that your comments blew me away. It seems as if we share a similar interest. You mentioned a Jewish pal of yours and his Israeli wife. I'd love to know more about them. You said your daughter traveled to Israel. Tell me about all that."

"I'll give you the short version."

For the next fifteen minutes, Bobby regaled Arnie with his mini-memoir starting over fifty years before in an attic. He pointed out how the story began back in late April of 1945 with his dad, John Langford, fighting in southern Germany. Bobby detailed how his father had struggled to share with his family the painful story of liberating Dachau.

Arnie listened closely as Bobby described how he met Danny as a schoolboy and how a silly, snowy evening's tobogganing began a lifelong friendship. Bobby shared how his own Christian family came to appreciate the importance and righteousness of the struggles of the small State of Israel. His daughter Susanne was especially involved with Israel through their church and interfaith activities. Most members of their church, especially the pastor, would call themselves Christian Zionists.

In his recounting, he introduced Maya, Danny's wife, telling Arnie about her father Yonatan and his death during the Yom Kippur War. He told Arnie about meeting her mother Dahlia, and about Maya and Danny's son, Yoni, who became a lone soldier in the Israel Defense Forces.

Arnie listened intently. He didn't say one word. When Bobby finished talking, Arnie waited for even more details.

There was a brief silence. Arnie leaned back and said, "That is a remarkable story. I am so very grateful that you shared it with me. It was probably…" Arnie paused again, searching for just the right words. He eventually said simply, "It was a wonderful story."

Bobby glanced at his wristwatch and responded, "Arnie, I have to admit I am getting very tired. The drive down here and all the talking have done me in. Why don't you give me your short version for now, and we can make a plan to get together again?"

Arnie, still musing over Bobby's complex story, forged ahead. He, too, was wearing down. "I'll make it quick. And, yes, let's schedule another lunch. This has been great."

He described being raised in New York City in an actively Jewish, Zionist home. He told Bobby that his dad had been in the Marines and how in 1942 his uncle died in the North Atlantic transporting war goods to Murmansk. He added the specifics that a German U-boat sank the Liberty ship the *Robert Gray.*

Arnie downplayed his metropolitan New York story, thinking it was stereotypical and probably obvious. He detailed being raised along with his sister by conscientious parents, attending college at NYU, finding a good job in corporate finance, and then raising a family. Arnie perked up a bit telling how his wife Fran had been a teacher and had been so effective maintaining a Jewish home and raising their two children.

He talked about their growing involvement with friends and neighbors in both Jewish philanthropies and pro-Israel activism. He confessed that he might be too judgmental, leveling too much vitriol at those who didn't join in his efforts.

Arnie highlighted their six trips to Israel, including bar mitzvahs at the Western Wall and on top of Masada. Arnie regaled Bobby with tidbits about his favorite handshakes with dignitaries and poignant presentations by soldiers, survivors, and immigrants on the organized trips they took part in. He raced through visits to hospitals and schools, archeological digs, and military bases.

Arnie was also running out of energy. He promised that the next time they met, he would bring pictures to help illustrate his story.

Bobby politely applauded and praised, "Arnie, you have so much to be proud of – really terrific. I appreciate your sharing all that. You have accomplished a great deal, and I'm sure there's more to come, more good times for you and Fran."

The sun had now passed over the restaurant, and the mid-afternoon heat was overtaking the sea breeze. It was time to go, but Bobby was fascinated by Arnie's travels.

Bobby decided, "Next time, let's start with your pictures from Israel. I've never been there, although our daughter has." Somberly, he added, "Now, I'm not sure it's in my future. Let me enjoy your travelogue."

They paid the bill, and the two walked side by side on the pier, past the conical covered pilings, and back into the air-conditioned restaurant. On their way to the parking lot, both moved slowly, fatigued by a long day and their illness. Standing in the shade of the porte cochere, Arnie and Bobby prepared to shake hands and head out into the steamy sunlight to their cars.

Arnie offered, "Look, when we get together next time, please tell me more about Susanne and her interest in Israel. She sounds like a special young woman." He shuffled for his keys. "I'll call you. Let's try to meet next week. Is that okay?" He qualified, "I know we can't plan too far ahead. Sometimes I can't plan any further than the next trip to the bathroom."

Bobby yawned, "Yes, that'd be great. And don't forget to bring those pictures from Israel."

In the bright sun, Bobby proclaimed as he walked toward his baking car, "Next year in Jerusalem. Next week with Arnie."

25 Coffee Table

Only a few days after Arnie and Bobby had met for fried fish sandwiches, they talked over the phone and planned a dinner at a local sports bar. Bobby had promised the joint had great burgers and great French dip.

Arnie parked his car and walked in from bright, late-afternoon sunshine. His vision was impaired as his eyes adjusted to the sports bar's dim light. The eight big-screen televisions silently entertained the customers and illuminated the darkened room with auto racing, soccer, tennis, and baseball competitions. All were muted but the flat screen behind the bar showing the soccer match. It received the full attention of the six patrons hunched over on their bar stools, as well as one skinny, tattooed bartender.

In unison, they grunted and groaned as the ball ricocheted near the net, as scoring kicks were attempted, and as the goalkeeper made heroic saves. Apparently, the seven were rooting for the team with yellow jerseys who were momentarily, and ineptly, on offense.

He guessed that this wasn't the World Cup, but perhaps a Latin American soccer league match. He squinted, looking for his new friend Bobby in the dimly lit room. He didn't see him and thought, *no luck, probably too early.*

There were several booths open, and he chose one to sit down and wait. The middle-aged waitress in a black and white striped referee jersey soon came by introducing herself. "I'm Lizzie. Hon, are you waiting for others, or you're alone tonight?"

Arnie answered, "I'm expecting my buddy…he'll be here in a few minutes. I saw you had Blue Moon on tap. I'll take one now, please. Do you have a menu?"

Lizzie obliged. "Be right back with the beer and menus."

She headed to the bar to fill the order. Arnie figured he could at least read the menu as he waited for his dinner companion to show up.

It was six o'clock, and Arnie was a little early. He sat back indifferently, watching the hotly contested soccer match from his booth. The Blue Moon was served with its traditional orange slice hanging on the glass's edge. It was his favorite beer, and the first golden gulps were, as always, deliciously refreshing.

Arnie casually watched the soccer match, as it was shown on the TV that required the least turning of his head. Truth be told, he was a little sleepy, still fatigued from the recent chemo and the longer-term effects of the surgery, so, he just relaxed waiting for Bobby.

After forty-five minutes, Arnie began to worry. He puzzled over whether he had the right place. Was the date correct? Arnie knew he was more forgetful lately, and some details were lost or scrambled. He thought enough time had passed that he could phone him without sounding like a worrywart.

After ten rings, a woman answered. "Hello. This is Robert Langford's phone, Andrea speaking."

Arnie responded with surprise, "Hello. I'm Arnie Krakow. We met a few weeks ago. I was waiting for Bobby to join me for dinner tonight. We're friends. New chemo buddies. Is everything okay?"

There was a momentary pause from Andrea. "Well, unfortunately, Bobby had a bad day yesterday, and we had to take him to the hospital."

Arnie quickly responded, "Oh, no, so sorry."

"I guess he just forgot to mention your dinner. He's stable now," Andrea reassured. "I don't want to wake him."

Arnie was taken aback by the disappointing news. "I'm glad he's doing better. We had met at the chemo center weeks ago, so I understand the setbacks that go with it. Please tell him to feel better and to call me when he's up to it."

Andrea promised she'd pass along his message.

Arnie mechanically finished the Blue Moon, paid his bill, and slowly walked back into the still sunny parking lot to his car. He sat back with the motor running and felt the air conditioner jetting a cooling breeze across his face and chest. He was disturbed by the call. He, of course, knew Bobby was ill with lymphoma, and fully displayed the range of chemo side effects: nausea, sweats, dizziness, weakness, and on and on.

He knew that when you are undergoing chemo, your body chemistry is altered and nothing is guaranteed, but he was still shaken by the disruption of what he thought would be a pleasant dinner and conversation. He slowly realized the flaw in thinking that, for a little while today, he and Bobby were just two regular guys, two men in control of their lives, two guys not battling cancer. He wanted them to be two guys whose big decision was what kind of beer to drink or which cheese to add to their burgers.

Damn it, he thought to himself, *tonight it was just beers and burgers, nothing wild or dangerous. We should be able to enjoy a few hours beyond a malignant sword of Damocles.*

Just then, in the middle of his self-pitying funk, his phone rang. He answered, "Hello, Arnie here."

"It's Bobby," His friend softly emitted. "Hey, pal, so sorry for the screwup. I had trouble yesterday. Passed out. Anemia. Ambulance. The whole thing."

Arnie answered, "Absolutely no problem. Hope you're feeling better. When are you going home?" He purposely didn't ask for any more medical information on what happened or how serious it all was.

Bobby replied optimistically, "I'm doing much better and hopefully going home tomorrow. Why don't you come on over when I get out and keep me entertained? Andrea's burgers aren't bad, but no French dip."

Arnie chuckled and agreed, "Sure. Call me when you're out of the hospital, and we'll make plans."

It had taken Bobby longer to rebound than he had expected. Almost two weeks passed before Arnie and Fran pulled onto the Langfords' crosshatched concrete driveway. Their compact, one-story Spanish-style home, surrounded with queen palms, was not too different from his home. He guessed it had three bedrooms and a lanai in the back.

Arnie rang the doorbell. A moment later, Bobby opened the door, stepping into the afternoon light that spilled out across the grey and tan foyer. "Arnie and Fran, so glad you could drive over. I know you already met my wife and head nurse."

With a knowing smile, he clarified, "Arnie, she really is a nurse, a full pediatric RN. I'm now her full-time toddler."

The Langfords escorted the Krakows deeper into the house. The guys separated from their wives, who took a tour of the home. The men stayed in the entrance, making small talk about the ambulance ride and the nearby golf course they had passed on the drive over.

Andrea and Fran didn't mention anything about their husbands' problems, but simple gestures and timid smiles revealed to each other the never-ending worries. Each could imagine the other's shock at the initial diagnosis and disappointment over setbacks. Each knew the fear and anguish that had to be managed, so it didn't overwhelm and distort the relationship between the inflicted and the caregiver.

Even though the Krakows were older, it seemed both the Krakows and the Langfords had arrived at a similar point in life's struggle. All still believed that good years lay ahead.

Arnie and Fran talked about their son Sam and daughter Karen, describing where they lived and what their respective spouses did for a living. Sam had two children, and Karen had a baby girl. The Langfords told them about Susanne and Meredith. Susanne was in graduate school. Meredith had married her high school sweetheart and recently had a baby.

The home's great room was bounded on one side by the kitchen and on another by wall-length bookshelves. Already, a tray with a tower of glasses, along with pitchers of iced tea and lemonade, was sitting on the near corner of the large beveled-edge glass coffee table that dominated the room. Arnie and Fran sat down on the corner of an L-shaped leather sofa, flanked by the Langfords.

On the far side of the coffee table was a trove of family pictures. Behind glass, family and friends were captured in groupings in front of porches, national parks, and lakes. Some were recent, and others were yellowing, now decades old. Arnie scanned across the honored collection.

Arnie's eyes were drawn to one photo, like it was a light bulb shining a little brighter than all the rest. It was a landscape-oriented picture of a smiling young girl with chestnut-colored hair, wearing a white blouse and tan slacks. She was standing by herself, arms by her side, in the plaza in front of Jerusalem's Kotel. In the background was the western retaining wall of the Second Temple's foundation. An Israeli flag curling in the breeze added a touch of blue and white to the golden hues of the Herodian stone blocks.

When the conversation paused for a moment, he pointed to the picture and asked, "The picture from Israel, from Jerusalem, is that your daughter Susanne?"

Andrea responded cheerily, "It sure is. It's her at the Kotel. It was at the very end of her church trip, just after her sophomore year in high school. She loved every minute of it. She's still very much involved with our church's Holy Land and pro-Israel projects."

Arnie simply smiled back, appreciating Andrea's use of the Hebrew word Kotel, not the Wailing Wall or even the Western Wall.

Even though Arnie and Bobby had spent time together only twice, the four shared a relaxed, unguarded interchange of their shared interests in Israel. The Langfords took turns telling Susanne's story about her Christian outreach trip to Israel. Ping-ponging their way through Pastor Ed's selection surprise, pre-trip preparation, and the itinerary, they added poignant anecdotes. It was as if Susanne was with them telling the tales herself.

Andrea was especially animated when she told the Krakows about the volunteer work that Susanne did in some of Israel's poorest communities. It made her so proud that her daughter cared about giving back, especially given her own history of mission work in third-world countries.

As they vicariously enjoyed the second-hand telling of Susanne's stories, Arnie easily visualized Susanne's personal journey. Sitting there on the comfortable couch, he imagined walking along the Tel Aviv promenade. He could imagine her surprise at the juxtaposition of the city's sprouting skyline and the millennia-old Jaffa port. He pictured her wide eyes as she stepped through the exotic Old City *shuk* or watched Shabbat shoppers crowd the covered Machane Yehuda marketplace.

He dreamily thought back to his own trips to Israel. Arnie and Fran, too, had walked by the Sea of Galilee, and they saw Christian pilgrims being baptized at the Yardenit in northern Israel. They had sat on the steps of the fourth-century Church of the Holy Sepulchre in the Christian Quarter of Jerusalem and watched the parade of visitors. He had learned from guides that it contained the last four stations of the Via Dolorosa.

Over the next forty minutes, Bobby and Andrea, using their coffee table pictures as props, introduced Arnie and Fran to their entire family. Little vignettes made the stills come alive. They talked about both of their children at various ages and shared a picture of Meredith's new baby boy.

Bobby reached forward and into the middle of the array to lift out a larger family photo and handed it to Arnie. Bobby pointed to the older man in the corner. "That was my dad, John. Mom's next to him," he said. "I told you how in 1945, my dad, Sergeant John Langford, helped liberate Dachau. It was something that meant so much to him. It influenced us all.

"Here's one more," pronounced Bobby. "This is my pal Danny and his wife Maya, and their two kids, Yoni and Orly. It's a few years old. We talked about them briefly at our lunch. You remember I mentioned Maya, she is Israeli born. She's a *sabra*." Bobby said proudly, "Yoni is a lone soldier."

The Krakows had to rely on several small wallet-sized photos of their children and grandchildren, and Fran promised more pictures for their next visit.

Arnie sat back, sinking into the sofa, while letting their family's puzzle pieces fall into place. Meeting Bobby had added an unexpected dimension to his life, a validation to his lifelong passion for Israel. There were good friends, Jewish friends, whom he worked with on political action initiatives, but somehow this budding friendship, an out-of-left-field confluence of lives, was reassuring. It added a broadened footing to a world that always felt as if the odds were against him.

Bobby stood up to pour an iced tea from the glass pitcher, now covered in dripping beads of condensation. He asked if there were any other takers. Only then did Arnie notice that Bobby looked thinner and less steady. He struggled with the sloshing weight of the iced liquid and had to steady himself with one hand on the coffee table before sitting back down.

Bobby checked his watch and suggested that he and Arnie sit outside in the screened-in lanai while Andrea and Fran prepared dinner. On their way past the refrigerator, Bobby grabbed two beers. He pulled the glass sliding door closed and turned on the slow-moving ceiling fan as they settled into canvas-cushioned chairs.

From the lanai, they looked over a small kidney-shaped lake circled with mid-sized Florida oaks. Rising above thick foliage silhouetted against a darkening sky, the grey cumulonimbus clouds were tinted pink by the setting sun. This pleasant western view must have been very familiar, yet Bobby stared without saying a word. For the first time, there was an awkward silence.

"It's been a tough time," Bobby ruminated. "I think you know where I'm coming from. Even with all of the treatments and all the doctors, I still feel I'm on a slow steady decline. It's like jet lag all the time."

Bobby lowered his voice so Andrea couldn't hear. "I'm not packing it in or anything like that, but I'm realistic about my outlook. Andrea and I can look forward to more great days, fun days, but I'm not so sure about the years. I'm no longer buying the big box of anything at Costco," he lamented with a half-smile. "I don't have too many choices left, not too many decisions about how to live my life. Sure, there are always medical options, experiments, and miracles. But I mean, I'm talking about how to live, really live in the time I have left."

Arnie listened carefully as Bobby talked. He was ready to respond, not with an argument or a pep-rally speech, but with a sympathetic confirmation that he understood it all. He could validate Bobby's need for realism.

Bobby raised a finger, asking Arnie to hold his thought and to let him complete his plaintive confession. He took a deep breath and shared, "I've come up with an idea. Maybe it's a crazy notion. No, really, it's more like a request." Wondering how Arnie would react, Bobby blurted out, "What do you think about us all taking a trip to Israel?"

26 Bus Stop

With her mocha skin, angular face, bright white teeth, and huge eyes, Orit looked like a fashion model. Even in her green uniform, with a backpack over her shoulders, hoisting a deadly automatic weapon, and wearing the same fox and sword insignia that Yoni wore, she was stunning. Even though she was crammed into a bus stop with fifteen other Givati Brigade soldiers trying to avoid the dusty winds and strong afternoon Negev sun, Yoni thought she could be strutting on a fashion show runway and she would have had all of Paris or Milan clambering to wear a backpack, purple beret, and black boots.

For now, on this early spring day in 2008, she was lighting up the bus stop just beyond the entry gates to the IDF army base in southern Israel near Mitzpe Ramon. He wondered where she was going. Most were headed to their parents' homes for Shabbat. As a lone soldier, he felt lucky to have plans for the next two days. What was her family planning for her?

They all waited for the regional bus heading north. Every time a car or a truck from one of the nearby farms or wineries rounded the turn, they alternately shushed each other and whooped with excitement, hoping that this was their ride. Each time they were wrong, they'd get back to telling jokes and stories, laughter ricocheting among them.

Ravi, a bulky, bearded soldier from the Galilee, said, "If you ask me, in one word, to describe my commander, it would be 'good.' In two words, 'not good.'" Those in earshot laughed out loud.

Of the fifteen soldiers, two were from Ethiopian families and three were from families of the recent Russian absorption. Five were women, and the rest were men. They chatted about the upcoming Shabbat.

Amir shared, "My extended family from Hazor will be dropping by, and I'll finally get to meet my Orthodox cousin's latest baby girl." Looking for a laugh, Amir said, "It's her fifth child. They are very, very fruitful, my cousin and her husband. Who knows? Maybe she's pregnant again. Anyway, I hope my pile of grimy laundry is kept separate from the baby's," Amir opined. "I'd hate to get baby crap on it."

They all laughed. While they hungered for some homemade food, having their *immas* wash their clothes for them came in a close second.

One of the two Ethiopians describe the *dabbo* his mother promised to cook for the ten family members coming over for dinner. He claimed her nearly two-foot-wide and nine-inch-high crusty oat bread was the best in all of Ramla. He promised to bring back a big wedge.

The casual talk of home-cooked food continued. Family dishes would all compare favorably to the army kitchen's limited provisions. While they all claimed to be going home to the best meal, they would have been happy to devour any of the meals described. Each gave such detail that the rest could almost see the food just down the road, piled high on a table, like a mirage in the desert.

Along with the food, they conjured up the sights and sounds of the kitchen, the rounded bellies of fathers, the bantering that picked up between siblings as if they had never been apart, the loving eyes of mothers reciting prayers over their warrior children's heads, drinking in the sight of their boy or girl, home for now, safe for now.

At the bus stop, their stomachs growled. "Listen everyone," one of them hollered out. "When you come back, bring some spices, some peppers, some *schug, amba*, and *shipka*. It'll liven up the sawdust we are given."

These soldiers would be home for just two days, so every minute counted. Before they went back, their families would finish their laundry and tuck into their bags some extra packages with goodies to eat. In Israel, because of the proximity and the good transportation systems, it was common for a soldier to come home every other weekend. They came trudging home late Thursday or early Friday and headed back on Sunday morning. Of course, if there were border tensions or other conflicts, then Shabbat leaves were much rarer.

Yoni felt affection for his fellow Israeli soldiers, but he couldn't help but envy them a little, or sometimes a lot, for their easy access to their families. He was one of over two thousand lone soldiers in the army. Although he received twice the salary of regular soldiers, as well as other benefits, no one complained; they knew the value of having family nearby.

Rounding the turn, the bus finally arrived and hissed to a stop. The doors swung open and all fifteen piled in, grabbing seats and stashing backpacks on the shelves above. Most kept their weapons on their laps or between their legs. Yoni was nearly last on the bus, and as he walked down the aisle, he kept a watchful eye on the empty seat next to Orit, hoping it would stay that way until he got there. He breathed a sigh of relief when the last of his comrades settled in, and he stowed his backpack over Orit's head.

Looking down, he said with the imagined accent of a Jewish-American cowboy, "This seat taken?"

She looked at him straight-faced and said, "Yes, it is." He shook his head thoughtfully and proceeded down the aisle, hoping she was playing with him. When he heard her laugh, he turned and plopped down next to her.

He didn't know anything about her, not even her name, but it occurred to him that she and he were the only ones at the bus stop not telling stories about their *abba*'s onion pie or their *imma*'s *shakshuka*. Perhaps, she too, was a lone soldier. Israelis who came from families who for whatever reason would not support them could also be treated as lone soldiers. He didn't want to pry, but if she was a lone soldier, that would give them something more in common. Part of him realized how pointless it was to make a connection, since there were rules prohibiting romantic relationships with fellow soldiers. But he looked at this woman, and he thought, *I just want to make conversation, that's all. It's not like I'm trying to escort her to the homecoming game.*

"I'm Yoni," he said.

She looked away from the window and met his eyes. "Orit," she crisply replied.

"I'm going to Petah Tikvah. I'll be with my friend Doron and his family. Where are you headed?" He left open the possibility that she, in fact, was going home to be with her family.

Orit's Hebrew, learned fourteen years before in the absorption center, was now flawless. Immediately, she knew that her seatmate was an American who had chosen to come to Israel to serve in the IDF. His Hebrew was limited, with odd inflections and awkward grammar. Like all other Israelis, she respected lone soldiers and was inspired by their selflessness and commitment to Israel. She knew that many had already or would eventually make aliyah.

Her army story was very different from his. While his was one of choice, for some Israelis, family challenges made their experience harder. Not all soldiers had an intact family to support them.

The children of these stressed families needed and often got help. It wasn't uncommon for Ethiopian families to have socioeconomic challenges that so often come with immigration. The Ethiopian parents who had been revered and treated with great deference in Ethiopia faced many cultural challenges upon their arrival in Israel. Over a short time, because the older generation was slow to learn Hebrew and to find employment, their status eroded.

She answered Yoni in English, "I'm Orit Negalla. I'm going to Yemin Orde for Shabbat." She wasn't sure if he knew about this special, religious boarding school and added, "It's a youth village in Mount Carmel. It's just southeast of Haifa. It's a long trip, but it will be great. Some of my old classmates will be there."

Her answer still didn't confirm or deny whether she'd be with her family, and her parsimonious description about herself left Yoni with questions about her possible lone soldier status.

The myriad Israeli immigration storylines, often including movie-quality intrigue and great courage, amazed Yoni. It seemed every third person had family that evaded the British or traveled overland across hostile lands like Turkey, Syria, and Lebanon. Some had escaped from dangerous Middle Eastern countries, leaving behind every possession. Some families traced back six generations to the beginnings of Jewish villages in the early twentieth century, some into the nineteenth century. Some families had lived in Israel for dozens of generations.

Now, the more recent Ethiopian rescues included the same elements of loss, risk, redemption, and renewal as earlier waves of immigrants.

A few weeks before, Yoni's friend from his platoon had recounted part of his parents' miraculous and harrowing passage from Ethiopia to Israel in the early 1980s. The family's elders had to negotiate and plan the dangerous journey. They walked mostly at night from their village, through the northwest mountains and through Sudan to a safe location where Israeli agents would arrange the final leg of their travel.

He described this ragtag band, carrying all that they possessed, with women holding infants on their backs, and with little knowledge of the world outside theirs. They had almost no food and not much water.

One night, as the family huddled in the cold air at the edge of the scrubby Sudanese desert, the family leader was told by the suspicious contact that no guide would go with them on this crossing. Instead, he told them that they would have to follow a donkey. The animal, by repetition, supposedly knew the way across the forbidding terrain. He was told that the donkey would lead them for three days to the next small village to find his dinner of straw and a pond with fresh water. There, they were told, the important agent would be found. The contact said there was no other choice. The contact also warned that they would have to guard the donkey and protect it from hyenas and lions.

It was the donkey or wait there for some other miracle.

His friend poked at the ground between himself and Yoni with a stick. He then looked up at Yoni, winked, and said, "He chose the donkey."

It had been a very long day, and Orit and Yoni rode along for miles in silence, dozing or relaxing with eyes closed. They passed rough-hewn desert limestone and sandstone cliffs and the ancient city of Avdat. For thousands of years, Avdat had been part of the old Nabatean spice route empire, extending from the Indian Ocean and the Arabian Sea to the Mediterranean. Soon, they'd drive by Sde Boker and the large, growing desert city of Beersheva, home to Ben-Gurion University.

While Orit came in and out of sleep, she drifted back to remembrances of her young life in Ethiopia, Beersheva, and the youth village. Faint images flashed by of her village in Ethiopia with her dad's glowing blacksmith fire and her family's few sheep and cows. She remembered the absorption center's too-small apartments and her new classmates at Yemin Orde.

When they passed Beersheva, she saw Yoni was awake and gazing out the window. She told Yoni, "We're close to the Nurit Absorption Center. That was my family's first stop in Israel sixteen years ago. I think a few minutes ago we passed the road that leads to it."

Yoni was glad that Orit had continued the conversation. He pivoted around to see where the exit was.

She went on, "Following the Operation Solomon airlift, we lived there for almost eighteen months. There were over fourteen thousand of us flown to Israel within thirty-six hours."

"I've seen pictures of the arrivals at the airport," Yoni interjected with sincere interest.

Orit nodded. "At the absorption center, all our needs were taken care of, and we learned Hebrew at the local ulpan. That was very difficult for my mother and father. They weren't illiterate, but they spoke only Amharic. We were taught about the Israeli way of life and what to expect in the schools. My parents didn't have a shekel, didn't have a job, and didn't understand anything about modern living. The Jewish Agency and the workers provided training and guidance. When we left Nurit, it was still very difficult."

Yoni was thrilled that Orit, who was clearly out of his league, was paying attention to him. Aside from that, though, he was fascinated by her story. "How did your family travel from Ethiopia to Israel?"

Orit answered, "We left our home in the Dembiya region of Ethiopia and moved together to the Jewish Agency compound in Gondar. We were there for thirty months. My brother Yitzhak had to live with other relatives until we were ready to travel to Addis Ababa. There we found another Jewish Agency center. They provided schooling on Israeli customs and lifestyle."

With a smile that dimpled her cheeks, she added, "It all sounds impossible, but my uncle came to Israel earlier, part of the covert Operation Moses in 1980. He walked across the desert to Sudan." Her expression hardened. "His brother died. Many perished along the way from sickness and bandits. Those were the pioneers for the rest of us."

Yoni and Orit made eye contact for an extended moment until Yoni looked down and laughed. "Well, I'm afraid your life story is much more interesting than mine. I'm just your typical American lone soldier."

"No, no," Orit reassured. "It's interesting too. Where are you headed for Shabbat?"

"I'm going to stay with my friend Doron, an Israeli I met when I came for the summer after high school. We stayed in touch ever since. He's married now, and they have a really cute baby."

"Nice! So, what's your story? How did you end up in Israel?" Orit inquired.

"I grew up in the United States, in Indiana. It's in the middle of the country. My mom was born in Israel, after her mother and father escaped the Holocaust in the 1930s."

Orit listened, but Yoni wasn't sure she could picture his childhood that was so different from hers. Could she imagine the American Jewish experience that was free from threats? Yoni wondered if she thought all American Jews strongly identified with their heritage like lone soldiers did and if she had any ideas about problems of assimilation and intermarriage. He hoped she didn't know about the apathy of all too many of his acquaintances. Instead, he focused on his trips to Israel as a child and his admiration of IDF soldiers from a young age.

Orit looked over Yoni's shoulder at a landscape that had changed from the stony desert's mix of tans and yellows to the organized, precisely planted fields of fruit trees, grains, and vegetables. The more frequent highway exits evidenced the increasing population density.

After Yoni wrapped up and they sat in silence for a moment, she cautiously volunteered, "Both my parents are alive, and I see them once in a while. They don't live together."

Shifting on the bus seat and squaring her shoulders toward him, she said, "Life in Israel has been a struggle, especially for my father. Anyway, I can go home to Yemin Orde anytime." With her gorgeous dimpled smile, she told him, "I stay in the Blue Roof housing; it's for returning graduates. When you arrive as a new student, it's important to know you will always have a place to return to. Lots of graduates go back, and we see Yemin Orde as our second home."

She wistfully added, "Once in a while, I visit my brother. It's fun. I really like his wife and kids."

Their talk moved to more neutral ground as they chatted about their lives in the army. Soldiers had such intense shared experiences that it was a cliché for their friends outside of the army to nag them to stop talking about it. Although soldiers were frequently complaining, whether they'd chosen to serve or not, most felt the passionate pull of Jewish history and the reality of defending their homeland.

Orit and Yoni's bus continued north until it stopped at the Central Station in Tel Aviv. Yoni gathered his backpack and hoisted his weapon. "Orit, it was wonderful to learn your story. Thanks for sharing. I'll see you back in Mitzpe Ramon. Have a great time at Yemin Orde."

Orit smiled. "Thanks! You enjoy your friends. Nice talking to you as well. Have a good time. Shabbat shalom, Yoni."

Orit made two more bus connections as she traveled north on Route 4 through Israel's narrow eleven-mile-wide waist, hemmed in by pre-1967 borders on one side and the Mediterranean on the other. As soon as the bus left the coast road, heading east on Route 7111, she watched for the familiar sand dunes. They passed fish farms and net-covered banana groves. She rode up the narrow winding roads into thick forests of pines, past the artist community of Ein Hod. Very soon, Orit would enter the Yemin Orde campus.

She walked into the oversized dining room. Like firecrackers going off, up popped residents and counselors who greeted her.

"Orit, Orit, ORIT!" they shouted out like the right answer to a TV game show question. Shabbat would be sweeter with Orit back as part of the family.

27
Shabbat

It only took one knock on the Meirs' apartment door before Naomi, Doron, and knee-high Reuven greeted Yoni. Yoni lifted up Reuven to give him a high five, which Reuven had recently learned how to do.

Stepping into the cramped apartment, Yoni smelled a delicious tomato sauce.

Naomi announced in her best English, "Tonight is Italian night. Yoni dear, I'm betting you have had enough Israeli salad and soggy eggplant."

Yoni added, "And not enough greasy schnitzel."

"Sorry, can't help you with that. We're having spaghetti and meatballs. No Chianti, but a nice Israeli red. It will be our Shabbat in Rome."

Doron had met and married Naomi during their year of travel between army and university. As was normal in Israel, they became parents during their degrees at Tel Aviv University.

As promised, the dinner was a much-needed change of culinary pace. While the produce in Israel was varied, plentiful, and fresh, the endless repetition of army meals bored Yoni's American tastes.

Tonight, the combination of candle lighting, prayers, pasta, vino, and friends was just what he needed. Yoni updated the Meirs about the two weeks since he'd seen them last. With a shy smile, he recounted his bus trip with Orit. "She was really stunning, with such an interesting life story. She's up in Yemin Orde for Shabbat."

Naomi could see that this girl had made a big impression on Yoni. He hadn't spoken to them about any girls since he made aliyah.

Doron shared news from Arieh and Dov. They were both doing well and working hard in new jobs.

Just after Shabbat dinner, Yoni sank down into their sectional sofa and pulled the phone onto his lap. Yoni, similarly to Doron and Naomi, identified as a "traditional" Jew; he kept kosher to an extent, went to synagogue sometimes on Shabbat, and participated in holidays. He liked the traditions, but he didn't observe all the laws, which included not using electricity on Shabbat.

He called his parents back in the United States. His cell phone plan included overseas calling, which he took advantage of frequently. Since he'd made aliyah, he called each and every Friday. His sister Orly was off at college, so he kept in touch with her mostly by texting.

He would keep his parents up to date on his adventures. When those included combat or border operations, there were security considerations; he had to be discrete about the particulars of time, place, and purpose in case his call was tapped. But all conversations would end with Maya reciting the blessing parents give their children at Shabbat dinner and a breezy "Shabbat shalom."

Today, Yoni focused on his conversation with Orit. "Guys, on the bus ride today, I sat next to a really beautiful Ethiopian girl from my base. She was heading to Yemin Orde, not too far from Haifa. Do you know it, Imma? She didn't explain why she went to a youth village, but I'm guessing her family situation is not good. She's going through basic training. It was really interesting, she told me about how she was part of Operation Solomon."

Yoni realized that he might have talked too much about a girl. It was one thing to keep his parents informed; it was another to provoke their natural interest in his social life.

After Yoni finished recounting his week's highlights, Danny took the lead. "Yoni, we might be seeing you sooner that we had planned. Maybe in the next six months." Yoni could hear Danny's slow breathing and hesitation. It was enough to alert Yoni that something in his parents' world had shifted. Danny explained, "I think you know that my good buddy Bobby has been undergoing chemotherapy treatments. I'm not sure it is all going well."

Danny took a deep breath. "I haven't seen him for a few months, but from our conversations, it seems that medical problems keep popping up. There are setbacks. I really love the guy…it is so painful to watch him suffer. Maya has talked with Andrea, and her takeaway is that the treatments are now more about maintenance and less about a cure."

Maya chimed in, "Honey, his form of lymphoma is very hard to eradicate. He was in remission, but then it flared up again."

Yoni sighed, "Sorry to hear that. I know he is such a good guy. You've been friends for so long."

"Thanks, Yoni. He really is. Anyway, a month ago Bobby met a fellow patient while undergoing chemo. The guy – I think his name is Arnie – is Jewish, and he's a pro-Israel political activist. He's been to Israel five or six times. As I understand it, our good Evangelical pal Bobby surprised the hell out of his new friend with his knowledge and love of Israel, and he actually suggested taking a trip there with him. Bobby didn't say it, but the trip is kind of a last hurrah. We are likely going to join them. Bobby needs the help."

Yoni asked excitedly, "Mom, what do you think?"

Danny answered for her. "She is very interested. Maya is very fond of Bobby and Andrea and wants to be helpful. Your mother's Hebrew would be invaluable. Plus, she'd get to see you."

Maya interjected, "Yes, I want very much to be part of their adventure. I know I can help with all of the little problems that may arise."

Danny continued, "So, Yoni, I will keep you posted. We haven't made any travel plans and we are working though the medical issues. Also, I haven't yet met Bobby's pal Arnie. We're scheduled to all meet in a few weeks. They're all really looking forward to talking to you as a lone soldier. You wouldn't need to be with us all the time, but I'd like you to be with us for some of it."

Yoni knew that his availability depended on the IDF. It had been several years since the 2005 unilateral withdrawal from Gaza and Hamas's election victory, and the region was in a state of unrest. Givati was the main combat brigade that dealt with the Gaza area. He could be drawn into action.

Yoni decided not to get into the what-ifs and told his parents what they wanted to hear. "Of course."

28
The Old City

Bobby had slept through a large part of the flight and was greatly relieved when it was over. Their overhead carry-ons seemed to get heavier, and he had to ask for help from younger passengers. Stiff, dehydrated, and tired, tagging behind Andrea, he dragged himself through a plane now littered with magazines, too-small pillows, and crumpled blankets.

Walking through Ben-Gurion Airport behind the Krakows and Baransons, Bobby and Andrea were wide-eyed, taking in their first look at Israel. The chiseled golden Jerusalem stone blocks gave them a foretaste of the eternal city's lustrous hue. Walking the corridors from the plane toward customs, Bobby saw informational signs written in a Hebrew-English-Arabic triad and thought about Israel's geopolitical complexities.

Arnie, Fran, Danny, and Maya watched Bobby and Andrea take it all in. They enjoyed watching the Langfords see Israel for the first time. They'd be sure the Langfords didn't miss anything, but they'd avoid force-feeding. They'd err on the side of letting Israel come slowly to them.

The jumble of cultural and religious denominations all trying to complete aviation's steeplechase of bag retrieval, clearing customs, and finding local transportation or transferring to yet another flight entertained Bobby and Andrea. A very tall Russian Orthodox cleric wearing a black cape, skufia hat, and a carved gold cross and chain towered over them on the passport line. While waiting for luggage by the conveyor belt, Bobby watched as young ultra-Orthodox Jewish families herded children forward. Boys raced around with long locks of hair flying in front of their ears as their parents hauled bulging suitcases, strollers, and hatboxes for their traditional fur hats. Women in burkas, men with keffiyehs, and West Coast hipster entrepreneurs kept one eye on the conveyer belt and one eye on their cell phones.

To Bobby and Andrea, it was a little like the cantina scene from *Star Wars*.

They traveled smoothly by van on Route 1 from Ben-Gurion Airport, winding their way upwards to Jerusalem. The fertile plains gave way to small rolling hills, and then the road curved higher through steeper cuts where small terraces barely held the grass for grazing animals, crops, and olive trees. Arnie pointed out places of historical significance. Heads pivoted around to see Latrun, the site of multiple battles during the War of Independence and the cluster of memorialized armored trucks used in 1948 to break Jerusalem's siege. About halfway was Abu Ghosh, an Arab town known for restaurants serving excellent Middle Eastern cuisine.

The group hired a driver and guide who came highly recommended. He'd give them a professional's narrative and provide hassle-free transportation. If everything went as planned, Corporal Yoni Baranson would also join them. Now, in the late summer of 2009, his Gaza battle wounds were healing nicely. He was given time off to visit with his family.

Danny and Maya hadn't seen him since before his injury, but Yoni vigorously reassured them that the broken arm and leg weren't too different from a bad fall on a ski run in Utah. He had sent pictures from the hospital, and they could see his smiling face as well as the traction frame supporting his encased leg. Maya's cousins went to visit him and make sure that he was okay.

Approaching Jerusalem, the traffic thickened as they passed near the Israel Museum and Hebrew University campus, turned onto Ramban Street, Agron Street, and finally King David Street to arrive at the splendid hotel.

The three couples had made reservations to stay at the aristocratic six-story King David Hotel. It was expensive, but they all agreed it would be a treat to join the long list of celebrities, diplomats, and heads of state who had also stayed there. The taxi pulled into the circular driveway under the stone porte cochere. Arnie watched as Bobby and Andrea eyed the armed guard. They would have to get used to the ubiquitous security checks at the entrances to malls, museums, and hotels. The young female soldiers toting heavy weapons back at the airport fascinated Andrea.

The six walked through the revolving door into the lobby. It had been designed back in the late 1920s to reflect a composite biblical style. With gold, taupe, and turquoise touches detailing the generous space and the bold rectangular columns, it was magnificent. Bobby took a quick scan around the high-ceilinged lobby and its sitting area. He requested, "Can you folks give me a little while to recover? I need a couple of hours to catch my breath. I'll be ready for dinner after I can rest a bit."

Arnie affirmed, "You're doing great. Rest up. Let's meet around seven."

Before dinner, in the cooling evening air, they gathered on the veranda for a drink. They quietly looked out at the unmatched panoramic views of the Old City's crenellated walls. The Tower of David and the Jaffa Gate were visible to the far left, and the St. James Cathedral could be seen to the far right. The golden-hewed walls built and rebuilt by a succession of conquerors, including the Crusaders, Saladin, and Suleiman, glowed from the ground lighting. All around, the sparkling home and streetlights hovered above the dark hilly contours, and in spite of the never-ending conflicts, they gave an atmosphere of heavenly peace.

Sitting around a glass-topped table, they talked about an agenda for the next few days. Danny smoothed out a folded map of the city and the country. Already marked with a felt-tipped pen were the locations where the guide would take them. In a different color were places they wanted to explore on their own. He added, "We expect Yoni to join us tomorrow morning.

Andrea thoughtfully asked Maya, "Are you sure he's going to be able to join us? I thought his arm and leg were still healing."

"I know, I keep asking him that, but Yoni always just tells me his brigade's motto is 'anywhere, any time, and any place.'"

Just after a sumptuous breakfast buffet, Maya and Danny returned to the lobby and spied Yoni walking through the hotel's revolving door. They both noticed a slight limp, the result of his leg crushed by the heavy, falling Gaza balcony. Both broke into a trot to give him a three-way extended hug. Moments later, they pulled back to see their uniformed son. He looked taller but thinner than they had remembered, and fulfilling their prayers, there were no other signs of his war injuries. For Danny, no matter how many times he had seen armed IDF soldiers in civilian settings, seeing his son with his weapon slung in front of him was still a shock. Yoni had always dreamed of doing this, and here he was, doing it.

Maya held on firmly to Yoni's arm as Danny made introductions. "Arnie and Bobby, and Fran and Andrea, please let me introduce you to Yoni." Danny corrected himself, "Corporal Yonatan Baranson."

Standing there in his uniform, he captured their full attention. He thoughtfully answered their stream of questions about the IDF, the lone soldier experience, and even the operation in Gaza, but he encouraged them to begin walking so that they could meet the tour guide near the Jaffa Gate.

They made their way up the pathways to the Old City's imposing sloped outer ramparts. Only four months after Yoni was injured, he was fit enough to return to his unit. Because of the jet lag and an infirm Bobby, he led more slowly.

They passed through the thick, arched Jaffa Gate, one of eight gates to the Old City and the only one positioned at a right angle to the walls. The prearranged guide, Zvi Rosen, had no trouble finding them as they waited in the crowded plaza next to the Tower of David. Introductions were made, and off they went into the Christian Quarter of Jerusalem's Old City.

Over the next two hours, Zvi led the group on a walk along the Via Dolorosa following the path of Christ's suffering and then to explore the Garden Tomb. The uneven but smooth stones, buffed from the shuffling feet of millions of visitors over two dozen centuries, had to be carefully traversed. The late morning heat challenged Bobby, and Arnie, Danny, and Yoni took turns supporting him between holy sites.

They exited the Old City and walked to the Garden Tomb. Yoni wanted Bobby at his absolute best so he could appreciate the tranquil beauty of the rock-cut tomb discovered in 1867, believed by many to be the site of the burial and resurrection of Jesus.

Bobby walked cautiously down from the street level to the little plaza in front of the tomb's opening. Sitting on stone steps next to wooden planters with red flowers, he was moved to tears, sensing the overwhelming significance of the location. He and Andrea were given time and privacy to absorb the blessing of being there together.

Bobby shared, "Susanne's descriptions were so good, so impassioned that I feel like I have been here before."

Danny quietly suggested, "She's such a great advocate. It's hard not to be moved by her words."

It was time for lunch and a rest. The crew trooped through the narrow, colorful Arab *shuk* and into the Jewish Quarter. In spite of the summer heat, the high stone walls provided shade and trapped cool air. They walked past the sixth-century Roman Cardo. Ten minutes later, with Bobby's energy running on empty, they plodded up the steps into Arnie's favorite Old City restaurant, the Quarter Café.

The two ebullient brothers who in 1975 opened the unusual restaurant at the end of Tiferet Street benefitted from an unmatched vista facing east. Diners have a magnificent view of the Mount of Olives, the tower from the Church of the Ascension, the Al-Aqsa Mosque, and the scalloped Intercontinental Hotel. Arnie introduced his friends to the owners. The buffet included pan-fried Saint Peter's fish, salads, blintzes, and hummus and falafel plates. He prodded his friends, "Grab a tray and pick anything. It's all great."

They ate gazing out at the view of a neighborhood so much in dispute. In the clear air of the Jerusalem hills, the dramatic landscape made it hard to concentrate on food or conversation. Each of the visitors found themselves alone with their thoughts.

After a prolonged lunch and a well-earned rest, they walked down to the Western Wall cobblestone plaza and passed through the security check. They stood together taking in the Kotel, the rampart to the Muslim-controlled Temple Mount, and the many flapping Israeli flags.

Zvi told everyone a bit about the Kotel. The Langfords were very curious to learn that the Kotel was not part of the original Temple, but rather, it was a supporting wall. The Temple stood on top of it before it was destroyed in 70 CE. The reason it was often hailed as the holiest spot for Jews is because the western retaining wall was the closest to the Holy of Holies, the central part of the Temple. The Temple Mount itself, then, was technically holier, but there were complex agreements that prevented Jews from accessing it.

Bobby confessed that after the prayers at the Western Wall, he would need to head back to the hotel for a nap. Zvi promised to escort Bobby and Andrea to the Dung Gate and to a taxi. The others would wait for Zvi to return. He would lead them to the nearby archeological excavations. Yoni would happily stay with them until after dinner, and then he would head back to his base.

With their game plan in place, the group separated toward the men's and women's sides. Yoni, Arnie, and Danny guided Bobby down a small ramp through the crowd of Orthodox men and tourists, past the high wooden tables placed there for religious services.

Andrea, Maya, and Fran went to pray in the women's section. It was smaller than the men's section, and given that it was tourist season, it was hard to find a spot by the wall. Eventually, three women left, leaving open a spot wide enough for them to stand together. They stood there alone with their thoughts, but together as loving friends.

Bobby and Andrea had been advised of the tradition to write down personal prayers to God and insert them in the crevices between the wall's huge limestone blocks. The notes typically called for divine support for personal matters, including longevity, health, children, marriage, financial security, and happiness. Religious Jews would recite the traditional millennia-old prayers for the reconstruction of the Temple, the return of the Jewish nation to its homeland, the coming of the Messiah, and peace.

Andrea folded her paper and placed it carefully into a crevice of the Kotel.

In the men's section, Yoni, Arnie, Danny, and Bobby slowly fanned out to find their own spots next to the sixty-two-foot-high ancient wall. Arnie rested his head against his forearm that touched the warm stones and recited his prayers. In the presence of the holiest place, struggled over for millennia, he felt time slowing. Tears ran down his cheeks as he tried to control a flashback of faces, events, and past prayers. There was his father, once again young…Fran in her wedding gown…caps and gowns at graduations…his kids were hip-high and chased a black Labrador retriever.

Danny was standing next to a young, blond Hasidic boy who buzzed through his prayers energetically. He noticed Yoni to the left of the boy. He wondered if he had stood at this exact spot once before. Did the golden stone with the diagonal crack immediately in front of him look familiar? For just a few moments, Danny forgot about his three traveling companions and felt completely at home, alone with his thoughts. He inserted his prayer note, being careful not to displace any other. Danny whispered the Shema: "Hear, O Israel: the Lord is our God, the Lord is one." He prayed for his family and thanked the Almighty for the survival of his soldier son, Yoni.

Yoni prayed for the safety of Israeli soldiers, especially for his brothers in Givati.

Everyone prayed for Bobby.

Bobby found his own space next to the wall. He rested his forehead on a warm, chiseled stone. Bobby felt at peace. Eyes closed, he took the time to look back over his life's major events and all of his good fortune. He saw the faces of his smiling children, and he was swept back to Route 231, hearing the resonant sound of his father's voice. He resisted addressing his affliction. From his left shirt pocket, he withdrew a small folded triangle of paper containing his messages to the Lord. He wedged his note in with dozens of others in a niche where a small bush managed to take root and grow into a bold sphere of green.

The Village

Carrying his small, canvas backpack chock-full of Israeli tour guide essentials, all five feet and seven inches of Asher Hagai walked into the dining room of the Carmel Forest Resort and Spa. This was the last stop on the crew's journey in the Holy Land. They'd spent the last four days seeing the highlights of northern Israel, including witnessing a baptism in the Jordan River. Tomorrow, they'd return to Tel Aviv and board a midnight flight back to the United States.

The six tourists had been kind enough to arrange for their guide to also stay at the luxury hotel, as they did at all of the other hotels. The dining room was almost empty, and in spite of his simple tastes in food, Asher made a survey of the inventive array of breakfast options laid out at multiple serving stations. The Carmel Forest Spa was known for its excellent and healthy food. He took a plate and piled on cubes of local cheese, a dozen olives, a stuffed grape vine leaf, and a croissant from an industrial-sized wicker basket of breads. With his free hand, he snatched a pear from the pear pyramid and sat down at a table for four along the floor-to-ceiling windows. Asher began to eat before his troop came in. This way, he could explain the day's agenda or answer questions without having to talk and munch at the same time.

The contemporary white stucco hotel was built on the side of a mountain. When the Baransons, the Langfords, and the Krakows awoke, they could draw back the drapes, look out over the lawns and pool below, and gaze further across the mellow vistas of the Carmel

Forest nature preserve. They could also walk out onto their terrace and breath in the cool, clean air of northern Israel. When they were ready, they would dress and join Asher in the dining room.

The Krakows were the first to join Asher. They walked over to him and were quick on the draw to say, "*Boker tov.*" Asher slid his tortoiseshell glasses down from his forehead, stood, and returned a dramatically bright "*Boker or.*"

This simple exchange of good morning greetings tickled Arnie and Fran. They loved Asher's little Hebrew snippets that gave them a taste of the everyday Israeli banter. Just listening to casual street talk delighted them, even though they could never understand Hebrew.

About ten minutes later, Danny and Maya arrived. They walked behind Arnie and Fran's chairs, patted their shoulders, and greeted, "*Boker tov.*" Placing hats, cameras, and pocketbooks at an adjoining table for four, they saved space for the soon-to-arrive Langfords.

Maya, before selecting her breakfast, plopped in next to Asher and asked in quiet Hebrew, "*Ma nishma?*" He told her he was doing fine. Although Asher's English was perfect, Maya chose to speak to him in Hebrew in the interest of discretion. She needed to alert him to her earlier phone conversation with Andrea.

Asher knew about Bobby's lymphoma and constant fatigue in Jerusalem. In fact, even before they arrived in Israel, he had thought through the challenges of guiding two older men suffering with cancer and feeling the side effects of chemotherapy. It only took a call or two to his old army buddies before Asher spoke to several doctors to learn what might become issues and what to do if they needed medical support. He knew what extra foods to have aboard, and he had all the phone numbers scribbled in a notepad.

"Andrea called our room earlier," Maya told Asher in Hebrew. She warned that Bobby had a rough night and hadn't gotten much sleep. "Andrea told me he's intent on going ahead with today's drive through the north. He knows it's a full day with lots of driving."

Asher nodded and said, *"Ein be'ayah*, no problem. Let's let him have some breakfast, and we'll do our very best to help Bobby have a great day."

After a few minutes, Bobby and Andrea appeared at the restaurant's doorway. Bobby wore a Purdue baseball cap, representing his alma mater. Asher spied them and waved them over. Even Asher, who was a lovable combination of a gentle older brother and a tough once-upon-a-time IDF paratrooper, was taken aback by Bobby's appearance. It seemed to him that, overnight, Bobby had shrunk a few inches, and his color had gotten markedly grayer. But Asher didn't let it faze him.

"Bobby," he said, "*Achi*, my friend, there's still a few crumbs left for you and Andrea. Please eat."

Bobby looked back passively at Asher, as if any response would have taken more energy than he had to give. His stomach ached. On a scale of one to ten, his ability to think clearly was maybe a six. He just nodded hello and walked carefully toward the buffet. Andrea, too, was resolute, and she shadowed him through the food selections.

Bobby enjoyed the touring and the time with Danny and Arnie, so he just wanted to keep pressing ahead. He had the grim determination of a marathoner waiting for his second wind, fighting through the burn at the twenty-second milepost. He kept his mind focused on the task of completing the journey.

Bobby hadn't said it, but his private motivation was a vision of returning home, settling into the old sofa, and reminiscing with Susanne about his trip. He could imagine her voice. *What did you think of the Garden Tomb? I hope you walked atop the Old City ramparts. Who was with you at the baptism? Did you feel Jesus's presence at the synagogue in Capernaum?*

He could easily remember her excited descriptions from the time she had spent in the Galilee visiting the sites of the miracles. Bobby knew their experience in the Holy Land would bring them closer together. Together, they could discuss the scriptures with reference to their geographic and historic setting. He hoped that Meredith and her family would someday share the experience, too.

When Bobby finished his modest breakfast of oatmeal and fruit, he nodded to Asher. Holding hands with Andrea, Bobby arose and joined the others climbing into the van.

It was late in the afternoon when their Toyota van pulled onto the roads of the Yemin Orde Youth Village. The passengers dozed while Asher carefully steered the van around the mountain switchbacks. He slowed as youngsters walked along the road and crossed from one pathway to another. Students purposefully walked in groups of two and three, just as you'd see on an American college campus.

Since 1953, these seventy-seven acres had been home to thousands of at-risk kids. Sad combinations of trauma, anti-Semitism, or abandonment brought them there. For over half a century, they had arrived at Yemin Orde as the product of world events, demographic shifts, and the global flow of refugees – a microcosm of Israel herself. Some were orphans; some had parents still in their native countries. Now, many came from Ethiopia, the Former Soviet Union, Eastern Europe, and South America.

Behind the physical reality of the village was a social structure and educational philosophy unique to Israel. The Yemin Orde staff provided a warm, nurturing "family." Its director and educational leader, Chaim Peri, called for a "mending of the heart," and he believed that his village could instill in its children "a recognition and pride in their past, a sense of direction, and security about the future." For the residents, it would be forever a place that they could call home.

"Hello! Wake up, boys and girls. Good afternoon," Asher called out.

As the van slowed, they awoke to a beautiful scene. In his best tour guide voice, Asher instructed, "Please look, on the right, at their pretty synagogue. Its roof looks like a jewel, maybe a crown. Some say a collection of tents. It is a place of safety in a world of change. A famous architect designed it." The usually encyclopedic Asher had to admit, "Just now, I forgot his name."

Maya and Danny were the first to leave the van. With a cry of pure joy, again, they raced to their son, who met them there.

"Yoni, Yoni!" they kissed and embraced him.

As he juggled his belongings, they hugged in a tight stack of three.

Asher helped the Langfords and the Krakows off the van. As they slowly regained their walking legs, they joined the three Baransons. Asher handed each an icy bottle of water. Danny threw an arm around Asher and pulled him over to meet Yoni.

Asher said, "We love our lone soldiers. They're amazing." He took a look at Yoni's purple beret. "Givati, very nice," Asher noted with a clap on the shoulder.

Orit walked out of the women's dormitory with three younger girls trailing closely behind. She wore her army uniform; they wore skirts, sweatshirts, and sandals. In spite of her radiance and dramatic appearance, Orit was clearly one of the residents. As the four stepped out of the shadows cast by the building and the thick shrubbery, they chatted animatedly. After a few more steps, Orit took control of the conversation, and the girls listened attentively. Before they walked away, the girls smiled and thanked her. "*Todah rabah.*"

Earlier in the day, the girls had shared their problems with Orit. Aviva's parents were trying to drag her back into their vicious fighting. Her mother had pleaded with her to come home, because her father quit his job as a packer at a fruit cooperative. Now, they might not be able to pay the rent for their dismal apartment in Hadera. Their beloved grandfather, who was the mastermind of their family's trek through the Sudanese desert, was not well and needed constant help.

The second girl, Luleh, hair tied up with a purple scrunchie, was failing in her attempt to reason with her brother who was edging toward crime. Would he ever be able to join the army?

The third young woman, a Russian émigrée with blond hair hidden under a bandana, had come to Israel without her parents. She was living with her grandmother, who suffered from emphysema and more recently was diagnosed with heart failure. It was her grandmother's Jewishness that qualified them to join the mass migration.

Orit, before leaving them, hugged each and reminded them that only so much can be controlled. She told them that fear and shame are normal to experience. She wanted them to remember that they were part of the village family as well as their own.

Yoni and Orit took steps toward each other and met with a high five. Before Yoni led her to meet his parents and his family friends, Orit briefly explained how she was acting as a big sister even though she no longer was a resident. Head down, he listened.

Over the past few months, Orit had shared her own history with Yoni, including the disintegration of a family that had suffered the loss of a baby in the Ethiopian Jews' camp while waiting for the flights to Israel. She told him how her first years in Israel were overwhelming for both parents, and they felt isolated from her extended family. In school, Orit felt the shame of being different, not speaking Hebrew, her cultural practices, and her dark skin. She came to Yemin Orde as a ninth-grader; she left as a confident young woman, with excellent matriculation scores and a quality placement in the IDF. Yes, she still saw her mother, two brothers, and sister, but even she knew it was in her best interest to stay close to her Yemin Orde roots.

Orit turned first toward the small crowd by the van, walking half a step ahead of Yoni. She knew that they would assume she was Yoni's girlfriend, and she would do nothing to confuse them. She and Yoni were not dating, and these Americans should see them as two army buddies, nothing more. She could tell that Yoni thought that she was very pretty, but she worked hard to keep army friendships platonic. The horror of her parents' economic woes haunted her, and she was determined to rely on her intelligence and not on her beauty. After the army, she would attend an excellent university.

The six travelers greeted Yoni and Orit in a crisscross of handshakes, hugs, and introductions. As impressive as Yoni was, Orit, a stunning Ethiopian woman in an IDF uniform and with her Tavor, mesmerized the group. The otherwise gregarious group, for a moment, could not generate a question for her.

Asher stood off to the side and let Yoni and Orit share their specialized perspective as soldiers. Yoni's unaccented English was a pleasant break from their tour guides' heavy accents, and Orit's English was more than adequate to respond to their inquiries.

At a momentary lull in the conversation, Asher suggested, "Let's walk a little further to a more comfortable location. We can sit down, and I want to tell all of you a little story."

Walking around several of the village's buildings, on well-worn paths and tired, patchy grass, they climbed up a slight hill to a set of outdoor tables and chairs. There, they were shaded from the sun by pines, and they could enjoy the magnificent view of Mount Carmel flowing gently down to the sea. The patchwork of tilled land butting up against rocky outcroppings and yellow-green meadows spread out before them.

Asher passed around more water bottles, trail mix, and Bamba, Israel's trademark peanut butter puffs. He sat down while they ate and gulped, and he dug though his backpack.

Asher began, "We're at the Yemin Orde Youth Village. We have talked about its history as a boarding school for children. It means 'In memory of Orde' for Charles Orde Wingate."

As they rested and enjoyed the breeze, quick exchanges between Danny and Bobby confirmed that Bobby was surviving a grueling afternoon.

Bobby winked at Danny. "I may be hurting, but remember our drunken toboggan run? You know that I can hang in there."

Danny patted his shoulder and laughed, "Yes, sir. I still recall the whiskey, the snow, and the hospital."

Asher opened the travel bag on his lap and withdrew a book wrapped in brown paper. The book's cream-colored jacket was torn in two places, and he handled it gingerly, "Look at the name of the author: Christopher Sykes. Do any of you recognize the name?" With a finger wag, he admonished, "Arnie and Fran, don't say it if you know it."

The group shook their heads. He lectured, "He was the son of Sir Mark Sykes. He was a Brit. He and François Georges-Picot of France, in 1916, negotiated a secret deal that effectively divided up the Middle East. It set the rough boundaries of Syria, Iraq, Lebanon, Jordan, and Palestine, assigning each to either British or French rule. It came into effect after the defeat of the Ottoman Empire. The agreement set the stage for the Balfour Declaration. Anyway, back to Christopher Sykes, Sir Mark Sykes's son. He wrote this grand book about Charles Wingate in 1959."

Gently holding his first-edition copy, he went on. "I cannot tell you his entire story, not his early years with his birth in colonial India in 1903, and not his schooling in England. We don't have time. So let me focus on Major-General Wingate and his time in Palestine."

With two hands clasped together, Asher instructed, "When you get home, find out who is the only non-American buried in Arlington Cemetery." Asher winked. "It's our very own Charles Orde Wingate."

Over the next fifteen minutes, Asher colorfully recounted the story of the eccentric, religiously aware British officer Wingate. He came to Israel in 1932. In short order, he fell in love with the Jewish pioneers working the land and building a country.

He laid out for the group how Wingate became politically involved with Zionist leaders and became an ardent Zionist himself.

Asher described how he taught the nascent Haganah troops, including Moshe Dayan, and how guerrilla warfare with special night squads effectively kept the Arab marauders under control. Asher noted how Wingate's pro-Zionist positions led to his reassignment away from Palestine in May 1939.

Shuffling through more papers stuffed into the book, he fished out a well-worn page. He said, "For the ladies, let me tell you about his beloved wife, Lorna."

He read, "They married in England in 1935 and moved to Palestine one year later. Seeing Jewish farmers in the Jezreel Valley and the Galilee laboring on the land of their biblical ancestors rang true to both of them."

In a near whisper, he told them, "In late 1947, after her husband's death, she was keenly aware of the Jews' struggle at the United Nations for a vote in favor of a partition of Palestine. She corresponded directly with Emperor Haile Selassie, reminding him of her husband's service to Ethiopia. She asked for him now to support the partition of Palestine into an Arab and a Jewish state."

Asher's eyes sparkled. "Ethiopia abstained instead of voting against, and on November 29, the two-thirds vote, 33-13, prevailed."

He took a swig from his water bottle. "And here we are now at Yemin Orde. We are sitting here with Yoni and Orit, two soldiers from two faraway countries, as one group of Jews and Christians, like Orde and his Jewish pioneer friends."

He paused to let the thought sink in. "We're here in a village that heals the broken. The wonders of Israel's story still thrill me. As you Americans like to say, 'You can't make this stuff up.'"

Asher saw that his travelers were wearing down. In spite of their rapt attention to his presentation, he pleaded, "Please, let me finish by reading to you directly from Wingate's order of the day issued to his troops in wartime Burma, February 13, 1943." Asher tried to use an aristocratic British affectation when he pronounced "order of the day."

Asher's voice grew serious. "I've come to know you – all eight of you – and your reasons for coming to Israel. I know that not every tourist feels as strongly as you do. Bobby and Andrea, it is with the deepest appreciation that we greet you and thank Christian Zionists like you and your daughter Susanne."

Asher looking around and made careful eye contact. "In his order, sixty years ago, written in what were desperate times and in the harshest of conditions – remember he died about a year later – there is a theme that speaks to us still today."

Reopening the book, he selected another worn page and proceeded to quote Charles Orde Wingate. "It is always a minority that occupies the front line. It is still a smaller minority that accepts, with a good heart, tasks like this that we have chosen to carry out."

Asher summarized, "Wingate knew what it was like for the few, the minority, to face the many. He knew that not everyone would step up when they should, and he was always an activist – a leader – on the front lines.

The group nodded, enamored by the story.

"By referring to a good heart, I can only guess what he meant. Maybe he realized that it was a blessing to be at peace, to accept a virtuous mission, no matter how difficult it is to complete."

30 Dixieland

When the doorbell rang, Danny was deeply asleep on the sofa bed jammed in the cool, darkened guest room. As he slowly opened his eyes, post-dozing tunnel vision limited his view. He sensed the front door open and close, and he heard fragments of an excited conversation that followed. But even with the disturbances, he lay back, still not ready to get up.

His earlier walk in the afternoon heat, pushing the baby stroller up the hills, had tired him out. Even though Maya had urged him to drink plenty, the Tel Aviv humidity in the Lev Ha'ir neighborhood coupled with the physical effort had taken its toll. Thankfully, the baby stroller was high tech with big, thick wheels. In spite of the weight of Matan, the baby paraphernalia, and the groceries they bought, he made it back to the apartment.

Looking around the room as he lay on his back, he glanced at Yoni's dinged, industrial metal bookcase holding several of his college textbooks, still wrapped in their Indiana University dust jackets. Danny was amused that in this Israeli apartment, in a growing Jewish city perched on the edge of the Mediterranean, the Hoosiers were represented.

On Yoni's desk next to the bookshelf was a brown, elbowed fluorescent lamp that used to sit on his childhood desk. Just next to the lamp's heavy base was a framed photograph of Yoni and Orit on their wedding day. Their loving focus on each other conveyed the deepest commitment, and Orit was a stunning bride.

In the dim silence of the room, Danny thought about all of the reasons he had given Yoni for not becoming an IDF lone soldier. Just as he had worried, Yoni had endured battlefield wounds. He couldn't even stop worrying yet, because Yoni still had reserve duty. But if he had been convincing, would he have prevented Yoni and Orit from ever meeting? Would he have upset the cosmic plan for his glorious grandchild and their happy home?

He remembered how sure he had been that Yoni's Zionism had gone too far and that graduate degrees and a good American job in an electronics or software firm would have been the right way to go. He never admitted to Maya or Yoni that his fears for his son were a constant source of nightmares and anxiety.

Images of border skirmishes, gutted buses, suicide bombers, and terrorists haunted him. He didn't confess that he quietly blamed Maya, and even her deceased father whom he had never met, for Yoni's early interest in Israel and the IDF. He knew on some level that even he probably contributed to the decision by traveling with Yoni to Israel so many times.

Danny cleared his head and tried to get control of his ruminations. He remembered the 50-50 rule. It suggested that fifty percent of what you think is good for you isn't, and fifty percent of what you think is not good for you actually is.

In a few more moments, he sat up and took another look at Yoni's desk. There was a group photo from the trip with the Langfords and the Krakows, taken with Yoni and Orit at Yemin Orde. Danny was pleased that this photo had earned a space on Yoni's crowded desktop.

With a little more effort, he put on his shirt, buttoned his trousers, and went to see who had come to visit.

Sitting in the cramped living room were Maya, Orit, and to his surprise, Susanne. They were chatting quietly as little Matan, just a few months old, slept in his baby swing. A tiny bubble of saliva hung on the corner of his precious mouth. Their fiber art wall hangings brightened the room, and colorful woven baskets stood in corners accenting the neutral tile floor.

Questions, answers, and opinions flew back and forth, and only Orit looked up and noticed Danny standing in the hall's archway. She grinned and said in her best English, "Sabba, did you have a nice nap?" Danny smiled at being called grandpa.

Seeing Danny, Susanne bounced out of her chair and gave him a huge hug. Danny was so excited about the surprise visit, in Israel of all places. He babbled in a wave of excitement, "Wow, so nice to see you! It's been so long! What brings you here? How are your mother and Meredith?"

It had been four years since Bobby passed away. Danny and Maya often visited Andrea in the months after the funeral, but they hadn't seen Susanne over the past two years. Both Danny and Maya had been so focused on the wedding, then on Orit's pregnancy, and then on Matan's birth that they had less time for everyone else. They talked by phone with Andrea frequently and learned that Susanne had traveled to Israel several times on behalf of a pro-Israel Christian organization headquartered in Jerusalem. She was drawn to the organization because of its virtuous stand in support of Israel and through practical projects such as assisting in aliyah to the Jewish homeland and building bomb shelters.

Danny had been with Bobby up until the day he died. In the dark of the room where Bobby fought his final battle, he had fed him ice chips. Bobby lay still in the rented hospital bed set up in the downstairs living room. No words were spoken, but they were together for what they both knew was to be the last time.

Arnie and his wife Fran were at the funeral. Bobby had been an uncomplaining trooper, and his only request was to spend his final days and hours in his own home. He died quietly and peacefully surrounded by his family.

Susanne stepped back from her embrace with Danny and quietly reported, "Mom is doing just fine. She's adjusting, and we're all keeping her busy. I think you know that she sold our home. It was just too big."

Danny gave Susanne a pained look, followed by an understanding nod. "It's so hard to think of returning to Dawkins and not going to their home," he mused. "But I know it was the right thing to do."

As the two of them talked about family, Maya joined the reminiscing. Maya and Andrea had actually kept up more frequent correspondence than Danny and Bobby had. Over the years, the two had become like sisters.

Orit hadn't had the opportunity to learn much about Bobby and Andrea, as their meeting at Yemin Orde was too brief and with too many distractions. She had never met Susanne. Over the past few weeks, Maya had shared with Orit the story of Bobby and Danny's childhood friendship. Maya also talked about the difficulties Andrea had faced as a young girl and how she persevered without parents. She went on to describe the Langfords' two daughters and talked about Susanne's involvement with Christian Zionism.

Orit, circumspect about her family's aliyah and all of their subsequent travails in Israel, was drawn to Andrea's history. She was taken with Andrea's resilience and mission work in third-world countries and was glad to meet her daughter Susanne.

Orit had arranged for Maya to meet her mother Yalem for lunch that day. The two had met at the wedding, but they didn't get a chance to really talk. Yalem now lived with Orit's brother's family in Ashdod, a short bus ride from Orit and Yoni's apartment in Tel Aviv. Orit saw her mother on occasion and had a generally positive relationship with her, but Maya took it upon herself as her mother-in-law to emotionally support Orit in the ways her mother could not.

Maya rose to greet Yalem at the door and gave her a warm hug. Danny shook her hand and introduced her to Susanne in terrible Hebrew, which Maya promptly corrected. Yoni had to work that day, so Orit sent his regards.

Underneath Yalem's hardened, aged exterior, it was clear that Orit had inherited her beauty from her mother. She carried herself with a humble, modest formality that hinted at the challenging life she had endured.

Urged on by Orit, Yalem told her story of early life in a small village not far from Gondar in hilly, rural Ethiopia. Like all the Jews of Ethiopia, they lived isolated from the general population, not able to own land but connected to an extended family and led by the *qes*, the spiritual leader. She told the story of the secret relocation to a slum near Addis Ababa not far from the Israeli embassy.

The family had connected with the Jewish Agency in Ethiopia, and in a few months, they were whisked away in unmarked planes. Yalem choked on her words as she recounted the steps down the plane's walkway onto Israeli soil. Everyone was emotional and captivated. When Orit translated, Susanne's eyes welled with tears.

Orit and Yalem talked about the confusion and challenge of the absorption centers, the dispersion to unpopulated cities, and the transition into high-tech, fast-paced Israeli society. As children, Orit and her two brothers quickly mastered Hebrew and witnessed the slow, grueling progress of their parents and grandparents. Her parents struggled with the practical complexities of Western life. Orit avoided talking about unemployment, poverty, and the loss of self-respect that had led her father to leave the family. Yalem reengaged in the conversation, explaining why it was so important for Orit and her brothers to go to the Yemin Orde village.

While grandmothers Maya and Yalem had little in common other than fluency in Hebrew, both had experienced the trauma of relocation and personal loss. Now, little Matan was a shared joy. At Orit and Yoni's wedding, the Baranson and Negalla families enjoyed rituals and customs from both traditions.

Only when the front door opened and Yoni stepped in did the subject change. In one fluid motion, Yoni dropped his leather briefcase and gave Susanne a bear hug. He pushed her back to arm's length and exclaimed, "How are you? It's been forever! Congrats on your engagement!"

Susanne sized up Yoni, proclaiming, "Look at you! New *abba.* Lucky husband. Mr. Israeli innovator."

In the flurry of greetings, Yoni found his way to the baby swing and looked down at his little boy, who was now stirring. Maya and Danny watched as Yoni picked up his squirming son. He and Orit simultaneously kissed him and then shared a hello peck.

Over the next two hours, they all enjoyed a simple but tasty dinner, enlivened with hectic conversation and two bottles of an Israeli Sauvignon Blanc. Yoni updated Susanne on the new software enterprise that he had begun with several of his Garin Tzabar friends.

Susanne described how she had remained close to her Christian church and had dedicated time to support the International Christian Embassy Jerusalem. She was here to learn more about their latest project to build bomb shelters for border communities facing periodic rocket attacks from Gaza and from the northern borders. She'd return ready to raise awareness among the other local American churches. Maya, especially, was impressed by how Susanne balanced these commitments with her career as a journalist and now planning a wedding with her fiancé, Luke.

With Orit now back from checking on Matan, Yoni stepped over to his laptop and switched the music selection from the Israeli vocal duo with a guitar accompanist to his Dixieland jazz collection.

Yoni had learned to enjoy Dixieland music. It was Danny's favorite, and now Yoni was a true fan. Danny felt that it was the most authentically American form of music. He thought the spontaneity – the "let's make it up as we go" style – reflected the youth, exuberance, and innovation central to the broader American story. He appreciated the performers' skills in musical composition, and a carefree demeanor often masked instrument expertise.

The first song up was "Sweet Georgia Brown." Yoni had turned down the sound so that now-sleeping Matan would not be awakened. Even so, the clarion trumpets and chirping clarinets riffing around the tinkling piano and the deeper, steadier trombones and bass added an authentic American flavor to the decidedly Israeli apartment.

After dinner, they all relaxed on the couches. Susanne, pinned into the corner of the sofa, asked Yoni, "Please hand me my backpack."

He grabbed its strap and swung it around to her. He guessed she was looking for her phone. Danny was the first to notice that the usually effervescent Susanne had lost her smile. She rustled through the bag's contents, finding by touch what she sought.

She looked at Danny and announced solemnly, "I have something for you."

She labored to find the right words. "It's a sort of gift, I suppose. It's something you should have."

All of the other conversation quieted and then stopped, and only the soft jazz in the background filled in the silence.

Susanne cautiously and deliberately explained, "We talked before about my mother having sold her home. You can imagine that she had to make some very difficult decisions as she downsized into her new apartment. She wrestled with every choice. What should she keep, what should be sold, what should be given away."

Danny sympathized as Susanne struggled to talk about this painful topic and consoled, "Susanne, we can so easily picture your dad and Andrea in their home. It's painful to think someone else lives there now." He tried to lighten the mood by reminiscing. "It's where we enjoyed the prettiest Christmas trees and best spiked eggnog." But his words only added to the somber tone.

Danny accepted the seriousness of the conversation and allowed himself to get emotional. "I miss your dad, I really do. It was our great joy to be in Israel with him." He reached for Susanne's hand and said, "Bobby couldn't stop talking about his seeing what you saw, feeling what you felt, and he told us all what it meant to you. It meant so much to him that you felt connected to Israel."

Susanne nodded in appreciation. She continued, "When mom was nearly done packing, after so many heart-wrenching decisions, she handed me something that was very dear to my dad." She added, "In his last days, he asked us to deliver this to you."

With that, Susanne handed Danny a light blue translucent plastic folder. Danny loosened the flap as all watched in silence. In the single-pleat folder was a brittle paper envelope. Danny opened the plastic folder so he could peek in without touching the contents. Down in the folds of the paper envelope was the torn, coarse fabric swatch, grey and blue striped, once part of a prisoner's tunic sleeve. Sergeant John Langford had brought it back from Dachau.

Susanne, crying now, choked out, "Danny, I know you are familiar with the story of my Grandpa John liberating the concentration camp in 1945, and how my dad found out about it."

She caught her breath and continued. "Dad knew that his life was altered by the box in the attic and his talks with Grandpa John. We all felt the significance of Grandpa's actions and his values. It rippled through the lives of all the Langfords."

They all sat silent. The street noises and the muffled jazz were all that could be heard.

A few moments passed as everyone regained composure. All had been moved by Susanne's presentation. There was deep appreciation for a daughter carrying out, so elegantly, the wishes of her dying father.

Yoni, just an arm's length from his laptop, leaned over and carefully raised the sound just a bit. After a few concluding bars from the song "Twelfth Street Rag," during the momentary transitional silence, Yoni narrated, "Pete Fountain's Dixieland rendition of the gospel music classic 'Just a Closer Walk with Thee' is about to play."

As the aficionado of the genre, Yoni noted, "The next selection is a traditional spiritual adapted to a Dixieland jazz motif. Many artists have performed 'Just a Closer Walk with Thee,' sometimes in a country style, sometimes jazz, but this one by Fountain is my favorite."

They all sat back enjoying the fluid, soulful, throaty artistry of clarinetist Pete Fountain and his six accompanists.

Some in the room closed their eyes as they listened. The simple four-verse song was embellished with collective melodic variations played around the gentle religious theme.

Pete Fountain's stellar clarinet improvisation soared and danced weightlessly around the major chords. Midway through the song, Pete segued into another deeply spiritual standard, "Amazing Grace," and after forty-five seconds, he flawlessly returned to the pure melody of "Just a Closer Walk with Thee."

While Pete Fountain and his band played the sentimental dirge, no one spoke.

As they listened, Susanne was drawn back to Indiana and all the Dr. Peppers drunk with Pastor Ed while sitting next to his overloaded wooden desk. She was reminded of his optimistic, loving view of a not-so-gentle world.

Susanne, comfortable among her new and old friends, modestly offered, "My pastor told me the theme of this song derives from 2 Corinthians 5:7. It tells us, 'We walk by faith, not by sight.'"

Yoni paused the music so Susanne could finish.

Susanne told them, "He said it helped him understand his life's unpredictable journey."

They reflected on the generational odyssey that had brought them together from across continents and religions. They saw how they all fit into a larger puzzle. Sitting in Yoni and Orit's Israeli home, they reflected on the divine paths that had led them all there. They looked back to those who were no longer with them, and they pondered how their story would continue.

Acknowledgments

“Days pass and years vanish, and we walk sightless among miracles,” begins an old Sabbath prayer. It finishes with a plaintive wish for illumination and appreciation for the miracles all around us.

In writing *Good Heart*, my goal was to craft a storyline that entertains and also shares enough about Israel’s history, culture, and people that it would be an invitation to learn more. As the characters emerged and the plot developed, I found that four compelling modern-day miracles form the foundation for the tale. These are the sacrifice and courage of Israel’s lone soldiers, the rescue of the Ethiopian Jews, the passionate support of pro-Israel Christians, and the establishment of the modern State of Israel. These wonders illustrate what David Ben-Gurion famously observed about Israel: “In Israel, in order to be a realist you must believe in miracles.”

I’ve organized my acknowledgments of the generous support received in writing *Good Heart* according to these four miracles.

First, I had the opportunity to explore the unique, worldwide phenomenon of lone soldiers’ commitment to the Israel Defense Forces. Gene Kroner, a Sar-El leader, and Ben Goldstein, a tireless IDF advocate, facilitated my connection with two lone soldiers, Brett Kaplan and Jason Barnett. Brett and Jason generously shared their experiences with me.

For nearly two decades, my wife Phylis and I have been active supporters of Ethiopian Israeli education. Their steadfast Jewish observance while in isolation for twenty-four hundred years is an unparalleled demonstration of dedication and perseverance. We take great pride playing a small part in their steady advancement into Israeli society. Grace Rodnitzki and Roni Akele, leaders of the Ethiopian National Program, helped me shape the story's Ethiopian characters and vignettes.

Today, in both political advocacy and philanthropic initiatives, the energy and urgency of the pro-Israel Christian community is a vital part of Israel's advocacy network. Working closely with Sandra and Bill Callahan, Bill Emerson, Emily McLarty, Pastor Tony Crisp, and Susan Michael, I was better able to develop the characters of the Langford family.

The capstone miracle is the rebirth, after two thousand years, of the State of Israel. While the challenges of regional peace remain unsolved, the beauty of the land and the uplifting spectrum of her people's achievement never cease to amaze our family. Phylis and I have been blessed to share many joyous visits to Israel with our children, Jonathan and Evan. More recently, we watch in awe as our grandchildren, Aviv and Gavriel, discover Israel's magic. In our photo albums, we see the faces of family members who are no longer here but who stoked our love of Israel.

I want to also call out Orly and Chris Popik, Shelley and Gabe Grossman, Rick Fisher, Peter Fass, Richard Newman, and Seymour Bosworth, who helped with specialized expertise. Arthur Schreibman, photographer extraordinaire, created the cover art that captures the temporal and geographic arc of *Good Heart*. A special thank-you to Emily Wind, whose thoughtful editing contributed so much to the final product.

Lastly, without the continuous collaboration with my beloved Phylis, *Good Heart* couldn't have been created. I want to also praise the inspiring energy and comforting warmth of all our many wonderful friends who join us in the good-hearted support of pro-Israel activism and healing-the-world philanthropy.

Glossary

abba. Hebrew for father.

chuppah. A canopy under which the bride and groom stand during Jewish wedding ceremonies.

Gaza, disengagement. Gaza is a strip of land on Israel's southwestern border that Israel won in the Six-Day War of 1967. In 2005, Israel unilaterally disengaged from Gaza, removing all Jewish residents and all Israeli military presence.

Givati. A combat brigade in the Israeli army, predominately responsible for operations on Israel's southern borders.

Hamas. A terrorist group founded in 1987 that is in power over Gaza and committed to Israel's destruction.

"Hatikvah." Israel's national anthem.

"Hava Nagila." A traditional Jewish song that is danced to at celebrations.

hora. traditional Jewish circle dance for celebrations.

imma. Hebrew for mother.

kibbutz. A small socialist village in Israel. Today, most kibbutzim are not truly socialist anymore, but they retain strong communal values.

Kotel. The Western Wall or the Wailing Wall, which remains from Judaism's holiest site, the destroyed Temple in Jerusalem.

lone soldier. A status given by the Israeli army to soldiers who do not have family in the country, usually because the soldier has immigrated alone in order to serve. They receive special government benefits.

Qassam rockets. Rudimentary rockets fired by Hamas into Israel.
Rosh Hashanah. The holiday celebrating the Jewish New Year.
sof maslul. The ceremonial, rigorous trek marking the end of army training.
Tanakh. A Hebrew acronym that stands for the Torah, Prophets, and Writings, this canon is also known as the Old Testament.
tefillin. Two small leather boxes that contain verses from the Torah, worn during prayer on the head and on one arm and held in place by leather straps.
ulpan. An intensive Hebrew immersion program.
Yom Kippur. A Jewish holiday focused on repenting for sins.

About the Author

Alan Newman is a pro-Israel activist and retired from a career in financial services. He was born in rural Pennsylvania in 1944. He attended Pennsylvania State University and New York University, graduating with degrees in aerospace engineering and business. He holds several US patents. He retired to West Palm Beach, Florida in 2005.

Mr. Newman's philanthropic and pro-Israel activities include AIPAC's National Council and board positions at American Friends of Ben-Gurion University, Friends of the Ethiopian National Project, and Jewish Family Services.

Alan's wife Phylis is a Jewish educator and a volunteer to help children and adults with special needs. They have two sons, Jonathan and Evan, who are both pro-Israel activists, and two grandsons. Their worldwide travel has included sixteen trips to Israel.